Surrender My Love

The Bradens
at Peaceful Harbor

Love in Bloom Series

Melissa Foster

ISBN-10: 1941480241
ISBN-13: 978-1-941480-24-3

SURRENDER MY LOVE
All Rights Reserved.

Cover Design: Natasha Brown & Elizabeth Mackey

WORLD LITERARY PRESS
PRINTED IN THE UNITED STATES OF AMERICA

A Note to Readers

When I first met Cole, I couldn't help but feel his enormous heart and desire to love and be loved. The moment I met Leesa I knew that Cole was truly the right man for her, and she was exactly the woman he needed in his life. I hope you enjoy their love story as much as I enjoyed writing it.

The best way to keep up to date with my releases is to sign up for my newsletter (and receive a free Braden/Remington short story!)
www.MelissaFoster.com/newsletter

If this is your first Braden book, then you have a whole series of loyal, sexy, and wickedly naughty Bradens and sexy, sassy heroines waiting for you. All Love in Bloom books are written to be enjoyed as stand-alone novels or as part of the larger series. The characters from each series (Snow Sisters, The Bradens, The Remingtons, Seaside Summers, and The Ryders) make appearances in future books so you never miss an engagement, wedding, or birth.

Be sure to check out my Reader Goodies page, where you can download a family tree, reading order, series checklists, and more. Pick up the essential Love in Bloom Series Guide to keep track of family and character growth.
www.melissafoster.com/reader-goodies

Happy reading!
Melissa

For Les, my very own hunky hero

Chapter One

COLE BRADEN INHALED the sweet aroma of specialty coffee and baked goods as he walked into Jazzy Joe's Café. It was finally Friday, which meant a lighter patient load at his orthopedics practice, and at least this week, time to help his father and brothers with the sailboat they were refitting. But all he could think about right now was a French vanilla maple cappuccino and a low-fat cranberry walnut muffin, Jasmine and Joey Carbo's specialty. The twins only made them on Fridays, and after performing a difficult surgery on a patient with a broken tibia, Cole deserved that deliciousness.

"Welcome to Jazzy's," Jasmine called out from behind the counter where she was serving a line of customers. Her curly dark hair was tied back in a ponytail, trying its best to bust free from its tether as she pushed a bag across the counter and waved to Cole.

"Joe's," her tall, dark-haired twin added with a smirk. They greeted everyone at the café with the bright, cheery welcome. Sometimes Joe got his welcome out first, *Welcome to JJ's*, or *Welcome to Joe's*, but they never said, *Welcome to Jazzy Joe's*, and it was one of the things that never failed to make Cole smile. As a physician, his days were about methodical diagnoses and precise treatments. He enjoyed the siblings' tag-team greetings.

Cole made his way around the colorful, oversized chairs, where customers sat chatting, and around a sofa, where a couple sat holding steaming mugs. At the self-help station, he filled a to-go cup. He could practically taste the sweet liquid as he moved to the side to grab a lid and a pretty blonde stepped up beside him. She flashed a shy smile and quickly averted her eyes to the machine. Cole's eyes drifted down her clingy tank top, over her skimpy blue running shorts, to her incredibly sexy ass and lean legs.

"Cups?" She said it so quietly he thought she might be talking to herself.

Cole reached above her, brushing against her side in the process. She smelled as sweet and fresh as summer rain. He handed her a cup. "Here you go."

"Thanks. I never would have thought to look *up*." She blinked at him long enough for him to notice the grassy hue of her eyes before returning her attention to the coffee machine.

He pointed to another shelf below the counter, where more cups were stored. "They like to keep the customers guessing."

She nodded and started the machine. Cappuccino streamed into her cup and then quickly fizzled out. She sighed, her shoulders dipping slightly.

"They have other flavors." He pointed to the other machines.

"Thanks. This is my friend's favorite. I'm not sure what else she likes." She furrowed her brows, her gorgeous green eyes filled with concentration.

"Here, take mine." He handed her his cup. As the eldest of six, he'd been raised to take care of others first, and for this beautiful blonde with the kissable lips and wisps of silky hair falling in front of her eyes, he'd happily give up just about anything.

"No." She waved her hand. "I can't do that."

"Please. I don't mind." He set the cup in her hand and she smiled tentatively, like a kitten unsure if the outreached hand was safe. He was used to women taking, taking, taking, seemingly without a care of who they were taking from. Her cautiousness intrigued him.

"Thank you. That's sweet of you." She took the cup. "Are you sure?"

Cole smiled. "Yeah, I'm sure. I'll just grab a muffin. I hope your friend likes it."

He walked toward the pastry counter to grab a muffin and she followed him over. Her eyes sailed over the muffin labels as Cole snagged a piece of wax paper and reached for the last of his favorite muffins.

"Oh, I need to find the low-fat cranberry walnut muffins. That's Tegan's favorite."

He stopped midreach and laughed softly. *Are you kidding me?* If she weren't so sexy and sweet, he might not relinquish his favorite treats so easily. "Really? Cranberry walnut?"

She trapped her lower lip, reining in a guilty smile, and nodded.

He placed the muffin in a bag and handed it to her.

"Thanks, but now I feel even worse. First I take your coffee, and now..." She looked down at the bag and pushed the coffee cup back into his hand. "Here, you take this and she can have the muffin."

"No. Don't be silly." He put a low-fat blueberry muffin into a bag for himself. "You've got one lucky friend." He followed her into line. "I haven't seen you in here before."

"I'm just here for a few weeks." She eyed the coffee and bag again and said, "Unfortunately, for you, I guess, since I'm taking your goodies."

Now, there was an idea. He'd love to share his *goodies* with her.

"Hardly." He held her gaze until Jasmine cleared her throat, indicating that they were holding up the line. The blonde's cheeks flushed as she stepped up to the counter and set the items down.

Jasmine rang them up and smiled at her. "That'll be eight forty-nine."

The blonde patted her butt, like she was searching for her nonexistent pocket.

"Ohmygod."

Cole shook his head as she turned a deeper shade of red. "I've got this, Jasmine." He set his bag on the counter and pulled out his wallet. "You should probably tell me your name. I don't usually buy breakfast for women I don't know."

She covered her face with her hand and a cute groan slipped through her fingers, making Cole wonder what she might sound like if those groans were moans of pleasure instead. He couldn't remember the last time he'd been interested in a woman right off the bat like this, but this flustered blonde with the killer figure piqued his curiosity.

"Um…" Her eyes coasted over his face, as if she were weighing her answer. "Leesa, with two e's. Thank you so much…?"

"Cole."

"Cole, thank you. If you tell me where I can reach you, I promise to repay you."

"Now, that's a great pickup line," Jasmine said with an arched brow as she handed Cole his change and then turned her attention to the next customer.

"No," Leesa said quickly. "Really, it wasn't a pickup line. I went for a run at the beach and I was driving by and thought I'd bring my friend something, and I must have left my money at home."

"Thanks, Jazz." Cole handed Leesa the coffee cup and bag and they headed for the door. "Relax. She's just giving me a hard time. We went to school together."

He held the door open for her, squinting against the harsh sun, and checked his watch. His appointments began in ten minutes. He had to get back to the office.

"Let me see if I have my purse in the car." She pointed to a yellow Cabriolet convertible.

"Cute car, but I think I can handle spending a few bucks on you."

"On my *friend*," she corrected him.

"On your friend. *Right*. You think I'm still buying that?"

"Ohmygod. It's *really* for her."

He liked the way her cheeks pinked up and her eyes went hot when she got flustered. He debated asking for her number, but he wasn't in the habit of picking up tourists around his small hometown—even beautiful ones.

He leaned in close, trying to ignore the heat simmering between them, and said, "Relax. I just like how you look when you're riled up. It was nice to meet you, Leesa with two e's. Enjoy Peaceful Harbor."

AN HOUR LATER Leesa and her friend Tegan were sitting in the waiting room of Peaceful Harbor Pain Management Center, waiting to have Tegan's cast removed from her ankle. She'd broken her ankle while playing with her niece at a park several weeks ago, and Tegan had made no bones about the inconvenience of the darn thing. Not that Leesa minded. They'd been college roommates and had been each other's sounding boards about everything from schoolwork and men to shoes and, eventually, their careers. Tegan was like the sister she'd never had, and she was thankful for her friendship and support. Listening to her bitch about a cast was nothing compared to the hours Tegan had endured listening to Leesa over the weeks before she'd come to visit.

Leesa flipped through a magazine, trying to quiet her mind. She had taken a cold shower after her run-in with that smokin'-hot guy Cole, but it had done nothing to temper her quickening pulse at the thought of him, and it was driving her crazy. Her life was completely upside down at the moment, and she definitely wasn't looking for a man. But that didn't stop thoughts of his smoldering dark eyes, his deep voice, or his low laugh, which sounded so genuine that it made her smile, too. She hadn't had a reason to smile in weeks, and she had to admit that when she'd felt his heated gaze on her and he'd looked at her like she was an attractive woman when most of the people back home wouldn't even look at her, it felt utterly fantastic.

"You look like you're off on cloud nine," Tegan said as she flipped through a magazine. "Still thinking of Mr. Tall Dark and Helpful?"

"No," she said too sharply. Tegan's exaggerated eye roll told her that she wasn't buying it.

"Annalise."

Leesa scowled at her and whispered, "*Leesa*, please." She'd been using the name *Leesa* only since she'd arrived in Peaceful

Harbor. Despite Tegan assuring her that no one here would have heard about what she went through back in Towson, Annalise wasn't taking any chances—and so she'd become *Leesa*. At least for now.

"Okay, sorry. Then that can mean only that you're thinking about the loser kid who ruined your life." She closed the magazine and set it aside. "Want to talk about it?"

"I'm sick of talking about it, Teg. I've lived it for too long already. Weeks of investigations, interviews, endless questions, defending myself against something I didn't do. I didn't just lose my career. I also lost the Girl Power group I ran, and you know how I loved that." Girl Power was a confidence- and self-esteem-building group for girls, which she'd run a chapter of for several years. She missed the girls terribly. Thankfully, her friend Patty, who had helped her run the group, had taken it over. Leesa wished she could forget the last few weeks of her life, but how could she when she'd worked hard to become a teacher and then one false accusation from a twelve-year-old boy had stolen it—and her almost two-year relationship with Chris Megraw—away. She felt sick even thinking about being accused of fondling a student.

"Yes, you did, but you won. The charges were dropped," Tegan reminded her.

"I'm not sure there's any winning or losing in that situation. In the eyes of everyone in Towson—the town where I grew up, for God's sake—I'm forever tainted." Leesa had built a great reputation as a seventh-grade English teacher, had a strong support system of friends and peers, and she'd thought she had a boyfriend who loved her. What a farce *that* was. She'd been put on administrative leave and endured an invasive investigation. By the time the investigators declared the accusations unfounded and the charges were dropped, enough seeds of doubt had been planted that she saw questions in the eyes of even her strongest supporters—or she thought she did. She was smart enough to know that what she'd gone through could have just screwed up her perception. But really, she wouldn't blame anyone for wondering. It was the boy's word against hers.

Tegan took her hand and gave it a gentle squeeze. "That's why you're here. To start over."

"I don't know if I'm actually *starting over* here. I still have the offer for the position in Baltimore to decide on, but I'm hoping a few weeks of being here will give me some answers. I just need time to breathe. To process it all and put some space between me and what happened."

"You're *starting over*," Tegan insisted. "I know they offered you another teaching position in Baltimore, but, Anna— *Leesa*—you don't know anyone in Baltimore. Here you've got me." She batted her eyelashes, and Leesa's heart tugged at how much Tegan's belief in her innocence meant to her. "Besides, no one here knows about any of that, and they won't care, because you weren't guilty. That little prick tried to ruin you, but he didn't. You're here, you're whole, and you're starting over."

She cringed at the words *little prick*. Andy Darren, the twelve-year-old boy who had accused her of inappropriately touching him, had never admitted he'd lied, but Leesa still didn't harbor ill feelings toward him.

"It's not Andy's fault. He's a kid. He had no idea about the impact his lies would have on my life."

She was angry at the situation, but Andy had opened up his young heart to her and admitted that he'd had a crush on her, and she'd turned him away. She'd done it in a professional, kind manner, but still, it had probably stung. Maybe if she *could* have hard feelings toward the boy, it would be easier for her to move past what happened, but she simply couldn't muster them. She'd begun tutoring him after a car hit him and left him with two broken legs, broken ribs, a fractured hip, and a fractured hand. He had a long recovery time ahead of him. He was going through a treacherous time, set apart from all his friends, unsure about regaining his ability to walk and the full use of his hand, while trying to maintain his grades. He was angry and depressed, and Leesa had been so focused on their private tutoring sessions, helping him remain on grade level so he wouldn't fall behind his friends in school, that she hadn't thought he was serious when he'd told her that she'd *pay* for turning him away. She'd thought he was just upset and would get over it by their next session.

Now she worried that the guilt from lying would eventually take a heavy toll on him. This wasn't a tiny lie, like eating the last cookie and blaming it on the dog. This was a lie that had the force of a tsunami, and it had wiped away her life. She couldn't imagine that a lie like that would sit well inside anyone with a conscience, and she knew Andy had a good conscience. Even after his accident he had worried about the people in the car that had hit him as much as he'd worried about himself. She carried the worry over how the lie would affect Andy with her on a daily basis. No one else would worry about that, would they? Even his parents wouldn't know to look for signs of guilt eating away at him. After all, she and Andy were the only ones who were there that afternoon, and they both knew the truth, despite what he'd said to the investigators.

She tried to push away thoughts of Andy and focus on the part of her life that she hadn't expected to lose in the aftermath.

"And I lost Chris."

She and Chris had been dating for almost two years. When she'd first told him about the accusation, he'd been livid with Andy, but Chris taught at the same middle school, and as the investigation became public, he'd quickly begun worrying more about what his association with Leesa would do to his own career and less about what she was going through. Within a week, he'd ended their relationship, shattering not only her heart, but her belief in trust, loyalty, and love—all the things she'd relied upon her whole life. And to top it all off, two years earlier she'd lost her father, who was the one person who had always been there for her. He'd been her rock, the epitome of a man she could trust, whose love and loyalty were ever-present. But she'd lost him to a brain aneurysm that had led to a stroke.

"Another little prick," Tegan said with anger in her blue eyes. She must have seen the hurt in Leesa's expression, because she added, "Chris never deserved you in the first place. What kind of man puts himself above the woman he loves? I'm sorry, but that's not true love, and you know it."

A nurse entered the lobby from a hallway beside the registration desk and called Tegan's name.

"Come on." Tegan rose from the chair. "Check out the hottie doctor who put my cast on. I promise you, *he* will delete Chris's face from your memory forever."

They followed the petite nurse into an exam room, where Tegan promptly sat on the exam table, the paper beneath her crinkling loudly.

Leesa paced, still thinking about all she'd lost. She'd been in Peaceful Harbor for the past two weeks, and she'd already found a waitressing job at Mr. B's, a microbrewery down by the marina, which Tegan wasn't thrilled about. She thought Leesa should jump right back into something that had to do with teaching, but Leesa wasn't ready to be anywhere near children. She'd waitressed throughout college, and she enjoyed the contact with people and the less rigid hours. Besides, surely as a waitress she couldn't be accused of doing anything inappropriate. She was right out in the open where everyone could see her at all times, and she really liked the people she was working for. She cringed inside at the reality that she even had to think about being *seen* as inappropriate.

Maybe she'd been stupid to tutor Andy in his home, but she'd loved teaching, and she'd loved all of her students, and she knew with the right guidance Andy could keep up with the class. She also knew that the thought of having to repeat the year was devastating to him and certainly to his overbearing father. His mother was quiet as a mouse, and Leesa never knew what to think of her.

"Sit down. You're making me nervous." Tegan patted the paper covering the exam table. "Want to sit next to me?"

She laughed. "No. I'm not ten years old, thank you very much. I just wish we hadn't talked about all that stuff. I need to put it behind me."

Tegan's eyes skipped to the door as it pushed open and the tall, broad-shouldered, impossibly handsome man who had given Leesa his coffee and muffin earlier that morning walked in, sucking all the air from the room.

His dark eyes lifted from the chart he was reading. "Tegan, nice to see you again." His gaze shifted to Leesa, and a slow, sexy smile curved his full lips and sent her stomach into a tizzy. "Well, I'll be...Leesa with two e's, how are you?"

It took her a second to realize he'd said her new name, and she could have sworn she heard a hint of desire in the way it slid

11

off his tongue. She silently chastised herself, knowing that was not only nuts, but also something she should not be thinking about. Hadn't she learned her lesson with Chris? Cole didn't need a woman with a past like hers in his life—and if he ever found out, he'd probably tell her that himself.

"So, Leesa. Are you stalking me? Because lunch isn't for a few hours yet, but if you're hungry and need a few bucks..." He reached for his wallet and smiled with the tease.

Tegan's eyes darted between them. "You're the guy who bought my breakfast?"

"You're the woman who ate my breakfast?" He arched a brow, and Leesa was struck by the glint of humor in his eyes.

"I guess so." Tegan slid a look of approval to Leesa that Leesa had seen hundreds of times when they were college roommates.

Leesa pulled her wallet from her purse. "I have money to pay you back." She thrust a ten-dollar bill toward him.

Cole eyed the money and said in a low, entirely too seductive tone, "As I said, it was my pleasure. Hold on to your money." Their eyes held long enough for Leesa's mind to catalog his thick dark brows, sharp jawline, and angular nose. His cheeks held the dark shadow of manliness that she imagined would scruff up deliciously by dinnertime. Even with his dress shirt covering his body, she could see he was athletically fit without being overly muscular. His dark slacks hung to a pair of black leather shoes, classy but not too flashy. She wondered what he'd look like in a worn pair of jeans with bare feet, and with that thought, she realized she was staring and tore her eyes away.

As if he realized he'd crossed an invisible line with a patient present, he cleared his throat and set the chart down on the counter. When he looked up again, his gaze was as professional and serious as it had been when he'd first entered the room.

"So, can we get this thing off?" Tegan asked.

Leesa shoved her money back in her purse as Cole turned his attention to her friend.

"Yes, let's get this puppy off of you and see how you've healed up."

Breathe, Leesa, breathe.

She listened to Cole and Tegan discuss how her ankle was feeling as a nurse came in and began removing the cast. Cole told Tegan about the physical therapy she'd need to strengthen her ankle and leg again.

"Leesa's staying with me," Tegan said. "She can help me with the therapy."

"You really need a licensed physical therapist to work with you," Cole said, then smiled at Leesa. "No offense, but proper care is important."

Tegan sighed. "She took massage therapy classes during college. Doesn't that count?"

Leesa scoffed.

"Probably, if you're looking for a good masseuse. We recommend working with licensed physical therapists. But if you're really against it, I can have our therapist give you a list of the exercises to do at home."

Leesa admired his professionalism as he answered Tegan's questions about whether she could drive, dance, and exercise.

"You were lucky. You had a simple, barely displaced oblique fracture of the distal fibula. Your PT time shouldn't be too long, but you need to go easy until you strengthen your muscles again. I'd hold off on doing anything too strenuous for the next few weeks." He glanced at Leesa, his eyes serious again. "It was a simple fracture, but pushing any injury through recovery can lead to other issues."

She tried to concentrate on what he was saying, but how could she when his eyes bored into her and the whole room heated up every time their eyes met. "I'll make sure she takes it slow." *What? I will?* She had no idea why she was even speaking.

He smiled again and his eyes warmed, as if she were talking about them instead of Tegan's injury. Embarrassed by the thought, she glanced at Tegan, who was looking at her with a curious grin. God, what was wrong with her? This was Tegan's *doctor.* She had no business even thinking about him in that way, especially given where she was with her life right now.

Leesa spent the rest of the visit trying not to notice Dr. Cole Braden's super-fine ass when he leaned on the counter to write in the chart or the way his eyes lingered on her until she had no choice but to meet his gaze.

"So no dancing at the annual bachelor auction? That should be fun." Sarcasm dripped from Tegan's voice.

Cole laughed under his breath as he'd done in the café. It was a nice sound, masculine and playful, and it made Leesa smile.

"I'm sure the bachelor you win won't mind slow dancing," he assured her. In a more serious tone, he said, "Tegan, use the walking boot, and if you have any unusual pain or questions, call the office." He turned to Leesa and said with a hint of wickedness in his eyes, "And if you need breakfast tomorrow, I'll be at Jazzy Joe's early."

When he left the room, Leesa exhaled the breath she'd been holding.

"What the hell did I just witness?" Tegan asked as she reached for the door.

"Nothing." *Everything.* She shook her head to try to clear the image of his handsome face from her mind. She couldn't afford to be focused on anything but getting her life back together.

Chapter Two

COLE SET ASIDE his computer and rose from the chair where he'd been reviewing patient files. Concentrating was a futile effort. He hadn't been able to stop thinking about Leesa since he'd met her at Jazzy Joe's. He looked out over the deck of his waterfront home, wondering why she was still on his mind. He'd worked all day, spent two hours sanding the sailboat with his father and Sam, one of his younger brothers, and still she was front and center in his thoughts. She was beautiful and incredibly cute when she was nervous, the way she blinked up at him from beneath her wispy blond bangs, and she had a killer body, not stick skinny like so many women around the harbor. She had hips he was dying to feel beneath his hands. But there were plenty of women with nice bodies; that wasn't something that usually held his attention this long. There was more to her. He'd felt it the first time they'd met, when he'd caught sight of her intelligent green eyes, which held a strange mix of caution and seduction.

He pulled his vibrating cell phone from his pocket and read a text from Mackenna Klein, the woman he'd dated for two years before he'd left for medical school.

Can't we forget the bad stuff and catch up? For old times' sake?

She'd texted him a number of times over the last few days, and he had yet to respond with more than a few words, none of which should encourage a get-together. He hadn't seen her in years, and he wanted to keep it that way. He had no idea why she was coming back to Peaceful Harbor, and hoped it was a temporary move. He'd thought she was *it* for him. The woman he'd love for the rest of his life. But she'd shattered that hope the summer before he left for medical school, when she'd said she wanted an open relationship. She wanted to sow her wild oats and wanted him to do the same. The problem was, Cole hadn't started dating her until he was twenty, and he'd had his fill of fast women and too much to drink. He wasn't looking for more of the same. His heart had been wrapped up in Kenna— but somewhere along the way, she'd forgotten about her heart altogether.

Cole had no interest in being someone's fallback plan.

He shoved his phone in his pocket without responding to the text and walked down to the beach. He loved the sounds of the waves at night, the cool sand beneath his bare feet. He'd grown up in Peaceful Harbor, and he'd always known that he'd return and settle down in the small town, with its community days, fall festival, and winter wonderland carnival. His parents owned a microbrewery in town, along with several others on the East Coast, and each of his five siblings had also settled in the area. Although his youngest brother, Ty, a professional photographer and world-renowned mountain climber, traveled so often they only caught up between trips.

He walked down toward the water and sat in the sand, watching the moon's reflection dance across the rippling water and thinking about his life. He had a good life, a warm and wonderful family, and an enviable medical practice. Hell, he even got along famously with his boisterous business partner, Jon Butterscotch, where many of the docs he knew weren't as lucky.

Cole wanted for nothing.

Almost.

The truth was, he missed having someone special in his life. He dated plenty of women, but something was always missing, and he was smart enough to know that when his brothers gave him a hard time about being too damn picky, they were probably right. That is, if wanting to find a woman who was as serious as she was funny, as intelligent as she was sensual, was too picky. He wasn't looking for a model. He was looking for a woman with a brain—a smart woman was a hundred times sexier than a sexy bimbo. Then he had the issue of finding someone who was intellectually stimulating and didn't want him for his status in the small town or for his family's wealth.

His phone rang, and he pulled it from his pocket, hoping it wasn't Kenna. She had yet to actually call instead of text, but he assumed that she eventually would, and he wasn't looking forward to that conversation. She never gave up easily.

He was pleasantly surprised to see the name of his youngest sister, Shannon, on the screen.

"Hey, sis, how's it going?"

"Really, really good, Cole, but I miss you guys." Shannon was a year younger than Ty. She was staying at their uncle Hal's ranch in Weston, Colorado, while working on a project monitoring red foxes, and she'd already been gone for several weeks.

"We all miss you, too. How's the project? Are you having fun with everyone out there?" Hal had six children, though only Rex and Treat lived in Colorado. Rex helped run their family horse ranch, and Treat owned several resorts all over the world. Treat was married with two children, and Rex had recently married his longtime girlfriend, Jade, and they were expecting their first child.

"Yes. It's great to see everyone, and I'm working with Jade's brother, Steve, on the project next month, so I'm looking forward to that, too. Oh my God, Cole, you have got to see Treat and Max's kids! I wish you guys would hurry up and get married and have babies so I could have nieces and nephews to play with." Shannon laughed, and Cole pictured her dark eyes wide with excitement. Shannon had a zest for life that came with a knack for nosing into her siblings' love lives. Cole had a feeling that if she could, she'd direct their love lives like a cruise director facilitated activities. He smiled at the notion.

"Well, Nate's on his way now that he and Jewel are living together. I bet they'll tie the knot before too long." Jewel, their brother Nate's girlfriend, had recently moved in with him. He'd been in love with her for years, but he'd also been her older brother Rick's best friend. Nate and Rick had enrolled in the military together, and when Rick was killed overseas, a piece of Nate had died, too. It had been a long road back for Nate, and Jewel's love had pulled him through.

"How about you, big brother? Any beach bunnies in your life?"

"You've only been gone a few weeks. Not much has changed, Shannon. Except Dad's sailboat. We're all working on getting it in shape." He rubbed his elbow, which was aching from the constant pressure of the sanding he'd done earlier. When Cole was in high school he'd been an all-star pitcher. He'd even contemplated going into pro sports rather than the medical field, but thanks to a coach from hell—and his own obsessive drive to be the best in everything he did—he'd given in to playing through a torn ulnar collateral ligament in his elbow. After rehabbing his elbow back into shape, he'd given up on the idea of pursuing a sports career, foreseeing more overuse injuries in his future and a short pitching career, and had gone into medicine instead. He figured if he couldn't play, he could at least heal those who could.

"I know. Sammy told me, and he also said that you're still working your butt off. Don't you remember the talk we had before I left?" The tease in her voice made him smile. She was always lecturing Cole about how he'd never find a woman if he was always working. "I swear, when I'm home for the charity auction, I'm finding you a date. Maybe we should auction you off instead of Sam."

"Yeah, that's not happening, sis." Every year the town held a bachelor auction fundraiser. Funds from the auction went to the local homeless shelter, and this year their parents were hosting it at Mr. B's, the microbrewery they owned by the marina.

"Well, Sammy hardly needs auctioning off. He's got women lining up to go out with him. You, on the other hand…"

As picky as Cole was, Sam was the polar opposite. His idea of a fun night was a blonde and a brunette for dinner and a redhead for dessert. He was smart as a whip, kind as the day was long, and though he was in his late twenties, he was as horny as a teenager. Of all his siblings, Sam was the one Cole expected would never settle down.

Cole rubbed his elbow and glanced down the beach, catching sight of a woman walking along the shore. She had something in her hand, and when she stopped to gaze out over the water, she hugged whatever it was to her chest. He watched her for a minute, feeling a tug of familiarity, and he realized it was hope he felt. Hope that it was Leesa.

Damn, she'd done a job on his brain. He shifted his gaze away and turned his attention back to the conversation with Shannon, who was saying that she needed to call Nate. They talked for a few more minutes, and after ending the call, Cole thought about what she'd said. His siblings were great at taking time off to enjoy life, but Cole didn't settle down easily. When he wasn't at work, he was thinking about it, researching, reading journal articles, staying up–to-date on the latest medical findings and treatments. It's what he'd always done—worked harder than everyone else to be the best at what he did.

He rose to his feet as the woman down the beach came into focus. *Leesa.* He felt as though he'd conjured her up and smiled at the coincidence. She froze, still as a stone, as if she'd just recognized him, too.

"Leesa?" He closed the distance between them. She was dressed in a pair of jeans, rolled up above her ankles, and a loose sweater. Her hair cascaded over her shoulders in natural golden waves, giving her a softer, even more feminine look than she'd had earlier in the day. And her eyes, those gloriously green havens of emotion, once again perplexed him as they darted away. He couldn't decide if she was shy or evasive.

"Hi." She tucked a notebook beneath her arm, slid her fingers into her pockets, and shrugged her shoulders. "Are you out for a walk, too?"

"I was out for a sit, actually." He pointed to his house on the dune. "I live there. How about you? You're staying with Tegan? Does she live nearby?" He realized that just seeing her again made his body thrum with desire. It had been too long since he'd been this attracted to a woman, and man, did he like the tripping of his heart and the heat coursing through his veins.

"She lives on Second Street." She pointed back the way she'd come. "It's not far from the beach." She shrugged her shoulders again with another tentative smile, and he realized that the look in her eyes was one of careful assessment rather than shyness.

"I know Second Street. I grew up here." He lifted his chin toward his house. "Want to come up for a glass of wine?"

She crossed her arms over her chest and shifted her gaze to the water. "Um, no, thanks. I don't think that's a good idea. I mean, I barely know you."

He smiled. *Careful, definitely careful.* "True. A walk, then?"

She looked up and down the beach, then back at him with a genuine smile this time. "Sure."

They walked in silence for a few minutes, and Cole tried to focus on the sounds of the breaking waves and the breeze as it tickled over his skin, instead of Leesa's sweet scent, but even the salty sea air that he loved so much couldn't distract him from his attraction to her.

"So, what brought you to Peaceful Harbor?"

She didn't answer for a few minutes, and although Cole didn't push her, he'd learned to read as much into what people didn't say as what they did. He wondered what she was hiding.

"I needed a change, and Tegan suggested I visit to see if this was someplace I'd like to move to."

"Where are you from?" Her brows knitted together, and he said, "You don't have to share that with me."

"It's okay. I don't really like to talk about myself very much. I'm from Towson."

He changed the subject to try to put her at ease. "What do you think of Peaceful Harbor?"

She stopped walking and stared out at the water again. "It's pretty here. A world away from Towson even though it's only a few hours away."

"Want to sit and talk?" He reached for her hand without thinking and felt her fingers stiffen.

She looked at their hands, then sank down beside him in the sand, leaving a good six or eight inches between them. She set the notebook in her lap and pulled her knees up to her chest. Sometimes Cole wished he didn't read so much into what the actions or silence of others meant, but that came with being a physician. He learned as much from a person's facial expressions and breathing as he did from their words, and Leesa's discomfort was palpable. He hadn't meant to make her uncomfortable, but he definitely wanted her right there beside him.

"Sorry for grabbing your hand."

She closed her eyes for a beat and sighed. When she opened them, she met his direct gaze. "I'm sorry. I'm not usually this weird."

"I don't find you weird. Guarded maybe. Beautiful definitely. But not weird." He smiled, and the tension in her face turned to embarrassment. Her lips curved up and she dropped her eyes again.

"What are you usually, if not who you are right now?" Cole asked, intrigued by her evasiveness.

IF I COULD *answer that, my life would be a lot easier. Wrongly accused ex-teacher? Defender of my reputation?* That's what she'd felt like for most of the past year, and even though she knew she was so much more than that, she was having a hard time separating who she'd had to become in order to survive from who she was at heart.

Not wanting to share her past, she told him what she knew to be true. "I'm a nature lover, a runner, and probably not the best friend in the world, since I left Tegan alone to come out by myself tonight. Oh, and a bookaholic."

"A bookaholic? That sounds like serious business." He bumped her knee with the tease. "Is that who you usually are, or just who you are now?"

It was an interesting question, but then again, this was Cole Braden, and in the short time she'd known him, she'd already realized that he wasn't like most men. He had a serious look in his eyes that even when he was flirting never seemed to disappear completely. She liked that about him.

"All those things are who I usually am, except the not-a-great-friend part. I'm usually a really good friend, but tonight I needed a little solitude to think—" Realizing she was revealing more than she was comfortable with, she cut her sentence short.

He leaned back on his palms and crossed his bare feet casually at the ankles. His gray shirt looked soft and cozy and fit snugly across his broad chest. She smiled at the fact that he was wearing jeans, and probably an old, favorite pair, considering the faded thighs and fraying hemline.

"Thinking is good," he said as he turned to meet her gaze and caught her ogling him. His mouth tipped up in a sexy smile.

She didn't shift her eyes away this time. She was caught. What could she do but own up to it? It's not like he'd say something about it. *She hoped.* The thought made her answer quickly, hoping to distract him from her stare.

"What about you, Dr. Braden? Who are you...*usually*, I mean?"

"Good question." He was quiet for a moment as he gazed out at the water, the breaking waves filling the silence. "I guess I'm a brother and son first, a doctor second. A runner, like you, and believe it or not, also a bookaholic. Medical books usually, but books nonetheless."

She liked the bookaholic part. Most of the men she knew were into watching sports on television. Even Chris always seemed to have ESPN on in the background while she read. She set her notebook beside her in the sand and stretched her legs out.

"That's interesting, the order in which you labeled yourself."

"Are you a psychologist?" His eyes narrowed, but he was smiling, and it was a startlingly enticing combination.

"No. A teacher. Why, does it bother you that I noticed that, *Doc*?"

He leaned closer, bringing a heat wave with him. "Bother me? Not in the least. I like that you notice me."

She tried to smile but knew it probably looked more like a nervous twitch.

"What do you think that says about me?" he asked.

"I think you know exactly what it says about you." Their eyes held, and she was glad they were sitting down, because her whole body felt like a wet noodle wanting to melt against him. Lord, he was gorgeous. His dark eyes moved slowly over her face, from her eyes to her mouth, where they lingered for a beat too long, making the heat in her belly coil tight and turn to lust.

He lifted his eyes to hers again. "That I'm a good brother and son?" His voice was low and deep, barely above a whisper.

Leesa felt herself leaning closer, wanting to kiss him, to feel his strong arms around her. She forced herself to lean back, needing the distance to pull herself together. *What the hell is wrong with me?*

"And probably a workaholic," she said as she set her notebook on her lap again, as if that could stop her from touching the man who looked more delicious than an ice cream sundae.

"Maybe so," he admitted.

"How about hobbies? Do you have any?" Hobbies were a safer subject than what was really on her mind, like touching her foot to his just to feel his warm skin, or inching her fingers on top of his in the sand, or pressing her lips to his to taste his mouth. She hadn't kissed a man since Chris, and her feelings for him had never been this intense. Wondering what Cole's lips would feel like—soft and giving or hard and demanding—she knew she'd think of nothing else until she found out.

Lovely. Wanting to make a pass at my best friend's doctor is not going to help my tarnished reputation. She should get up and go back to Tegan's, take an ice-cold shower, and go to bed.

But that thought made her think of Cole...*in the shower, in bed.*

Holy cow! Shut up!

"Right now I'm having a great time with this new hobby of trying to guess what's going on in your mind. Your cheeks are all pink and you're shredding the edge of your notebook."

She'd forgotten that she'd even asked him a question. She stopped fidgeting and set the notebook on the sand beside her.

"That's hardly a hobby," she said as she lifted her chin in feigned confidence.

"Maybe not, but it is fun." He sat up and brushed the sand from his hands. "What's with the notebook?"

She looked down at the notebook that she'd begun keeping with her shortly after being put on leave from teaching, when she'd needed to get thoughts out of her head, and for some reason, the truth came easily.

"My thoughts." She placed her hand on the notebook. His shoulder brushed hers, and when she turned, his face was so close that she could see flecks of gold in his dark eyes. "When did you move closer?"

"When you moved farther away," he said easily.

A tornado kicked up inside her, and he seemed as calm as could be, which made her even more nervous.

"Maybe you shouldn't have." *Seriously? Shut. Up.*

"Maybe not. But I did." He smiled again, holding her gaze. It took every ounce of restraint for her not to lean forward and kiss him.

"That's awfully forward of you," she managed.

"Yeah, it is. And it's awfully out of character for me, too." He leaned away, and she felt a wave of cold air fill the space he'd vacated. "Your thoughts." He nodded at the notebook. "Want to share?"

Never in a million years with anyone. "Not really."

"Okay, then I'll share mine." His gaze never strayed from hers. "I think you're incredibly beautiful, and interesting, in a guarded sort of way. And you should let me take you out to dinner sometime."

Leesa's entire body tingled with the urge to say *Yes!*, but her mind was smarter than the aroused area between her legs, and like it or not, she had to be smart right now. She was just off of the most miserable, terrifying time of her life, and she hadn't yet had a chance to catch her breath. She was still deciding if she was going to make Peaceful Harbor her new home or take the job in Baltimore. She couldn't date anyone—least of all the man Tegan called *one of Peaceful Harbor's most eligible bachelors*— until she sorted through her own situation and figured out if being seen with her would cause trouble for him.

As much as she wanted to accept his offer for dinner, she couldn't. She wasn't sure she'd ever be able to trust any man after the way Chris had abandoned her.

"I'm not really in a good place to date right now." She looked out at the sea. "Besides, I'm over promises of forever and all that." *Oh shit.* She hadn't meant to say that out loud.

A soft laugh escaped his lips. "I only want to promise you dinner."

"You're tempting. Sweet, generous, cute, easy to talk to...but I can't. Thank you anyway." *There, I did it.* Now she could go about her work at Mr. B's, where they were hosting a bachelor auction tomorrow night, and try to blend in. Become invisible. Invisible was so much better than the hell she'd just come out of. Her bosses, Maisy and Ace Braden, had told her that things would be crazy during the auction.

Oh shit. Braden. The realization spilled from her lips like an excuse.

"I think I work for your parents."

His smile widened. "My parents? You work at Mr. B's?"

"Yes. I'm waitressing there." Her pulse was racing as he nodded, as if he was going to accept that as her reason.

"But I thought you were a teacher." His eyes went serious again.

"Yes, but I'm not teaching. I wanted a change." She shrugged like it was what every woman did when her life fell apart.

He sat up a little taller, and his voice turned serious. "Why would you make such a drastic change? Didn't you enjoy teaching?"

"I loved every minute of it." *Until Andy Darren decided to ruin it for me.*

"Then why stop? You said you were only here for a few weeks. Are you vacationing?"

"Sort of."

"Sort of? Escaping a crazy ex or something?"

Or something. She lowered her eyes for a beat as she considered her answer. *Escaping craziness, yeah, that's it.* "No. That's a strange question."

He arched a brow. "Is it?"

She pushed to her feet, because what else could she do? Sit there and debate her life? No, it wasn't a strange question, but it wasn't one she wanted to answer, either.

"I should be going." What was she thinking, telling him she loved her job and in the next breath saying she needed a change. *Who did that?* People who were running from something or someone. Or hippies who lived life like tomorrow might never come. She was definitely not one of those people. She'd liked her predictable life before the nightmare began. Her morning runs, classes throughout the day, dinners by candlelight even when she was alone because it made her relax and savor the moment, and then hours of escaping into a fictional world.

Cole rose beside her and touched her hand again. This time she didn't pull away, although she knew she should now more than ever. But the look in his eyes was warm with concern as he stepped in closer and circled her fingers with his.

"Just tell me one thing." He searched her eyes, and her pulse quickened as she silently hoped he wasn't going to ask her if she was Annalise Avalon. "Is whatever—or whoever—you're not running from something you need help with?"

She felt her jaw drop open but didn't have a clear enough head to close it. Everything fell away except the kindness in his eyes, which seemed to swallow her whole.

He brushed her hair from her shoulder, and it was such a tender, intimate thing to do that it startled her back to his question.

She dropped her eyes in an effort to center her thoughts, because his eyes were dangerously alluring in a safe and seductive way, which made their threat even harder to escape. Especially since she didn't want to escape them.

But she had to.

For his sake.

"No," she finally managed. She blinked up at him through the cover of her bangs and withdrew her fingers from his grasp, instantly missing them. She had Tegan's support, and even though she had no family to fall back on, she hadn't realized how alone she'd felt in the nightmare that had become her life until that very second. She wanted this connection with this wonderful man so badly it frightened her.

He must have seen it written all over her face, because he gave her arm a gentle squeeze and said, "Okay, but I'm here if you need someone to talk to, or you just want to take a walk."

"Thank you." She took a step away, needing the space to gather her thoughts again. Her past was dangling off the edge of her tongue, trying to reveal itself. Did he have that trusting effect on everyone? She'd never felt so comfortable—or so disarmed—by anyone.

He slid his hands in his pockets and smiled. "Can I walk you back to Tegan's?"

Oh God, yes, please.

"No, thank you. I…Thank you for the offer." She felt his eyes on her as she turned and headed back the way she'd come, and at the exact second she stopped to thank him again, he called her name—her new name, which went along with her new life—*Leesa.*

She turned and found him smiling, his eyes still warm and welcoming. One hand slipped from his pocket, and he wiggled his fingers in a silent wave.

"Thanks for spending some of your alone time with me. Think about it. The date, I mean."

She couldn't find her voice but managed a grateful smile and a nod before starting down the beach again, wondering why walking away from Towson, where she'd lived for twenty-seven years, was easier than walking away from a man she'd just met.

Chapter Three

"FIFTY SHADES OF sweetness at your service." Jon Butterscotch, Cole's business partner, stood on Cole's front porch bright and early Saturday morning for their weekend run. His longish dirty-blond hair was still wet from his shower and finger combed, making him look more like a surfer than a doctor. They'd met in medical school, and at first sight—Cole, with his short-cropped hair and collared shirt, and Jon in board shorts and a tank top—were as different as could be. But they'd quickly learned that appearances didn't mean shit when it came to work ethic and motivation. They were as alike in their determination as they were in their career goals, and they'd been best buddies ever since that first meeting. Jon was as flamboyant as Cole was serious, and at the moment the bare-chested, overly tanned doctor was beating his fists against his muscular chest and grinning like he'd just found the treatment for cancer.

Cole shook his head. "Fifty shades of *way too early for this*, maybe."

"Shit." Jon scoffed. "I'm going to raise so much money for the homeless, you'll wish you'd been a slave to your body the way I have been to mine these last few months." He crooked his arms and flexed his biceps. "Go ahead. Touch 'em."

"Thanks, but I'll let you know when I get the urge to feel up a guy." Cole stepped off the porch. "Are we going for a run or what?"

"Hell yeah, we're running. I've got to be in prime shape for the auction." They took off down the dune to the beach and headed toward town for their six-mile run.

"I still can't believe you're doing that. Why don't you just donate like I do?" Cole had no interest in putting his body on display for a roomful of random women, most of whom he'd grown up with. Jon, like Cole's brother Sam, would take any and all attention he could get.

"What fun is there in that? You keep that killer bod of yours hidden all the time; you bury your nose in your books at night. When are you going to go out and get some snatch?"

"Snatch? Okay, Madonna. You've known me for how long?" Cole shook his head. "You know I'm done with one-night stands. I'm looking for more."

"Snatch *is* more."

Cole laughed as they ran down the beach. "Do people even use that word anymore?"

It was only seven o'clock in the morning, and already families were making their way across the dunes. Cole watched a young father spread a blanket out while his wife cradled a baby in her arms and a toddler sat in the sand beside her. That was what Cole wanted.

Jon rambled on about the glory of women's bodies and the young father yawned up at the morning sun.

"*That's* more, Jon." Cole nodded toward the family as they jogged past.

"Seriously? You're going to go from workaholic to married with children?"

"I've had my fill of game playing."

"That you have," Jon agreed. "But I've still got plenty of wild oats left to sow for the both of us."

He and Jon had gone carousing together more times than Cole could remember, but Cole's work had always taken priority over his social life. When he was in medical school, he'd studied every night and kept his social calendar to the weekends, having sowed enough wild oats for twelve men before dating Kenna. Since starting his practice, he'd been focused on growing the business, and now that he had a steady practice, he was ready to think about the part of his life he'd been ignoring.

They jogged past Mr. B's and the marina, where boats were leaving wavy wakes as they made their way out to sea, and continued toward the pier that marked the halfway point in their run. The morning sun, now high in the sky, beat down on their heated bodies as they headed up Main Street. Sunlight reflected off the windows of the shops. Joey was straightening tables in front of the café and waved as they passed by.

They talked about their practice and sports, falling quiet as they turned down Eighth Street and headed back toward Cole's house.

"Hey, check it out." Jon nodded toward Leesa, jogging half a block ahead of them, wearing a pair of skimpy blue shorts and another clingy tank top.

This was the fourth time Cole had seen her in two days. Was the universe trying to tell him something? *Guess what, God? You've got my full attention.* He watched her run. Her hair was pinned up in a ponytail, swinging with every footfall. Her strides were long and even, her tanned skin glistened with sweat, and Cole felt the blood in his head rush south.

"Now, that's one fine ass," Jon said.

The blood rushed back up to Cole's brain, kicking his possessive urges into high gear. He tugged Jon's arm and pulled him down the next side street.

"What the hell, man?" Jon snapped. "I was enjoying the view."

Cole debated making up an excuse and decided he'd be better off giving Jon a hard limit. Even though Leesa wasn't his to claim, he wanted that line drawn in Jon's mind.

"I asked her out last night."

"Ah, so you're not totally out of the game after all." Jon's brows lifted in quick succession.

This feels like anything but a game.

IT DIDN'T TAKE long for Leesa to fall into the swing of things at Mr. B's. She'd been waitressing there for a few days, and already she'd gotten to know a number of the regular customers. The brewery overlooked the marina, allowing Leesa to really feel the difference between working in Towson and working here. It was almost seven, and the restaurant was already packed. The other waiters and waitresses had warned her that by the time the auction started there would barely be room to maneuver between tables. She was glad for the distraction, after a fitful night's sleep. Last night, after she'd gotten home from her walk on the beach, she and Tegan had stayed up talking for hours. Tegan had pushed her to accept Cole's dinner invitation, and the more Leesa claimed not to be interested, the less Tegan believed her. Hell, the less she believed herself. Cole was handsome and charming, and he had the most compassionate eyes she'd ever seen. But she'd been down that path before, and she wasn't about to get tangled up with a doctor who would surely run the other way once he heard about her past.

She tried to push thoughts of Cole away as she served a young couple, and spotted Maisy Braden putting up the final preparations for the bachelor auction. Her thick, curly blond hair fell wild and free past her shoulders. Her long colorful skirt whipped around her legs as she hurried from one side of the restaurant to the other, setting up the tables along a wall of windows.

Now that Leesa knew Maisy and her husband, Thomas, who went by the nickname "Ace," were Cole's parents, she found herself searching for similarities. Maisy's eyes were sea blue and always seemed to be smiling. Cole clearly took after his father. Ace's dark eyes were serious as he watched her approach. Ace was as conservative as Maisy was artsy. Like Cole, he wore his dark hair cropped short and brushed away from his handsome face. Cole shared his height, broad shoulders, and strong features. And, apparently, his style, too, because like his son was wearing when Leesa had first met him, Ace had on dress pants and a white button-down shirt, with the sleeves rolled up, revealing thick forearms and large hands.

Leesa set an order slip on the pass-through for the cook, Roman. "Two BLTs and one tuna on rye, please." She turned to Ace, who was bartending, and he smiled, giving her a good idea of what Cole might look like in another twenty-five years. Leesa felt herself staring, and she shook off the momentary lapse of brain function and said, "Two gin and tonics, please."

"Coming right up." He pulled the bottles from behind the bar and began mixing the drinks. He walked with a slight limp as he moved in the tight space. "Everything going okay for you today?"

"Yes, thank you. The auction starts in an hour, and I can't imagine how we'll fit any more people in the restaurant. I don't know how Maisy set things up so fast."

His eyes followed his wife as she moved from one table to the next. "Maisy's got this down to a science."

Maisy, having heard her name, glanced over and blew him a kiss.

"Our daughters, Shannon and Tempe, will be along shortly to help her finish setting up." He handed her the drinks he'd made. "In fact, you'll meet our whole brood tonight, with the exception of Ty, our youngest. He's off on a photography assignment."

The whole brood? Her pulse quickened at the thought of Cole showing up. As if it weren't enough that she'd be serving half the town tonight and would surely mess up a handful of orders. She gulped down her anxiety and said, "I look forward to it."

Over the next hour the restaurant was so busy that Leesa didn't have time to think about how nervous she was. Men and women filled the tables and just about every space in between. Tegan was there with a few of her girlfriends, sitting at a table by the front of the room, where the auction was going to be held. Leesa balanced a tray with both hands, walking sideways among the crowd toward the booths in the back where she'd just taken a drink order. She broke through the crowd and lowered the tray as a hand touched her arm. She turned, and her breath caught in her throat at the site of Cole's smiling eyes. His mouth was moving, but she couldn't hear him above the din of the customers.

She held up a finger, indicating for him to hold on a second while she served drinks to her customers in the booth.

"Thank you," a handsome dark-haired guy said.

"You're new here," said a pretty blond woman.

"Yes. I just started a few days ago," Leesa answered. "Can I get you anything else?"

A brunette woman sitting beside the blonde smiled up at her. "I think we're good, thanks." Her eyes shifted to Cole, and she squealed and rose from the table. "Finally! You're here!" She stepped in front of Leesa and threw her arms around his neck.

Leesa barely had time to process the unfamiliar spike of jealousy that gripped her before she heard Cole say, "Hi, sis. I've missed you."

Relief swept through her. *Oh my God, what am I thinking?* She tucked the tray beneath her arm and turned to tend to another booth as Cole touched her arm again and leaned in close. He smelled like warm cider and man all wrapped up into one delicious scent, sending her stomach into a tizzy again.

"Hi," she said over the noise of the crowd.

He placed his hand on her hip and leaned in so close their cheeks touched. His voice was deep and intent. "It's nice to see you again. You look beautiful."

She felt her cheeks flush and wasn't sure if it was from the heat of being close to him or his words.

The brunette's dark eyes moved between the two of them, and when she smiled, the resemblance to her mother was uncanny. "Cole, aren't you going to introduce us?"

His hand remained on Leesa's hip, making her even more aware of his close proximity.

"Leesa, this is my sister Shannon. Shannon, this is Leesa." Cole waved his free hand toward the table, keeping his other hand on her. "These are my younger brothers Sam and Nate and my sister Tempest."

The blonde stood and extended a hand. "Tempe, please. It's nice to meet you. Mom and Dad have told me a lot about you."

Oh God. Really? Why would they talk about her to their daughter? "It's nice to meet you. Your parents are really great to work for."

To her surprise, Sam pulled her out of Cole's grasp and into an embrace. "Nice to meet you. Welcome to the Mr. B family."

Cole had a narrow-eyed glare locked on his brother. There was no mistaking the hands-off look he was giving Sam. It thrilled and worried her at once. She shouldn't even be contemplating getting closer to Cole, and yet here she was, reveling in the way he was staking claim to her. Sam's hand remained on Leesa a few seconds longer than necessary, and she could tell that was some sort of tease meant for Cole. She might have laughed when Tempe rolled her eyes and said, "Sammy," if it weren't for the embarrassment heating up her chest.

Nate, whose blond hair was a shade darker than Tempe's, tugged Sam backward with one hard yank and smiled at Leesa. "Ignore Sammy. He's a clingy dude. Nice to meet you." He shoved Sam back down to his seat and shook Leesa's hand over Sam's head. Sam was laughing like this was an everyday occurrence, and from the playful look in the siblings' eyes, she assumed it was. As an only child, she longed for that type of kinship.

"Wow, there sure are a lot of Bradens."

"There's one more. You haven't met our youngest brother, Ty, yet," Nate said. "He's on a photography assignment in Africa for *National Geographic.*"

"Your father told me about him. He must love his work. Are all three of you being auctioned off tonight?" she asked.

A man with sandy blond hair peered over Cole's shoulder

and said, "All four of us. Are you bidding?"

"Three, thank you very much," Cole corrected him. "Leesa, this is my business partner, Jon."

"Nice to meet you," she said.

Jon took her hand between both of his and said, "The pleasure is all mine."

"Ignore him, too," Cole said, placing a hand on Jon's shoulder and pulling him backward. "You'd think he and Sam hadn't ever seen a beautiful woman before."

"Way to embarrass her. Are you bidding tonight, Leesa?" Shannon asked as she sat beside Tempe again.

"Um, no. I'm working, and actually, I should get back to it. It was nice to meet you all."

Cole stepped between her and his partner. "I wish you'd reconsider my offer."

"I...I'd really like to, but I can't." She glanced over his shoulder at Jon and his siblings, who were watching them so intently it made her even more nervous. "I really should get back to work." She turned and headed for Tegan's booth, needing a familiar face to remind her of all the reasons why her insides shouldn't be quivering.

Tegan was sitting with Dina and Chelsea and a blonde Leesa didn't know.

"There she is." Tegan reached for her hand. "It's crazy in here, Annali—"

Leesa's eyes widened.

"*Leesa*," Tegan corrected herself. "How are you holding up?"

"Good, I think." She noticed Sam, Nate, and Jon walking toward the front of the restaurant, where Ace, the auctioneer for tonight, was waving them over.

"Cole?" his father said into the microphone, motioning with

his hands for Cole to join him.

Leesa watched Cole cross the floor, and her stomach tightened at the sight of all the other women watching him, too. He and his father leaned in head-to-head as they talked. Cole shook his head and turned to Sam with an angry expression on his face. Sam and Jon joined Cole and his father, and a heated discussion ensued. Sam and Jon each took one of Cole's arms and pulled him into the line of bachelors, where now three other handsome men had joined them. Cole's jaw clenched, his hands fisted at his sides, and if looks could kill, his brother and business partner would be flat-out by now.

"Looks like he got wrangled into the auction," Tegan said. "You need to bid."

"I am not doing any such thing." With her heart in her throat she tried to tamp down the jealousy that gripped her, sending her pulse into a panic.

"You like Cole?" the blond girl asked.

"What? No. I just met him."

"He's so sweet. I'm Jewel, by the way. Nate's mine." She grinned and said, "I'll bid every cent I have for him."

"Nice to meet you. Nate seems really sweet."

"He is, and so is Cole," Jewel said. "You should definitely bid on him if you like him, because I'm sure tons of other women will be."

Just what she needed, to be jealous of half the town over a man she had no business liking. Her eyes found Cole, turning the annoyance in his eyes to blazing desire. She wondered just how much extra cash she had on hand.

Chapter Four

"POP, I AM *not* being auctioned off," Cole said firmly.

His father held out the printed brochure for the auction, and sure enough, his name was listed as one of the available bachelors. His blood boiled as he turned toward his snickering brother.

"Seriously, Sam?" He closed the distance between them and stood eye to eye with the troublemaker. "Why would you do that?"

Sam's shit-eating grin made Cole want to pound it off of him.

"Everyone needs a little fun in their life. Besides, it wasn't all me. It was Shannon's idea, too." Sam's eyes shifted toward Leesa, who was serving a table of guys while they ogled her.

Cole's hands fisted by his sides as he turned back toward his brother. "This isn't my type of fun, Sam. This is your type of fun." He looked at Nate. "Why are you up here? You think Jewel wants you being won by some other woman?"

Nate winked. "I filled her purse with hundred-dollar bills. There's no chance she'll lose, and the homeless get a good donation from us."

Cole was beat and he knew it. His name was on the brochure; there was no backing out now.

"I'll be right back." He went to the hallway where the ATM machine was located and withdrew cash from two of his accounts, taking the max limit from each. Then he waited until Leesa was done serving the leering men and pulled her aside.

"Hi. Do you want me to get you a drink?" she asked with a teasing smile.

"No." He shoved the money into her hand. "But you can win me so I don't have to go out with someone else."

"What?" Her eyes widened. "No. I told you I can't go out with you."

That wasn't the response he'd hoped for. "You don't have to," he said, even though he hoped she'd change her mind. "Just save me from going out with someone else. I grew up with most of the women here. Trust me. You're saving me from a date I don't want. I'll owe you one." He squeezed her hand and walked away with a smile on his lips, leaving her with a gaping jaw and giving him a little more hope than he'd had when he'd arrived.

"What was that about?" Jon asked when he stepped in line with the rest of the men on the auction stage.

"That was about getting back in the game."

Leesa looked down at the cash in her hands and then back up at him. She shook her head, and he nodded and mouthed, *Please?*

A slow smile spread across her lips as she shook her head again, this time with less determination. She shoved the money in her pocket and turned away.

Ten minutes later his father stepped to the front of the crowd and held up a hand as he spoke. "Welcome to Mr. B's. We're proud to be hosting the twelfth annual Bachelor Auction for the Homeless."

Everyone clapped, women hooted and hollered, and guys whistled and cheered. Cole watched Jon and Sam hamming it up, waving to the crowd, flexing their biceps and flirting with the women in the front, who were waving money in the air. Nate blew a kiss to his girlfriend, Jewel, and Cole tried to locate Leesa, who was nowhere in sight.

"Tonight we're starting off with my own flesh and blood, Sam Braden." Ace motioned for Sam to step forward.

Sam made a show of whipping off his shirt and tossing it toward the outstretched hands of the women standing at the front of the crowd, who squealed with delight.

Ace shook his head and grinned, pride and amusement battling in his dark eyes.

"This is Sam's sixth auction, so most of you ladies are probably familiar with my boy here. Sam owns Rough Riders, a rafting and adventure company." His father read from a pad of paper, and Cole wondered what information had been given about him. "When he's not on the water, he's taking clients on wilderness trips or living the good life, as evident from his year-round tan and muscular physique." He rubbed his hand over his jaw and mumbled, "*Christ*, Sammy."

The crowd laughed.

"Just telling it like it is," Sam said.

"What did he write about me?" Cole whispered to Nate.

Nate shrugged, but the glint of humor in his eyes told him he did know.

"We're opening the bidding at fifty dollars," Ace said. "Do I hear fifty?"

"Fifty!" a redheaded woman yelled.

"Fifty-five!" yelled a blonde.

"Seventy-five!" the redhead hollered.

Sam flexed his muscles, then turned his back to the crowd and wiggled his ass.

Cole laughed and mumbled, "*Christ.*"

"He's just bumping up the bids," Jon said as the crowd cheered.

"One hundred dollars!" a blonde yelled.

Sam's bidding ended at five hundred dollars, and the blonde who won a date with him ran up to the stage wearing the tiniest miniskirt Cole had ever seen, a tank top, and a smile as wide as Texas. She dragged Sam away by a belt loop, accompanied by a loud round of applause.

"Lucky bastard," Jon said as Ace called his name.

Jon took off his shirt and spun it around over his head before tossing it into the crowd. He immediately began posing, as if he were in a bodybuilding competition.

"There's no shyness here, ladies. This is Dr. Jon Butterscotch's fifth auction. Jon is…" Ace consulted the paper again and furrowed his brow. "Who writes this stuff? Dr. Butterscotch is into medicine, fitness, and late-night fun."

"You've got that right," Jon said, laughing as he pointed to the women in the crowd. "Come on, ladies, bid me up!"

Cole spotted Leesa walking out of the kitchen carrying a tray of food. He lost sight of her again as the women in the crowd moved closer to the front, waving money and hollering out their bids.

"And we have a winner, for six hundred and fifty dollars!" Ace clapped as a brunette Cole recognized as having gone to school with Nate ran up to Jon and pulled him toward her table.

His father auctioned off two of the other guys, and by the

time he got to Cole, Cole was stressing out. He hadn't imagined that bidding would go so high, and he'd only given Leesa six hundred bucks. He stepped up to the front, and the women screamed his name and crowded in around him. Cole stepped back, trying to put space between him and the handsy women, while eagerly searching the crowd for Leesa.

"For the first time ever, my eldest son is on the auction box, and I'm not sure how I feel about that." Ace smiled at Cole.

"Me either," Cole mumbled. He recognized most of the women who were waving cash and reaching for him, and although they were attractive, none of them held a candle to Leesa. He finally spotted her standing by Shannon and Tempe, rubbing her hand over the pocket where she'd stowed the cash he'd given her. He silently pled for her to do as he'd asked.

Ace consulted the paper and began reading. "Dr. Braden enjoys sailing, reading, and—"

"Two hundred dollars!" a woman Cole couldn't see yelled from the back of the restaurant, but her voice sent a shiver of memory down his spine. *Kenna*.

He saw Shannon and Tempe both whip their heads in the direction of the voice, and Shannon's narrowing eyes told him he was right.

Another woman yelled, "Two fifty!"

Kenna pushed through the crowd, heading directly for the front, eyes locked on Cole. "Four hundred."

She was just as beautiful as she'd always been, with long auburn hair and big green eyes. Cole's gut ached, because he knew all too well what lay beneath that pretty exterior. A soul that knew nothing about love and loyalty. He searched for Leesa and saw her talking with Tegan.

"Four fifty!" another woman called out.

"Five hundred and fifty dollars." Kenna narrowed her eyes, and the right side of her crimson lips lifted in a smirk that would probably make another man fill with anticipation. It made Cole want to walk off the stage.

Shannon and Tempe pushed to the front of the crowd, looking at him with a question in their eyes. He knew they'd bid on him if he gave them a nod, but there was only one woman he wanted to win this auction, and she was still leaning over the table talking with Tegan and the other girls.

Cole needed to get her attention, and he knew of one sure way to do it. He gripped his shirt just beneath the collar and tore it off, sending buttons flying into the crowd and causing a ruckus of squeals and lewd comments that couldn't be ignored.

Perfect.

Leesa whipped her head around, and Cole grinned at the awestruck look in her eyes. He'd never had to resort to using his body to get a woman's attention, but hell if he wasn't about to do whatever it took. She walked nervously along the edge of the crowd. Cole's pulse kicked up with every step. God, she was gorgeous. She outshined every woman in the place, and she didn't even have to try, but apparently he did. He wasn't the posing type and couldn't stifle laughing at himself as he flexed his biceps and made his pecs dance. He kept his eyes locked on Leesa, so no other woman could mistake who he was posing for.

Leesa, now standing beside Shannon, gripped Shannon's arm, as if she needed to stabilize herself, and when she spoke, her voice was shaky. "Seven hundred and seventy-five dollars."

Kenna turned a venomous stare on Leesa and said, "Eight. Hundred. Dollars."

LEESA'S EYES FLICKED to Cole, standing before the group of hungry women with his Greek-god body on display, a face that should be on the cover of *People*'s Sexiest Man Alive issue, and a look of hope in his eyes meant just for her. Jewel had clued her in on his ex-girlfriend, Mackenna Klein, a few minutes earlier. She didn't know all the details about their long-term relationship or why they'd broken up, but she said there was no way in hell Cole would want to be won by that woman. When Cole had asked Leesa to bid on him, she hadn't been sure she would actually follow through, but after watching him up there in front of all those women and feeling his eyes on her, looking at her like she was the only woman in the room, she could hardly breathe. She hated the idea of not going out with him almost as much as she hated the idea of seeing his happiness deflate when she revealed her past, which she'd have to do if they went out. She couldn't keep something like that from him.

"I have two hundred," Shannon said.

"I've got the same," Tempe said.

The murmurs of the crowd filled her ears, and her heart raced like it never had before. She loved the way his sisters rallied and came to his rescue and quickly debated her next move. If she won him, everyone here would *expect* her to go out with him. Oh, how she wanted to!

She glanced at his ex-girlfriend, who was sending silent hate messages her way, then to Cole's father, whose thick dark brows were knitted, his hands clenched tightly around the paper he was holding, and finally, she shifted her gaze to Cole. The look in his eyes made her warm all over, pulling words she never expected from her lungs.

"One thousand dollars."

The other woman's jaw dropped open, and there was a collective gasp among the crowd.

"For charity," Leesa added with a nervous smile.

Every muscle in Cole's body flexed, but it was the way his smile reached all the way to his eyes that made her heart flip in her chest as his father announced, "And we have a winner!"

Ace took Leesa's hand and pulled her toward Cole. She nearly tripped over her feet as Cole gripped her hand in his and pulled her into his strong arms.

"Thank you. Thank you so much," he said before pressing his lips to hers.

When he kissed her with those soft, warm lips, she had a feeling it took him by surprise as much as it surprised her. It was only a few hot, perfect seconds, but it was enough to make her entire body ignite, not to mention short-circuit her brain. It had been so long since she'd had anything wonderful happen in her life, and this one moment, being cocooned in Cole's arms, feeling his lips against hers, his heart beating as strong and fast as hers, was absolutely marvelous.

When their lips parted, Cole gazed into her eyes, holding her tightly against him. It took a moment for her brain to kick into gear and for her to realize that everyone in the place was clapping and whistling and calling out congratulations. Everyone except his ex-girlfriend, who stormed out the front door.

Holy shit. She'd just bid *a thousand dollars* to win a date with this man.

And after that one perfect kiss, she knew she'd do it again, and again, and again.

Chapter Five

THERE WASN'T A chance in hell that Cole was going to let go of Leesa's hand. He laced his fingers with hers and held their clasped hands up between them, taking a bow and bringing Leesa with him before pulling her trembling body against him and leading her over to the side of the room.

"You're shaking. Is that from the kiss or nerves from being in front of the crowd?"

"Both." The sweet, nervous smile he'd seen earlier reappeared. "I wasn't sure if I was doing the right thing, but Jewel said…and your sisters…"

It felt natural to pull her in by her hips and hold her against him. Oh, those incredibly sexy hips! He *finally* got to touch them, and the way they filled his palms was even better than he'd imagined. She felt so right in his arms, her softness against his hard muscles, and that kiss…Her lips were supple and moist and so delicious that it had taken all his restraint not to deepen the kiss right there on the stage. But he'd been lost in it for too many luxurious seconds as it was, risking her embarrassment, and he knew he needed to release her.

"You did the absolute right thing. Thank you again. Come on, I'll get your cash." He took a step toward the hallway where the ATM machine was located, and she stood stock-still.

"No." She shook her head. "I wanted to bid. Your sisters offered me money, too, and...No. This was my bid. I'm paying for it."

"Leesa, I'm not going to let you spend four hundred dollars to go on a date with me."

"It's for charity." She searched his eyes, and he didn't know what she thought she'd find, but he hoped she saw how much what she'd said had touched him.

"You're not only beautiful, but you're generous, too. That's an appealing combination."

Leesa's eyes darted nervously around them. "Oh gosh, I need to get back to work. I...I'm sorry." She unlinked their hands and took a step away.

He reached for her. "Wait. What about our date?" He noticed his mother heading their way. Leesa must have thought she was coming to ask her to get back to work, but Cole knew by the smile on his mother's face that that wasn't the case.

"We'll figure it out. I have to get back to work." She disappeared into the crowd just as his mother arrived by his side.

"Wow, honey. A *thousand* dollars?" His mother touched his cheek the way she had since he was a little boy when she was happy for him. "I didn't even know you knew Leesa."

"We just met yesterday." He spotted Leesa taking an order from a table a few feet away. The auction was still going on, and women cheered and clapped as the final bachelor was brought up to the front. When Leesa was done taking the order, her eyes darted right to Cole, and he felt the attraction simmering through his veins.

"Uh-huh," his mother said with a knowing look. "There's only one thing a look like that tells a person."

"What's that, Mom?" Cole slid an arm around his mother's

shoulder.

She patted his bare stomach. "That my boy is growing up."

"I thought that's what I've spent the last ten years doing."

"Honey, see Sammy over there flirting with the tableful of girls? And see Jon entertaining all those young women who are eyeing him like he's the cat's meow?"

Cole laughed. "That's because he and Sammy *are* the cat's meow in our little town."

"No, honey. It's because Sammy and Jon haven't found their forever person yet, so they expend all their energy searching, reaching, entertaining, hoping. Oh, they'll never admit it, but one day, you'll see." She turned so they were facing Nate and Jewel, snuggled together in a booth, sitting with Shannon and Tempe.

"See Nate?" she said, ignoring the auction sounding off around them. "He grew up when he was in the military, but it wasn't until he finally let himself fall fully in love with Jewel that he really took that final leap into manhood. They're so perfect together. She pushes him in all the ways he needs, and she doesn't let him get away with hiding one single emotion. And he helps her remember how brave she really is. They're so well suited for each other. Your father and I knew it years before either one admitted it."

"I'm thrilled for them. I've never seen Nate so happy." His brother had loved Jewel from afar for many years, and after his best friend, Jewel's older brother, Rick, died, Cole worried that Nate might never tell Jewel how he felt about her.

"And I've never seen your smile look so...*full*." She leaned over and kissed Cole's cheek. "It's a nice look on you."

"I've got to admit, it feels good, too."

BY THE TIME the restaurant cleared out, it was nearly midnight and Leesa was second-guessing herself for bidding all that money for a date with Cole in front of the whole town while she was trying to remain invisible. Truth be known, she'd been jealous—wicked jealous—of his ex, who had been eyeing her like she'd eat her alive. Leesa had never been one to cower before a challenge, but now that she'd had time to think about what she'd done—and had been congratulated by just about every person in the place—she worried that she looked desperate for a date.

Since winning the auction, she'd been given more information about Cole from strangers than she'd ever hoped to know about a man before their first date. She knew he'd dated Kenna for two years and there was speculation as to why they broke up, though no one was sure. Rumors seemed to range from Kenna cheating on him with a handful of men to Cole not wanting to be tied down.

Leesa signed her time card and leaned on the counter in the kitchen for a moment before heading out. She breathed deeply, thinking about all the money she'd blown in one moment of jealousy.

A warm hand touched her back, startling her.

"I'm sorry. I didn't mean to frighten you." Ace took a step back. "Are you all right?"

"Yes, sorry. I'll get out of your way." She'd already told them about what had happened in Baltimore, and they'd been kind enough to still hire her. The last thing she wanted was to make them think she wasn't *okay*.

"Leesa, you're not in our way, and after spending a thousand dollars to win my son, I'd think that if you *were* in my way, well, I just might let it slide." Ace flashed that warm smile of his, which looked so much like Cole's. "How are things going for you here in Peaceful Harbor? Are you managing okay? I know this came on the heels of a difficult time, and if there's anything we can do to make it easier, Maisy and I are here for you."

"Thank you. That's really kind of you to offer. I'm managing okay." She was surprised that the owner of a microbrewery would be so kind to a new employee. Then again, she'd seen Ace with customers. He was sincere and warm with everyone.

"I know it's only been a short time, but in times of need, families are important. You must miss yours."

"I don't really have any family to speak of." Her heart squeezed with the ache of missing her father.

He cocked his head to the side. "No family? Why, everyone has family."

She shook her head. "I haven't had family for a while now." She walked to the lockers and pulled out her purse. "Tonight was fun. Thank you for letting me work this shift. I'd never been to an auction like that before."

His dark eyes held hers as he slid a hand into his slacks pocket, just as she'd seen Cole do earlier in the evening. "Why don't you stick around and have a drink with me and Maisy and the kids?"

"Oh, I don't want to impose."

He offered her his arm, as if they were walking down an aisle. Ace Braden was the type of man whose large frame and gentle voice contrasted, creating a sense of safety about him. Leesa had been without her father for only two years, but he'd been such a big part of her life, her biggest supporter in everything she did, that it felt like much longer, and she was drawn to Ace's comfort.

"There's no such thing as an imposition among friends and family." He pushed open the door that led to the restaurant. "And you're part of Mr. B's family now."

His words wrapped around her like an embrace, and even though she probably shouldn't allow herself to, she soaked them in like flowers soaked up the sun.

"Thank you." She glanced at the round table in the back of the room where his family sat. What a sight they were, all smiles and laughter and love so thick it practically created a bubble around them.

Cole rose to his feet, sporting a T-shirt with a Mr. B's logo on it, and nudged Sam, who was sitting beside him. Sam moved to the chair across the table, freeing the seat beside Cole for her.

"Hi," Cole said softly.

"Hi. Your father invited me to have a drink with your family. I hope you don't mind."

He placed a hand on her hip as he'd done earlier, and a streak of heat raced through her so fiercely, she was sure everyone else could feel it, too.

"If he hadn't asked you, I would have."

He pulled out the chair, and when she sat, he draped an arm across the back of her chair. She glanced around the table quickly, once again enjoying and worrying about his overtly possessive touch.

"So, you paid a thousand bucks for our big brother," Sammy said. "Leesa…what's your last name?"

Leesa swallowed the fear that clutched her and hoped no one would say, *Wait! I've heard of you! You're that teacher who touched a boy!*

"Avalon," she finally answered.

"Beautiful name," Cole said quietly.

"Leesa Avalon, sounds like an actress's name," Sam said. "I haven't seen you around town before."

"I just moved here recently. My best friend lives on Second Street."

"Who's your best friend?" Shannon asked.

"Tegan Fine. Do you know her? She was here tonight."

Tempe and Shannon shook their heads.

"I've heard of her. I think she went to South High," Shannon said. "We went to Peaceful Harbor High."

"She's friends with Chelsea," Jewel said. "Tegan works for her sister's photography company and also makes clothing accessories for Chelsea's Boutique. Tempe went to school with Chelsea," she explained to Leesa.

"Six degrees of separation," Nate said.

"What a crazy night," Maisy said. "Between the auction, profits that we're putting toward the charity, and the raffle Daddy held, we made a lot of money for the homeless. I'm proud of you all for doing your share." She held Cole's gaze, and Leesa wondered if there was something more behind her motherly smile.

Cole dropped his eyes for a second, and when he lifted them, he filled a wineglass for Leesa and held up his own. "To my first and last bachelor auction."

"Presumptive, aren't you?" Sammy asked.

Cole pointed at him. "You are in deep shit, little brother. I never should have been up on that auction block."

Sam snickered as Cole slid his hand from the back of Leesa's chair and onto her shoulder, surprising her with the intimate touch.

"Thankfully, Leesa saved me from the vultures." He smiled at her, and she felt her cheeks heat up.

"Vulture. Singular," Shannon said. She tucked her long dark hair behind her ear. "For a woman scorned, she was willing to pay big bucks to go out with you again."

"That's only because she's been texting and asking me to get together with her." Cole's jaw clenched, and his grip on Leesa's shoulder tightened. "Can we please not discuss this right now? This beautiful woman just spent a thousand dollars to go out with me—which reminds me." He caressed her shoulder, all the tension in his hand and face faded to sweet seduction. "When are we going on our date?"

"Wait, wait, wait," Shannon interrupted. "I want the details first. How did you two meet? How long have you been dating?"

"We're not dating," Leesa said quickly. The disappointed look in Cole's eyes cut her to her core.

"But you just paid a thousand dollars to go out with him," Tempe pointed out.

"Yes, but…That was to save him from his ex-girlfriend." She swallowed hard, feeling boxed in by the partial lie. She hated lies and quickly tried to backpedal. "I mean. It started out like that. To save him."

Cole smiled.

Sammy cleared his throat and eyed Cole.

"So, you aren't dating?" Shannon asked.

"Not yet," Cole answered with alluring confidence.

"Ah," Shannon said with wide eyes.

"I'm not looking for a boyfriend." *Ohmygod.* She couldn't believe she'd said that out loud.

Open mouth. Insert foot.

"That's okay, honey." Maisy patted her hand. "Our family can be a little overwhelming. You don't have to explain anything to us. We're just glad you're here with us."

"I'm glad I'm here, too. Thank you." Leesa felt Cole's fingers brush lightly over her shoulder and come to rest on her back.

They talked for a long while, and by the time she got up to leave, she felt like she'd grown up with the Bradens. Cole's siblings teased one another with reckless abandon, and he gave it right back to them. Although she sensed him being more careful than the others, never stepping over any lines that might cause them embarrassment and obviously very aware of his sisters' feelings in particular. His parents joked just as easily. They were a loving group, and Leesa found herself wondering what it would be like to be one of their inner circle.

"Thank you for letting me join you tonight," she said as she stood and slung her purse over her shoulder.

"I'll walk you to your car," Cole said, rising beside her.

The rest of his family stood, and one by one they embraced her. Leesa was a touchy-feely person and hugging people she'd only just met didn't surprise her, but the type of hugs did. There were complimentary hugs that people extended to strangers. Those felt a little tense and cold. And then there were hugs of affection. These were the latter and made her feel like she was already part of their close-knit group.

"Maybe we can get together for lunch tomorrow. I'm only home for a little while, but I'd like to get to know you better while I'm here," Shannon said.

"Um, sure. Okay."

"Can I join you guys?" Tempe asked.

"I don't work until late tomorrow, so if you don't mind one more person, I'd love to join you," Jewel said.

"Wow, really?" Leesa could hardly believe that they wanted to get together so quickly. "That would be fun."

"Why don't you girls have lunch here?" Maisy suggested. "You can eat outside on the deck while the guys work on the boat."

Ace put an arm around his wife. "Honey, they may want a break from us *and* from this place."

"Oh, right. Sorry." Maisy waved her hand. "Go wherever you'd like."

Tempe and Shannon exchanged a shrug.

"I think that sounds great," Shannon said. She turned to Cole, Sam, and Nate. "Are you guys working on Dad's boat tomorrow?"

Leesa caught Cole staring at her with that look in his eyes again, the one that sent shivers from her head to her toes.

"I'll be here, helping Dad," he said directly to her.

"I've got a big group coming in at Rough Riders. Sorry I can't be here, Pop," Sam said.

"That's okay, Sam," his father said.

Nate pulled Jewel against him and kissed her forehead. "I've got a few things to take care of at the restaurant in the morning, but I'll be by to help out by lunchtime."

"Good. Then we'll meet here around noon?" Shannon suggested. "Is that okay with you, Leesa? Or do you want to escape your workplace for an afternoon?"

"Oh no, I appreciate you guys letting me join you for lunch."

"We're joining you," Jewel pointed out. "It'll be fun."

They exchanged cell numbers, and then Cole walked her out to her car. The night air was cool and crisp, awakening all of her senses.

"I hope you didn't feel put on the spot back there."

"Not at all," she said honestly. "It's nice to be surrounded by people who actually want to be with me. Your family is so friendly. You're very lucky." She unlocked her car door, trying to ignore the nervous fluttering in her stomach, but all she could think about was the kiss they'd shared and the way it had left her craving more. She hadn't kissed a man in weeks, hadn't had time to think about anything more than making it through each day. Could she allow herself the freedom to enjoy herself a little? Surely she deserved that after everything she'd been through. She was an intelligent, well-educated woman, and on a cognitive level she knew damn well that she deserved to enjoy a date with Cole. But a nagging voice reminded her of why she was here in the first place, and the weight of what happened in Baltimore pressed in on her. A painful reminder of Chris and the way he'd chosen his career over her. The pain of that choice still stung more than she'd like to admit. Cole had a lot on the line career-wise.

"Thank you, but more importantly, when would you like to collect on your auction winnings?" He smiled and stepped in close, bringing with him a heat wave and a reminder that she'd not only used six hundred of his dollars to pay for the auction, but she'd forgotten to give the balance of the thousand dollars to the girl who'd collected the donations.

"Oh, gosh. I have to go back inside. I forgot to pay the additional four hundred dollars. I gave the girl who was collecting the money your cash, but I was going to get the rest from the ATM and I got sidetracked by a customer."

"I already took care of it."

"You—"

He pressed a finger over her lips. "Shh. I asked you out, remember? Twice."

"Cole," she said against his finger, fighting the urge to take that finger into her mouth and swirl her tongue around it. She pressed her lips together to keep from doing just that.

"Tomorrow night? I'll pick you up at Tegan's about six?"

She felt herself nodding, and when he leaned forward, placing a hand on her hip, and pressed a kiss to her cheek, she closed her eyes and soaked in the weight of his palm, the feel of his moist lips, the heat of his breath whispering over her skin. She had a feeling that this sweet, seductive man was going to test her resolve of invisibility, and she reminded herself that he had a lot to lose—and if she were honest with herself, so did she.

Chapter Six

SUNDAY MORNING COLE awoke before sunrise. He showered, did a quick Google search to find out Tegan's address, since he'd forgotten to ask Leesa for it last night, then worked out in his home gym. He had more energy than he'd had in months, and he knew it was because of Leesa. When he set out for his run, he hoped like hell he'd cross paths with her during her morning run. He ran with Jon only on Saturday mornings, which meant he was on his own—just the way he wanted it.

The sun peeked out from behind a fluff of clouds as his feet hit the sand and he ran down by the shore. He loved the beach any time of day, but early mornings were his favorite, before the town came to life, when birds scavenged and waves kissed the untouched sand. He ran farther than usual, passing the pier and running up a commercial street, then heading down Main Street toward Second. His nerves pushed him faster than usual, and when he hit Second, he slowed his pace to read the house numbers until he came to Tegan's home. It was a cute ranch-style home with well-tended gardens out front and a bright red front door. He wondered if Leesa was up, or snuggled in her bed still asleep.

He smiled with the thought. Of course, in his mind, she was lying in *his* bed. *Naked.*

Great, now he was aroused, and he felt like a stalker.

What was he thinking? That he'd time it just right to catch her as she left for her morning run?

He ran past the house and continued toward the beach, thinking about what an idiot he'd been. He was acting more like a teenager than a guy in his early thirties.

A few minutes later he crossed the road and hit the beach again, heading toward home. He pulled his shirt off and used it to wipe the sweat from his face as he slowed to a walk. At least he'd had a solid run.

"Hello?" Leesa came around the side of his house carrying a bag from Jazzy Joe's and two to-go cups, her neck craned as she peered up at his deck. She wore a sexy blue sundress that stopped above her knees, and her hair fell over her shoulders in gentle waves.

His hands instinctively opened and closed with the desire to tangle his fingers in her hair and kiss her again. He watched disappointment fill her eyes as they swept over the empty deck and down to the sand.

He jogged the thirty feet or so up the beach as she turned to leave and called out to her, "Leesa!"

She turned with a surprised look on her face as he joined her in the side yard.

"Hi." Her gaze traveled down his bare, sweaty chest, and her eyes heated. "I, um, I thought I'd bring you a little something as a thank-you for paying off my debt last night."

He wiped the sweat from his face with his shirt and pressed a kiss to her cheek. "You didn't have to do that, but I'm glad you did." He glanced up at the deck. "Join me to watch the day roll in?"

"Sure."

He followed her up to the deck. "Do you mind if I rinse off quickly?"

"No, not at all."

She set the coffees on the table as he went inside and showered, returning a few minutes later in clean shorts and a T-shirt. He found her spreading two napkins on the table and setting a cranberry walnut muffin on each.

"How did you manage this?" he asked as he took the seat beside her.

"I'm not above begging, and luckily, Jasmine seems to have a soft spot for her favorite doctor." She held up her coffee. "Cheers."

He touched his cup to hers and sipped the warm liquid. "Another favorite."

"I figured a thousand-dollar date better be worth it." She gazed out over the water, fidgeting with the edge of her dress, suddenly seeming more nervous than just moments before.

"I usually donate much more than that anyway, so please don't feel like you owe me anything."

She smiled, but her eyes dropped to her lap. "I...um. I wanted to talk to you about our date before we actually go out, in case you want to change your mind."

He set his coffee on the table and gave her his full attention. "Why would I want to do that?"

When she lifted her eyes to his again, they were clouded with worry. "Cole, last night was wonderful. Your family is so kind, and you're, well, I can tell that you're a real gentleman, not to mention handsome and obviously well respected and successful."

"My ego's liking your train of thought, but I hear a *but* coming."

"Yes." Her lips curved up in a nervous smile. "I'm a really honest person, and as much as I want to go out with you, I can't do it in good conscience without explaining what brought me to Peaceful Harbor."

"I sensed there was something more behind your move, but I figured you'd tell me when you were ready."

Her brows drew together, and knowing that whatever she had to say was weighing so heavily on her tugged at his heart. He couldn't imagine what would make her worry so much that she'd make a special trip out to his house.

"Ready or not, I want to tell you." She drew in a deep breath, and he noticed her hand was shaking.

He wanted to reach out and comfort her, but he had a feeling that might make her more uncomfortable.

"I'm not sure how long I'll be here or what I'll end up doing long-term. Tegan wants me to move here, and it's an option, but not a given. So, that's the first thing you need to know. I might only be here a short time. But more importantly, I might never have left Towson if it weren't for what happened there." She swallowed hard and met his gaze head-on. "I was accused of...Holy cow, this is much more difficult than I thought it would be."

Accused?

She gulped in air and blew it out slowly.

"You don't have to tell me anything," he assured her, despite his now piqued curiosity.

"Yes, I really do. It wouldn't be fair for you to find out some other way. Besides, I really don't have anything to hide. It's just terribly embarrassing. Life changing." She ran her finger along the edge of the table, concentrating on it as if it held the answers to some unspoken question. "Okay, maybe I do have something to hide, but only because of people who will judge me before they know me." She rose to her feet. "You know what? Never mind. Let's just cancel the date and—"

He stood and reached for her hand. "Leesa, whatever it is, I'm not going to judge you because of it. You can trust me."

"That's why I'm here. I got the impression that I *could* trust you, but I've trusted before and was sorely disappointed with the outcome."

"Maybe you trusted the wrong person. I've done that myself," he said, thinking of Kenna. "And I know how badly it can hurt to have your trust broken."

"Cole, this is very different from a cheating girlfriend or—"

"Mackenna didn't cheat on me." He was surprised at how easily that truth came, when he hadn't even shared as much with his family. But he was so drawn to Leesa, and the thought of her carrying around something that was obviously torturing her made his gut ache.

"Oh, well…"

"She wanted to," he explained. "She wanted an open relationship, threesomes, and that's not something I've ever been into." He stepped closer to try to ease the shock on her face.

"But don't all guys dream of that? Two women touching them, or watching two women make out? I thought that was every guy's fantasy."

"I don't share well," he said as he took her hand. He didn't want to talk about Mackenna, or his past. He wanted to help her through whatever was weighing her down. "I don't know what you were accused of, but there's a difference between accused and convicted, and I'm here if you want to talk about it. I'd much rather talk than have you walk out of my life over how you *think* I might react."

He searched her eyes and saw her resolve softening. He didn't know why he felt this strongly about her so quickly, but it had been forever since he'd felt anything this powerful that he wasn't about to let her go without trying.

"Give me a chance to hear you out. If you don't like my reaction, you can walk away and never look back, knowing that whatever you share with me will go no further than this deck."

LEESA HAD KNOWN the minute she woke up this morning that she had to be honest with Cole about her past *before* they went out rather than after, or even during, their date. The way her body reacted to him whenever he was near told her that even one date would bring them closer together. She wasn't a glutton for punishment. She didn't want to put herself in a position to be hurt again, and it wasn't fair to keep something that had the power to taint his career from him.

Now, standing here with her hand in his, his eyes pleading with her for honesty, and his promise of understanding vibrating through her, she fought for the strength to follow through.

"Okay," she finally managed. "But promise me that if I am honest with you, you'll be honest with me, too. If you want nothing more to do with me, you have to let me know, regardless of whether you think it'll hurt my feelings."

He nodded. "I promise."

They sat again, and Leesa drew her shoulders back, summoning the courage it had taken for her to get through the investigation. With her gut in a knot, she explained. "It's a strange feeling to know that I moved away so no one would recognize me, only to find out that I'm not the type of person who can live a lie."

"That says a lot about you." Cole reached for her hand again and she let him hold it for a few seconds, but her nerves were frayed. Even though he seemed understanding now, that didn't mean he would remain so after he heard the rest of the story. Rather than make him uncomfortable, or feel stuck, by holding her hand, she slid hers from his grip and rubbed her hands together.

"Thank you. Okay, well, here goes. In Towson, I taught seventh-grade English, and I loved it. I taught at the same school ever since I first became certified, and I got to know the kids really well. You know, kept up with older siblings when younger ones entered my classes and all that. I had a great group of peers, a wonderful principal, and all in the town where I grew up. In the middle school I had attended."

He smiled and said, "You returned to your roots, the same way I have."

"Well, I never left. I went to Towson State, too." She held his gaze, fighting everything inside her that was telling her to shut her big mouth and keep it to herself. She fought the edginess that made her want to bolt down the stairs and up to Tegan's house and hide there until Cole had forgotten she'd ever shown up. But the hardest fight of all was the fear that when she came clean, Cole would thank her for being honest and then tell her it was best to sever ties and go their separate ways. She thought she'd prepared herself for that before coming over this morning, but now stone-cold fear filled her chest and prickled her skin.

She tried to push that fear aside, but the shakiness in her limbs told her it wasn't going to budge. One look at his thoughtful gaze, and she knew he was worth the risk. She forced herself to tell him the truth.

"One of my students was in a terrible accident. He'd been hit by a car. It left him with two broken legs, broken ribs, a fractured hip, a fractured hand, and the worst part? It left him angry and bitter, and for a while I was concerned that he was going to try to…" Her eyes filled again, and she blinked the tears away. "I was afraid he was going to do something tragic."

Cole took her hand in his again and gave it a comforting squeeze. "Losing the ability to walk is hard for adults and children, but at that age, when kids are on the cusp of finding themselves, I think it's particularly stressful."

"Yes. It's good to talk to someone who understands. He has a really overbearing father who pushes him all the time. The type of parent who called the school every other week because his son, Andy, wasn't getting A's. His grades weren't great, but he was a smart kid. I offered to come to his home and tutor him so he wouldn't fall behind the other kids, at least not in English class. And, to be honest, I was worried about him. Emotionally, I mean. He was stuck inside most of the time, using a wheelchair because his injuries made it difficult for him to maneuver a walker or crutches—although he tried to use them."

"You did what any good teacher would do," Cole said. "Healing wounds has a lot to do with healing emotions, too."

"I thought so." She sighed with relief. "You'd be surprised, though. His father continued to push him, even with the injuries. It was like his father saw his injuries as an excuse Andy might use to get bad grades or something, so instead of showing empathy for his son, he basically ignored the injuries. And his mother is this meek woman whom I've never heard say more than a handful of words to anyone. Meanwhile, Andy's getting angrier and more evasive with his father each day, but he's working really hard to keep his grades up. I was proud of his efforts."

"It sounds like he was lucky to have you as a teacher," Cole said with a serious tone.

"Maybe, but you don't know the bad part yet, and that's the part that either makes people hate me or hate Andy, and honestly, I should tell you before I reveal what happened that I don't really blame him, at least not the way other people do."

Cole smiled, but it didn't reach his eyes, and she wondered if he was reserving judgment. He rubbed his thumb soothingly over her knuckles and said, "You're doing a good job of preparing me, but I've seen so much in my life, Leesa. I doubt you're going to say anything that will shock me."

She looked up at the sky and said, "Oh, you'd be surprised."

"Try me."

He kept his grip on her hand, and for the life of her she didn't want to pull away. Maybe this was all they'd ever have. One kiss and a little hand-holding. A few minutes together on his deck, sitting in the sun with the sea at her back and the scent of warm coffee and Cole surrounding her.

She took a moment to revel in that before continuing to open the window to her past.

"One afternoon when I showed up for Andy's session, he was acting nervous, not looking me in the eye, and fidgeting a lot. I could tell something was on his mind, and I thought maybe his father had said something unkind to him."

"Did his father ever hurt him physically?"

"No, at least not that I knew of. He's just a very gruff man.

Cold and determined, but I think he loves Andy. And, you know, everyone has their difficult days, and I can only imagine the strain it put on the family, dealing with his injuries. I think they were all under pressure."

Cole's jaw clenched repeatedly. His hand tightened around hers. "Go on."

She looked at him for a long moment before speaking, trying to figure out the best way to explain how things unfolded, but she knew that no matter what words she used, the end result was the same, so she just let it flow.

"That day, he told me he had a crush on me."

Cole raised his brows. "That probably happens often enough that it's not abnormal. We see it at every level, the nurses, docs, therapists. He's relying on you. It's not uncommon to see misplaced emotions."

"Yes, and my first thought was that it was cute and normal, and I smiled, you know, while I tried to piece together an appropriate response. I could see that he was anxiously awaiting my reply, so I said that it was very nice of him and that I was flattered, but I was way too old for him and that one day he'd find the perfect girl who was just his age."

"That's a reasonable response."

"Yes, or so I thought. But of course, I'm not a twelve-year-old boy who had his heart set on me telling him I was just as in love with him as he was with me."

Cole sat back and ran a hand through his hair. He blew out a breath and nodded. "How did he react?"

She turned her hand over, missing the feel of his against it. "He was upset. At first he clammed up, and I tried to talk about it, to reassure him that this sort of thing happens a lot. I gave him the spiel about misplaced feelings and told him that I care for him as a student but in the way that was appropriate for a teacher."

"Oh boy." Cole shook his head. "I bet that pissed him off even more."

"Yeah, it did." She crossed her arms, a barrier between her and the truth she had to reveal. "When I left that afternoon Andy told me that he hated me and that he never wanted to see me again. He said I'd pay for treating him that way. I honestly thought it would blow over." Tears welled in her eyes again, and she swiped angrily at them. "About an hour after I arrived at school the next morning, the principal called me down to her office."

Cole leaned forward and wiped a tear from her cheek with the pad of his thumb. "And what happened?"

"Several weeks of hell," she said flatly. "Andy said I touched him inappropriately, and it was his word against mine. At first my principal told me to stop tutoring him, obviously, and she gave me a letter stating the accusation. Everything moved really fast after that. I was put on administrative leave while the investigation took place. I think at first I was numb, in a state of disbelief. But the investigation was so invasive, there was no escaping it. They reviewed my employment files, which of course had no other complaints or accusations, but then they talked to other students, teachers, parents. I was so ashamed to have even been accused of such a horrible thing." Every word brought a painful reminder of the shame and embarrassment she'd gone through. "And my boyfriend of almost two years worried about what his affiliation with me would do to his career, because he was also a teacher, so we broke up."

Cole's hands fisted. "I assume he knew you were innocent?"

"Yes, of course he did. I thought he knew me better than

anyone, but what I realized was that we barely knew each other at all. It wasn't that he thought I was guilty. He was worried that parents would lose faith in him because of our connection. It was a nightmare." She paused, trying to remember how to breathe without allowing her heart rate to skyrocket, something she'd had to master to avoid passing out from anxiety during those first awful days. "I had a lot of supporters. All of my other students and my peers rallied around me."

"Family?" Cole inched closer, when she expected him to put space between them. He placed his hand over hers again.

She shook her head.

"They didn't support you?" He moved closer again, his inner thigh brushing her outer thigh.

"I never knew my mother. My father raised me, but he died of a stroke when I was twenty-five." She lifted one shoulder in a halfhearted shrug.

"Aw, Leese. I'm sorry that you've had to go through this alone and that you lost your father."

His tone was so sincere, it made her sad for herself, too, and the endearment *Leese* made her heart squeeze.

"I had Tegan and my friends, and that really helped. It took the investigators only a few weeks to see that there was no foundation for the charges, but by then the damage had been done. And those weeks? They were torturous. Every minute felt like a lifetime. I could feel everything I'd ever worked for—all the relationships I'd formed, the reputation I'd built with students and peers—being squeezed from my life like a wrung-out sponge. Even if people in town *weren't* looking at me with concern or mistrust, I felt like they were. That kind of stress does awful things to your confidence."

"I can only imagine. So you came here with hopes that no

one would know? You gave up your career?" He brought her hand to his lips and pressed a kiss to her knuckles. "That took a lot of courage."

"I think it would have taken a lot more courage to stay where I was. They offered me a job at another school, in Baltimore instead of Towson. I haven't made any final decisions. And don't call me courageous just yet. I am so frightened that someone might have read about it online or heard about it, that instead of going by my given name, Annalise, I go by Leesa, which is also new to me."

His eyes warmed. "Annalise. That's beautiful, and I still think you're courageous. To go through something like that for a day, much less longer? Of course your confidence has wavered. You'd have to be inhuman for it not to. I'd imagine your entire life was scrutinized."

It was all she could do to nod, as memories of the interrogations flew through her mind.

"In case you're wondering, I was honest with your parents. I couldn't mislead an employer, so I told them about what happened in Towson, and they were gracious enough to hire me anyway."

"Lee—Annalise, you were found *not* guilty of anything."

"I think you should call me Leesa. Just in case. And yes, I wasn't guilty, but that doesn't mean that anyone has to believe in my innocence. I truly appreciate your parents' willingness to take a chance on me, and after what happened with Chris, I understand if you want to put distance between us, too. If anyone found out—"

"I'd set them straight."

A lump formed in her throat with his response. How could he be so understanding? So confident in her innocence?

"But—"

He took her cheeks in his warm hands and gazed deeply into her eyes.

"Unless there's something more damning that you're not telling me, I can see no reason to put distance between us, when what I really want is to get closer to you."

"Cole," she whispered with disbelief.

"Annalise, did you do something inappropriate to that boy?"

She couldn't form the answer, not when he was so close that she could smell the coffee on his breath, see his pupils dilating, feel his heat warming her hotter than the sun ever could. Not when the vehemence in his tone told her that he believed her, trusted her. Instead, she shook her head.

He smiled again, leaning in so close his breath brushed over her mouth.

"Then may I please kiss you the way I've wanted to since last night?"

She nearly crumpled into his arms, unable to deny herself his touch any longer. "Ye—"

Before the word left her lips, his mouth captured hers. Passion radiated through her with every stroke of his tongue, awakening a burning desire inside her like she'd never experienced before. He slid one hand beneath her hair and cupped the back of her head, angling her mouth and deepening the kiss. She never dreamed that his touch would feel so gentle and powerful at the same time. He leaned in to her, and in the next second his strong arms had scooped her onto his lap, never breaking their connection. One hand slid hot and confidently along her thigh, and the other remained on the nape of her neck. A groan stole from his lungs, and she swallowed it down, feeling it vibrate through her as her hands discovered the thickness of his hair, the strength of his muscular back. Hypnotized by the most luxurious kiss she'd ever experienced, she was powerless to pull away, even as the nagging voice in her head tried to convince her to.

His touch, this kiss, was divine ecstasy, and she felt like she was exactly where she was supposed to be.

Which was crazy.

Insane.

Amazing.

"Annalise," he said against her lips, bringing her mind back to the present.

She became aware of his rigid length beneath her butt, his chest moving with heavy breaths, his strong, capable hands roaming along her back, and her tight nipples tingling beneath her shirt.

"Mm," was all she could manage, desperately wanting those delicious lips of his back on hers.

"Thank you for trusting me enough to share that part of your life with me."

The realization of how much she'd shared suddenly struck her, and he must have felt her body tense up, because he pressed a tender kiss to her lips and said, "It doesn't change anything. I just want you to know that what your ex did? It was wrong. No man should ever put himself before the woman he loves." He touched his forehead to hers. "He didn't know how to love you, and I'm sorry that he hurt you."

She closed her eyes against the familiarity of his words and felt a hot tear slip down her cheek.

"Leese?"

"My father used to tell me never to settle for a man who put himself before me. I thought that he was wrong, that men had to put themselves before the women they loved in order to maintain their careers. But when Chris told me that he wanted to end our relationship, I remember thinking about how my father had been right and feeling guilty for feeling that way."

Cole kissed away her tears. "There's no room for guilt when you care about someone. It sounds to me like your father was a wise man, and I'm sorry I never got to meet him."

They sat like that for a long while, with the waves crashing against the shore and their lives silently intertwining in the sweet summer breeze. Leesa wasn't fully aware of when the change occurred, but sometime between their kiss on the deck, making plans for the evening, and when Cole kissed her goodbye at her car, their date had become a given rather than a possibility.

Chapter Seven

LATER THAT AFTERNOON Leesa had lunch with Shannon, Tempe, and Jewel on the patio of Mr. B's overlooking the marina. It was a picture-perfect day, with sailboats crawling across the water in the distance, a young family fishing off of one of the piers, and best of all, Leesa had a clear view of Cole as he, Nate, and their father worked on the sailboat. She'd spent most of the morning trying to process his gracious reaction to her past. When she'd gone back to Tegan's, Tegan had been busy editing photographs for her sister Cici's business, which had left Leesa alone with her thoughts, giving her the opportunity to pick apart the emotions that swamped her. How could she already feel closer to Cole than she had felt to Chris after dating for almost two years? She tried to blame it on the relief that had come from her confession, but she somehow innately knew that even if she'd met Cole before her nightmare had begun, they'd still be drawn together like metal to magnet. By the time she met the girls for lunch, she felt like a week had passed, rather than a few short hours.

Now she tried to concentrate on her new friends, but it was difficult when Cole was just down the hill, shirtless, his tanned skin glistening in the afternoon sun. Sitting on his lap this morning, she'd had the urge to rip his shirt off and lie beneath him. To feel the hard planes of his bare flesh pressed against her. To feel him inside her. The quickness of those urges had surprised her. With Chris she'd waited a few weeks before they'd ended up in bed. *Weeks*. Not days or hours. Sounds of laughter carried up to where she sat. She glanced that way, catching Cole midlaugh, one hand on his father's shoulder, the other pointing at Nate, who was shaking his head. He was a beautiful sight, so unreserved and free. He was an intensely serious guy. That much she'd seen, and she liked that about him. But this. The unencumbered Cole tugged at her insides, too. She wanted to see more of both.

"So anyway," Shannon continued, bringing Leesa's attention back to the conversation. "A few weeks after returning to Weston, I'll be living in the wilderness to carry out the study."

"Living? Like camping?" Jewel asked. She tucked her blond hair behind her ear and scrunched her nose.

"Yes. I'm actually looking forward to it." Shannon sipped her iced tea. "I love nature."

"I've never been camping, but it's something I'd like to try one day," Leesa said.

"Never?" Tempe asked. "Our father believed that we all needed to master basic survival skills by the time we were seven. He was in the military for only a few years before he lost his left leg from the knee down after a jumping accident. It never healed properly and they had to amputate, but that didn't stop him from doing everything and teaching us to do it all, too." She laughed, bumping Shannon with her elbow.

Leesa thought of Ace's gait and the way he sometimes had a pained look in his eyes when he thought no one was looking. She had wondered if that look was caused by something emotional, like a memory, or physical. Now she had her answer.

"Once a military man always a military man," Shannon said. "Right, Jewel?"

"You're telling me? Nate is *always* prepared, and he watches over me to make sure I'm always prepared, which I never am." Jewel turned to Leesa and explained. "Nate was in the army with my older brother, Rick." Her eyes became hooded, and Tempe reached over and patted her hand. "Rick never made it home."

Leesa's heart ached for her new friend. "I'm so sorry."

"Thanks. It was really hard. We lost Rick just four years after we lost my father, and I have three younger siblings. It was tough." She pulled her shoulders back and smiled a resilient smile. "But we made it, and I'm glad Nate came back."

"I lost my father when I was twenty-five. I know how difficult it can be to try to move on." Sharing her life with the girls came easily, and as each of their faces filled with empathy and a collective *aww* surrounded her, their emotions were as genuine as an embrace.

"How did your mom take it?" Tempe asked.

"I've never known my mother. My father raised me. It was always just me and him." She felt the familiar thickening in her throat, remembering how alone she'd felt for the longest time after she'd lost her father. She couldn't count the number of times she'd reached for the phone to share something that had happened with him. And when she'd been accused of touching Andy, she'd wished he was there to tell her everything would be okay. It was one thing to hear it from friends, but her father had always been her rock, and ever since she was a little girl, if he said something would be okay, she'd believed him. Even now the emptiness inside her was like an arid well she visited often, hoping for a miracle. Her miracles came in the form of memories, and she cherished each and every one.

Shannon reached out and hugged her. "No one should be without a mother." She drew back and smiled at Leesa. "We'll just have to share ours with you."

Leesa laughed and Tempe smiled. "You laugh, but she's serious. Once she hears about your parents, she'll start to mother you like she does everyone else she thinks needs comfort in their life. It's one of her strengths."

"Or weaknesses, depending on who you ask," Shannon said. "When I was a teenager, she was super nice to even the creepiest boys."

"You only thought they were creepy because they all wanted to go out with you," Tempe said. "And you were too busy in the science lab to worry about them."

"Well, your parents have both been really kind to me," Leesa said as she glanced down at Cole again. He was sanding the deck of the boat, working head-to-head with Nate. "Your whole family has been wonderful. I love that you're all so close."

"It's kind of sickening, isn't it? Like a real-life Brady Bunch." The glint of mischief in Jewel's blue eyes told Leesa she was kidding.

"So, tell us about your plans, Leesa," Tempe said. "Mom said you moved from Towson. What did you do there? And do you miss it?"

Leesa's stomach clenched. She already felt comfortable enough with the girls that she couldn't imagine lying to them, but she was still nervous about sharing the truth, so she started small. "I'm not sure *moved* is the right word. I'm feeling things out right now, figuring out my next move. But I do miss the Girl Power group I ran."

"You taught Girl Power?" Tempe's eyes widened. "I'm a music therapist, and one of my patients was asking me about it. She said they have them all over Maryland but not here."

"What's Girl Power?" Shannon asked.

"It's a group for girls," Leesa explained. "Our focus was helping girls gain self-confidence and boost their self-esteem, which we did through group activities and friendship. Our meetings usually began with catching up on the good things that happened to each of the girls between meetings, and we talked about anything they were concerned about or had difficulty with. We usually did a bit of fun exercise, like take a walk, jog, play basketball, or other activities. We went on outings and basically tried to build the girls up about themselves and help them with the tools to handle whatever came at them." Thinking about the girls in the group made her miss them even more. "I ran the group with my friend Patty. Girls came and went—you know how that is. Girls could join at eight years old, and their interest waxed and waned as they got involved in other things, but we always had at least six or seven members."

"I wish they'd had that when I was growing up. Not that I would have had time for it, but it would have been fun to have a group of girls to do something productive with," Jewel said. "My younger sister Krissy would probably love that. Would you consider starting a group here? She's a total social butterfly. If only we could get her to focus on her schoolwork as much as her dance lessons and social calendar."

Leesa bit back the urge to offer to help Krissy with her studies. She'd been so wrapped up in getting over the pain of what had happened that she'd pushed away the ache of no longer teaching. She missed it.

"I could help you set up a group," Tempe said.

Shannon laughed. "You don't exercise other than using your delicate fingers to strum a guitar or play the piano."

"I could help in other ways." Tempe pulled a notebook from her purse.

"Here she goes." Shannon rolled her eyes. "She's going to write a song about Girl Power."

Leesa was too busy trying to figure out how to tell them she couldn't start a group to enjoy their teasing banter.

"No, I'm not," Tempe said. "I was going to make a note to look into it."

"Seriously, Tempe is super organized," Shannon said to Leesa. "If anyone could help you start something like that, it's her." She smiled at Tempe and said, "She could also write a kick-ass song about it, though."

"Do you really think the girls around here would be interested? Aren't they more focused on hitting the beach every afternoon?" The thought of working with kids again was terrifying. She hoped they told her she was right and that it was a silly idea. She felt like a transient hiding from a torrid past.

Shit. Her past. She had to be honest with them; otherwise she'd feel like she was abusing their trust. With her gut tangled in a knot, she knew she had to suck it up and come clean.

"Definitely," Tempe said. "They all want beach bodies, and everyone knows that girls need their confidence to be grounded in more than just their looks. I'd love to take part. I'm not at all athletically inclined, but I'm great with kids. I could, I don't know, talk with the girls, help organize. I would just love to be a part of it."

"You could be the water girl," Shannon suggested. When Tempe made a face that Leesa read as, *Very funny*, Shannon added, "I'm serious. Everyone loves you, Tempe. You're great with kids and adults, so the parents would probably feel good knowing that you were part of the group, too."

"Then it's settled." Tempe wrote something in the notepad. "We'll start a Girl Power group! I'm excited."

Oh shit. She had to nix this. She didn't even know if she was here to stay or not. She had to push past her fear and tell them the truth, but she was scared shitless. They'd only just accepted her into their inner circle. What if this changed everything? Her eyes slipped over each of their excited faces, and she realized that even if it meant losing her new friends, she couldn't lead them on.

"You guys are really great, and this all sounds really exciting, but I'm not even sure how long I'll be in Peaceful Harbor."

"Oh." Disappointment filled Tempe's voice.

"I have to tell you guys something." All eyes were on her. The anticipatory silence magnified in her ears, as if it had a pulse all its own. She explained to them what had happened in Towson, and when she'd told the whole story, including the part about losing Chris, she sat back and awaited judgment.

The look on their faces was something between empathy and disbelief. Leesa held her breath, unsure if that disbelief was about her or the situation.

"He left you?" Shannon said with a heated gaze. "What a dick."

"Yeah, he's a definite loser," Tempe said. "But more importantly, how are you now? Being accused of something so horrible must have made you feel awful. Especially after your boyfriend ended the relationship. And without your dad there to support you?" The sadness in her voice cut straight to Leesa's heart.

"I'm not going to lie and say it wasn't the hardest thing I've ever gone through. It was. It was worse than losing my father, because at least when he passed away, I could grieve. There's healing in grieving, as you probably know all too well," Leesa said to Jewel.

Jewel and Tempe both nodded in agreement.

"But with that whole mess, I couldn't grieve for my job or the students I had to stop working with. I was too busy trying to keep my head above water."

Shannon reached for her hand. "But you did, and you're here now, and that's what matters."

"Yes, now you can start over with a new support system," Tempe said. "Maybe moving here is the right thing to do. Your best friend is here, and I can help you get a job as a tutor with some of the kids I do therapy with."

Leesa's eyes dampened at her generosity. She glanced down at the marina, her eyes immediately finding Cole. Their parents must have done something right, because she'd never before met such accepting, supportive people. She looked at Jewel and felt an instant kinship from having experienced similar losses. Her future had begun feeling less bleak and lonely when she was with Cole earlier in the day, and now it seemed to bloom in the company of these amazing women.

"I'm not sure if I'm ready to jump back into tutoring again, and I have a teaching job waiting in the wings back in Baltimore," she explained. "But thank you for offering. To be honest, I'm still watching my back, waiting for someone to call me out. I'm trying not to get too comfortable or to let my guard down."

"Well, that's no way to live," Tempe said.

"What's the worst that happens? Someone says they heard about what happened and you explain that the accusation was unfounded." Shannon leaned back in her chair, her eyes and tone serious. "In today's day and age, false accusations like that seem to happen way too often."

"What happened with the boy who accused you?" Tempe asked.

Leesa shook her head. "I haven't seen him since that last tutoring session. I wanted to go see him, because he and I are the only ones who really know what happened, but my attorney and my boss advised me not to. I worry about him a lot, though. I can't believe that he would have done what he did if he ever thought things would go so far. He's just not a mean-spirited kid."

"With what you said about his parents, who knows what he faced once he made the accusation," Tempe said. "Given what you said about him, I'm sure it's affecting him in some way. It's a shame that it happened at all, especially to someone as nice and caring as you."

Leesa soaked in her compliment, but she didn't want to wallow in what shouldn't have happened, because there was no changing the past. There was only moving forward. And the hope of somehow building a new life. Her eyes sought Cole again and found him heading up the hill with Nate and their father. He had a shirt in his hand, and as his gaze met hers, he waved. Leesa watched as he pulled his shirt over his glistening body, covering up all those muscles that made her belly go a wonderful kind of crazy. She noticed Ace's limp again, and her heart ached for what he must have gone through when he'd lost his military career. She wondered again about the tightness in his brow as he climbed the steep incline, and when she realized the girls were watching her, waiting for a response, she brought her attention back to the conversation.

"It is a shame, but it's done, and I'm ready to focus on a more positive future. I'm not ready to start a Girl Power group here, because I don't even know how long I'll be here." Her stomach clenched again at the thought of walking away from Cole and her new friends. "Maybe we should wait a few weeks, just to be sure?"

Tempe waved a dismissive hand. "Life is way too short to spend waiting to be sure of anything. I think we should at least talk about it. In case you stay. You've got us behind you."

Cole stepped onto the patio, his eyes on Leesa. He leaned down and kissed her cheek, his hand settling on her shoulder as he said, "Hi, beautiful."

"Hi." She heard the breathiness of her voice and wondered if everyone else did, too.

"Looks like you've got Cole behind you, too," Shannon said with an approving smile.

"She sure does." Cole squeezed her shoulder.

Nate leaned down and kissed Jewel. "Hey, babe."

Jewel reached up and stroked his cheek. The love between them was palpable. Then again, the love between each member of this family was evident.

"It's nice to see all my girls together," Ace said as Maisy came out the door and reached for his hand, pausing only to touch Cole's back and blow a kiss to Nate.

"How's the boat coming along?" Maisy asked.

"She's getting there," Ace said. "The boys got hungry."

Maisy's eyes moved between Cole and Leesa, and an approving smile reached her blue eyes. "Sit and chat. I'll grab some sandwiches."

For the next hour, they talked and laughed like old friends while the men ate lunch. By the time Leesa left, she and Tempe had made arrangements to meet Friday to discuss putting together a Girl Power group even though she wasn't interested in doing it right away, and she and Cole, through hand-holding and stolen glances, had become impossibly closer.

Chapter Eight

WHEN COLE ARRIVED to pick up Leesa for their date, he was surprised to find her sitting on the front stoop of Tegan's house. She rose as he approached, looking sexy as hell in a white spaghetti-strap dress and a pair of sandals.

"Hi." He placed a hand on her hip and kissed her softly. "Everything okay?"

The bangles on her wrist slid up her arm as she pressed her hand to his chest and smiled. "Yeah, fine. I was just too nervous to wait inside."

He lifted her hand from his chest and kissed her knuckles. "I was nervous, too. It's been a long time since I've been nervous about going on a date."

Her long lashes swept over her green eyes as he laced their fingers together. The front door swung open and Tegan joined them on the porch. The physician in him did a quick visual assessment of her gait.

"Hey, Doc. How's it going?"

"Great, Tegan. How's your ankle?"

She lifted her walking boot and wiggled it around. "Almost good as new, thanks to the best doctor in town and a best friend who makes me do those physical therapy exercises. You guys make a great team."

Cole glanced at Leesa. "Thanks. I think so, too."

Tegan shooed them off the front porch. "Go on, get out of here. Bring her back late, or not at all, please. She needs to have some fun."

"Tegan!" Leesa laughed.

"Sorry," Tegan said to Leesa, then mouthed, *Late or not at all*, to Cole.

They all laughed as Tegan went back inside and he and Leesa walked to the car.

"You look gorgeous tonight."

"Thank you," Leesa said as he opened the car door. "I wasn't sure where we were going, so I hope I'm dressed okay."

"I'm not really sure where we're going either, so I hope *I'm* dressed okay." He waved at his jeans, then went around and settled into the driver's seat. "Hungry?"

"Always."

"Really?" He leaned across the console and kissed her, slowly at first, gauging her reaction. She tasted minty and sweet, and when he deepened the kiss, she wound her hands around his neck and met every stroke of his tongue with an eager stroke of her own.

"I could kiss you all night," he said against her lips.

"Sounds like a good plan."

He sealed his lips over hers again and felt himself getting lost in her as lust coiled inside him, thick and eager. When they drew apart, they were both breathing hard.

"Does this feel like a first date to you?" He pressed his lips to hers again before she could answer. He'd been thinking about her all afternoon, and the cold shower he'd taken before their date hadn't done anything to temper his desire to strip her bare and feast on every inch of her beautiful body. It took all his focus to stop kissing her again.

"We'd better go or Tegan's neighbors will start talking about the fogged-up windows."

She laughed, and it was a sound he wanted to hear over and over again. He'd hated hearing about all she'd gone through and wished he could have been by her side when it had occurred. The irrational anger he'd felt toward her ex-boyfriend lingered. He started the engine and drove down the street, pushing that anger away so he could focus on Leesa. "I thought we'd go to Nate's restaurant and grab some dinner."

He drove to the old train station that Nate had renovated for the restaurant, and on their way inside Leesa looked up at the sign and laughed.

"Tap It? Really? That's what he named it?"

Cole laughed. "He and Jewel's brother, Rick, came up with the idea before Rick was killed. That's what you get when you have two twenty-five-year-old guys planning a business together." He pulled her against him and kissed her, slow and deep, until he felt her body grow weightless and melt against him. God, he loved the way she felt. He reminded himself that she hadn't agreed to go out with him to be kissed senseless every few minutes and pried his lips away. The lustful look in her eyes made him think she was fighting the same intense attraction.

He held the door open, and they stepped inside the crowded restaurant. He had forgotten it was Sunday night, and now that they were there, he realized he should have taken her someplace much quieter. Weekend nights brought crowds in the tourist town. Music and chatter filled the bar area off to their right.

"Maybe this wasn't such a good idea," Cole said.

"Hey, Cole!" His brother Sam waved them over to the bar.

Cole lifted his chin, acknowledging that he'd seen Sam. "Sorry. I can't believe I forgot it was Sunday night. Usually the weeknights aren't bad, but weekends are another story altogether."

"That's okay. We can eat at the bar with Sam if you want."

"Is that one of those answers a woman gives a guy because she doesn't know how to tell him she doesn't want to do it?" He pressed his lips to hers again and then said, "We can go someplace else." Although this was probably safer than where he wanted to take her, which was right back to his place to be alone with her.

"No, really. It's totally fine. It'll be fun." She took a step toward Sam and said, "I really like your family."

When he'd seen her with his family earlier, it had done funny things to his stomach. It had been a long time since he'd wanted to introduce his family to a woman, and with Leesa, it was like the world was doing it for him. Bringing them together unexpectedly, seamlessly melding their lives together.

Sam stood from his barstool and hugged Leesa, then offered her his seat. "Great to see you guys." He gave Cole a manly pat on the back. Every barstool was taken, every table filled. There was barely room to stand, not exactly Cole's idea of an intimate dinner, but it was his own fault. He simply hadn't been able to think past seeing Leesa again to make a more careful decision.

"How's it going, Sam?" Cole moved behind Leesa's seat and draped an arm around her.

"All's good in my world. I'm only here for a few minutes." He nodded toward a tall blonde coming around the corner from the direction of the ladies' room. "We're heading over to Whispers. Want to join us?"

Whispers was a nightclub that had dancing and a live band.

It would be even louder and more crowded than Nate's restaurant. "No, thanks. I think we'll get a drink and take off if a table doesn't open up. I should have called Nate or made a reservation. I wasn't thinking."

"Okay, cool. Well, we're heading out. Have fun. Nice to see you, Leesa. Watch out for Cole with the trivia." He pointed up at the television behind the bar. "He knows every answer."

"Does he?" Leesa said. "Well, I'll give him a run for his money."

Sam waved and put a possessive arm around the blond woman on his way out.

The man on the stool beside Leesa rose to leave and offered his seat to Cole.

"Thanks." He sat beside her. "Sorry about this. Do you want to go someplace quieter?"

"No. This is fine. I'm looking forward to kicking your butt in trivia." The spark of determination in her eyes made him laugh.

"We'll see about that."

While the bartender filled their drink orders, Cole leaned closer and said, "So, you're a trivia girl, are you?"

"As an only child, I had to do something to keep myself occupied. Reading became my passion, and since it was just me and my dad, I read a lot of his old books and found myself drawn to topics like sports and war. Topics that are probably read more by men than women. So watch out, because my brain is full of so much trivia I'm surprised it doesn't leak out my ears." She smiled and sipped her wine. When she licked her lips, he couldn't resist kissing her again.

"Maybe if you're nice," she said, "I'll let you win."

They both laughed, and as the questions flashed on the

screen, they said the answers out loud, tripping over each other's words.

"You *are* good," he said as the bartender refilled their glasses.

"Told you. Let's play truth or dare instead so you don't have to lose."

He shifted on his barstool, bringing their bodies together from shoulder to hip. "That sounds like something we should play in private."

"That's what makes it so fun." She raised her brows in quick succession. "You want to go first?"

"Sure."

The bartender asked if they'd like to order food to eat at the bar rather than wait for a table, so they ordered a sampling of appetizers.

"Okay," she said. "Truth or dare?"

"Truth." He placed his hand on her thigh and said, "I have nothing to hide."

She narrowed her eyes and pressed her lips together. "Everyone has secrets. How old were you when you first kissed a girl?"

He laughed. "You have no way of knowing if I'm telling the truth."

"Sure I do." She pointed her index finger and second finger at her eyes, then pointed them at him. "Honesty is all in the eyes. Stop stalling."

"Thirteen, playing spin the bottle."

"Thirteen? You started young. With who?" She finished her wine, and the bartender was quick to refill their glasses.

"You only get one question. Your turn."

"Dare." She trapped her lower lip between her teeth as he tried to come up with a dare.

"Dare?" He drank his wine and arched a brow. "I dare you to—"

"Collecting on your thousand-dollar date?"

Cole spun around at the sound of Kenna's voice. Kenna eyed Leesa with a serious scowl, then turned a smile back to Cole.

"I never thought I'd see you hanging out here," Kenna said. "You sure have changed."

"Is there something I can do for you, Kenna?" Cole kept a hand on Leesa's leg as he spoke, and he felt Leesa's muscles tense beneath his palm.

Kenna rolled her eyes down his body in a way that intimated a relationship that hadn't existed in years and said, "I'd just like to talk. I thought we could clear the air."

"I think we've said all we need to say, and I'm on a date, so if you'll excuse me." He turned back to Leesa, hoping Kenna would go away.

"Cole, I'm back in Peaceful Harbor to stay. We should be able to talk like adults."

"I think I'll go to the ladies' room." Leesa stood, and Cole rose beside her, but before he could say anything, she hurried off toward the bathroom.

He huffed a breath and set an angry glare on Kenna. "What's so important that you have to interrupt my date?"

"I wanted to apologize. I know I hurt your feelings all those years ago—"

"You didn't hurt my feelings, Mackenna. Thank you for apologizing, but that's all water under the bridge. Let it go."

She touched his arm, setting a seductive stare on him the way she used to when they were dating. She was still beautiful, but she had an edge about her now. He'd seen it last night when she'd stormed out of Mr. B's, and he didn't like the snotty way she'd looked at Leesa a few minutes ago.

"But things have changed. I was hoping we could, you know, try to see if we could reignite the spark. We were good together, Cole. You know we were." She stepped closer, pressing her leg against his.

"That flame went out years ago. There's nothing to reignite." As he turned, she grabbed his cheeks and pressed her lips to his.

For a second he was too stunned to register what was happening, and then he grabbed her wrists and tore his mouth from hers. He threw cash on the bar for the drinks and appetizers and set his most threatening stare on Mackenna.

"It's over, Mackenna. There's not a chance in hell I'd ever go out with you again."

LEESA FROZE, TRYING to process what she was witnessing. She felt the kiss between Kenna and Cole tear through her chest like an ice pick. Cole broke free of the kiss, the look on his face one of disgust and anger. She fisted her hands at her sides, feeling more possessive of him than she ever had of Chris. Someone bumped her shoulder as they walked past, but she was too focused on Cole and Kenna to care. Cole said something she couldn't hear and stormed toward Leesa with fury in his eyes. His jaw was tight, his eyes dark with anger, but when he placed a hand on her arm, it was tender and warm.

"Do you mind if we get out of here?" There was no hint of anger in his voice, and Leesa wondered how he'd managed to keep the feelings she'd seen written all over his face under control.

"Yes, of course."

Outside the restaurant Cole's frustration was evident in his determined steps as they headed for the car. She knew he was trying to push past whatever was going on between him and Kenna, and being confined in the car was the last thing he needed.

"Why don't we take a walk?" Leesa suggested.

He ran a hand through his hair, eyeing the restaurant like it was a villain. "I'm really sorry about that."

She stepped in closer and touched his chest. His muscles were firm, but it was the frantic pace of his heart that she focused on. He was more upset by Kenna kissing him than he'd been when Leesa had told him about her past.

"Unless you initiated the kiss, you have nothing to be sorry for. And even if you did, we're not dating exclusively, so you still wouldn't need to be sorry. Unfortunately, exes are part of life, and yours was willing to pay hundreds of dollars last night just to get your attention."

"Mackenna has always wanted what she couldn't have, and I'm sure seeing us together makes me even more appealing to her." He cupped her cheeks and pressed his lips to hers. "More importantly, I'm with you tonight, so if I *had* initiated anything with another woman, I'd damn well better apologize. And let's rectify the other situation."

"Other situation?"

He smiled, and his eyes darkened seductively. "We should be dating exclusively, even though this is our first date, because the thought of you dating any other man makes my blood boil."

"Are you sure?" As the words left her lips, she silently prayed he'd say he was.

He pressed his lips to hers again in a kiss that drew her body against his and sent her mind spinning into the night. It was a passionate kiss, sending waves of pleasure through her as the kiss intensified, then eased. Like the tide rolling in and crashing over the shore, only to draw back and build pressure, then reclaim its place once again. A surge of lust had her gripping his back, pressing her fingers into his muscles in an effort to possess as much of him as possible in the dark parking lot. She tried to fight her mounting desires, but his hand on her back, in her hair, his kiss, and the masculine, greedy groan that tore from his lungs were too hot to ignore.

He drew back, leaving her tingling lips begging for more. "I'm more than sure." He pressed his lips to hers again, punishingly soft this time. "Tell me you'll date only me. I know this is fast. But I also know it's right."

Reality stilled her racing heart. "But being with me could hurt your career. I don't want to gloss over that. You've worked too hard to get where you are."

He kissed her again, his eyes dark and serious, his tone equally so. "I've already told you that I can handle anything."

Her throat thickened at his strength and fortitude and his desire to be strong *for her*. He was so different from the man who'd broken her heart that a fearful wave of disbelief washed through her. Could she trust him? Trust his actions, his words, his offer of support? When he cupped her cheek and brushed his thumb over her lips, she felt the difference in his touch.

"You can trust me."

The honesty in his eyes and the sincerity in his voice solidified his promise and erased her fears.

Chapter Nine

THEY HELD HANDS as they walked down the road toward the harbor. The air held the scents of the sea and the hum of sexual tension.

"It's been years since I've walked through Peaceful Harbor at night," Cole said as he draped an arm over Leesa's shoulder and pulled her in closer. "I couldn't wait to settle into a practice here, but then I got so busy that doing things like this never happened." He smiled at her and added, "Honestly, I haven't been with anyone here who I'd want to take on a walk like this. Until you."

Leesa's stomach fluttered with his confession. "When I first drove into town I was so scatterbrained from everything that happened that I didn't really take in my surroundings. Lately I've been taking walks at night, like the night you saw me on the beach. It's been cathartic, taking in the sights and stores and knowing the water is just minutes from Tegan's house. I can see why she loves it here. There's so much to this town that I wonder why everyone doesn't walk instead of drive." She pointed to the old-fashioned lampposts with big round globes that rained light over the sidewalk and the old-fashioned awnings that hung above storefronts. "This is nothing like

Towson. The streets here feel friendly and loved, and as much as I hate to say it, where I used to live, the streets felt lonely and neglected."

"Maybe that was the company you kept and not the streets." Cole squeezed her shoulder.

In just the few minutes that it took to walk from the restaurant down to the harbor, the tension in Cole's face had subsided completely. But Leesa couldn't stop thinking about Kenna and the anger she'd seen in her face last night and again at the bar. Something felt off to her, like more than just an ex-girlfriend who wanted to reconnect with a man.

"Can I ask you something personal?" she said tentatively. "You don't have to answer if you don't want to."

"Sure." He led her across the street toward the marina.

"Is there more to the story with Kenna?"

They crossed the parking lot, and Cole led her down a set of stairs to the docks below. The silence between them was cut only by the sounds of water splashing along the pilings.

"There is more," he finally said as they walked along the water. His eyes rolled over the sailboats, their masts standing erect against the inky sky. The farther they walked, the fewer boats they passed. Cole was quiet as he led her to the far end of the marina, where a beautiful boat was tucked into a slip.

"This side of the marina is private. We'll be alone here on my boat." An easy smile curved his lips, and she wondered if this was his way of distracting her from the question.

"It's a beautiful boat." Even though he didn't seem tense, she worried that he was trying to distract her, and now she felt bad for prying. "Cole, you don't have to tell me what happened between you and Kenna. I was just curious."

"Have you always been this careful with questions?" he

asked with wonder in his voice. "Or is it because of what you went through?"

"Oh. I…" *Can't believe you noticed that I'm careful.* She was definitely more careful now than she had been before her ordeal. "I think I'm more careful now. Having gone through something that I don't really want people to know about makes me more aware of others feeling the same."

"You don't have to be careful with me. Even though we just met, I feel a connection with you that's different from what I have with other people. I don't have anything to hide. I just wanted to be someplace where we could sit and talk uninterrupted."

He helped her onto the boat, and they settled in on the cushioned bench. Leesa turned to face him, and he draped an arm across the back of the bench.

"I haven't shared this with anyone else, so I'd appreciate it if you didn't share it with my family. Peaceful Harbor isn't *that* small of a town, but word can travel quickly if it falls upon the wrong ears. And strangely, I still feel sort of protective of Mackenna."

Leesa's stomach tightened with his admission, but if she was honest with herself, she still felt protective of Chris in certain ways, too. Even though she'd been devastated when he'd chosen work over her, once the ache and disappointment had subsided, she'd understood why he'd done it.

"We dated for about two years, and I guess you could say she was my first love. Or at least that's what I thought at the time. But now I'm sure it wasn't love, because in the two years I dated her, I never thought about her even one-tenth as much as I've thought of you over the past two days."

He paused, and Leesa was sure he could see the surprise and

delight she felt written all over her face.

His fingers brushed over her shoulder. "I'm not trying to say I'm in love with you. There's such a big difference in what I *do* feel, it made me realize that I *wasn't* in love with her."

"I'm sorry if I look surprised. I'm not, really, because I'm in the same boat."

He arched a brow and his smile grew as he tapped on the boat.

"Literally, I guess." She laughed. "I thought I was in love with Chris, too, but I now know I wasn't. I was attracted to him, comfortable with him, and maybe after two years I was ready to settle for him, too. I'm not sure about that." She thought for a second, and her father's words came back to her again. "I guess in a way I could say that if anything good came out of the mess I went through, it was that I got to see that side of him before we ended up married with children and something he didn't want to handle came up. It would be much harder to part with children involved. But I don't think anyone really knows what they can and can't handle until they've had to face it."

"Is that how you rationalize what he did?" His eyes grew serious again as he ran his finger up the length of her arm, sending shivers right through her. "Because I disagree. I think we know what we can handle, and we make choices based on those things. I knew I wasn't the type of guy who could share a woman. I've never been that person." He raised his brows. "Sammy? He'd rather share than be tied down any day of the week, and I get that. There are lots of guys who feel that way."

He gazed out over the water for a minute and said, "You asked if there was more to what's happened between me and Kenna, and there is. I told you the truth about why we broke up. She wanted an open relationship, and I didn't. It was what I found out afterward, the thing that, as far as I know, has been kept secret for all these years, that left the bitter taste in my mouth."

Leesa couldn't imagine what it might be, since he'd already told her that Kenna hadn't cheated when they were dating.

"You probably know by now how important family is to me," he said.

"Yes, you all seem very close." She thought of the way they teased one another and how Shannon built up Tempe's organizational skills. She loved seeing that type of support between siblings.

He smiled. "We are, but I never realized how important family loyalty was to me outside of my own circle until after Kenna and I broke up."

"I'm not sure what you mean." She was trying to concentrate on what he was saying, but he was absentmindedly brushing feathery touches across her shoulder, and her entire body was aware of each and every stroke of his fingertips.

"Mackenna and I broke up the summer before I started medical school, and that summer she went to stay with her sister, Beth, in Virginia. Beth and I went to school together. Mackenna's younger, Nate's age. I met her through my friendship with Beth. Anyway, a month after arriving in Virginia, Beth found out that Mackenna was sleeping with her fiancé."

Holy crap. "Oh, that poor girl. Beth must have been devastated. Her own sister's fiancé? I don't want to disparage your ex, but…that takes a certain type of person."

"Yes. I feel like I dodged a bullet, so if I seem harsh toward her, please understand that it's not just because we once dated.

Beth confided in me about what happened, but as far as I know, she never told anyone else. She didn't want to become the talk of Peaceful Harbor, so I never told my family, either. They really don't know why we broke up, and they don't know about what happened afterward. I told them that it just didn't work out, and they respected that. Although they're curious about the specifics."

"But if that's the case, then I don't understand why she's trying so hard to get you back," she said honestly. "I would never try to get back together with a man who knew that I'd done something like that."

His smile returned. "Like I said, Mackenna wants what she can't have. I'm sure that was the appeal of her sister's fiancé. And honestly, I'm not sure if Mackenna knows that I'm aware of what happened in Virginia. We haven't spoken since we broke up. And now when I see her, the frustration I feel is no longer for myself. It's not the fact that she threw me away to sleep with other men. My ego isn't that big." A soft laugh escaped his lips. "It's because of what she did to Beth. If family means that little to her, then she's not the right woman for me by a long stretch. I would give my life for my family, and I know they'd do the same for me."

His sense of loyalty spoke directly to her heart. She'd never longed for her mother, partially because she and her father had been so close, and so happy, that she hadn't felt like she was missing out on anything. And also because her mother had shown the unkindest hand of all. She'd walked away from her family and never looked back.

Leesa gazed into Cole's soulful eyes, feeling like she'd found someone who understood who she was at her core, with the same beliefs, the same ethics and morals, as she'd learned from her father. Someone who could live anywhere on earth but chose to build a life around the small town where he'd grown up and still made time for his family. A man who understood himself as well as she understood herself, and taught her that she'd been missing something after all. She simply hadn't known it until she met him.

COLE'S FINGERS DRIFTED over Leesa's warm skin. Goose bumps rose to meet his touch. Between the gentle rocking of the boat and the moonlight reflecting in her eyes, Cole felt himself moving closer to her. His body was drawn to her, so close their lips nearly touched.

"I would have done anything for my father," she whispered.

He brushed her hair from her shoulder, holding her gaze. "I could tell that about you when you first told me about him."

"In the days after I lost him, everything felt foreign and different. I live in the house I grew up in, and even that felt different."

"I can only imagine." He tucked her hair behind her ear, caressing her soft cheek with the back of his hand and feeling his emotions grow with every word she said.

"It was strange, trying to find my way without his silent strength behind me. I really miss him." She dropped her gaze.

"I can hear it in your voice. I'm so sorry." He pressed his lips to hers.

"I think that's one reason it's so hard for me to just pick up and move here. I feel like I'd be leaving part of him behind. But in so many ways it makes sense to start over, like Tegan wants me to."

"Like I want you to." Cole hadn't planned on admitting what was whirling around in his mind, but once the words were out, the truth of them thickened between them.

"You...?" She lifted her eyes to his, and he couldn't tell if she was surprised or hopeful.

"I do." He couldn't resist her a second longer. "Leesa, if there's anything else you want to know about me, I'll share the good, the bad, and the ugly. I'm no saint, no matter how much my siblings tease me about it. There's always bad with the good, but right this moment, I want—*I need*—to be closer to you."

He slid his hand to the nape of her neck and brushed his thumb over her heated skin. "Tell me if you want me to back off. I know you've been through a lot, and I don't want to rush you."

"I was determined to keep my distance from any man, despite Tegan's encouragement to get back into the dating pool." She touched his cheek and smiled, and that simple touch made his pulse kick up. She inched closer and her dress crept up, exposing her inner thighs and making him even more aroused. "And then I met you, and for two days I've tried to fight the attraction that I felt from our very first glance. But it's too strong. You waylay all my fears, and when we're together—"

"Everything else disappears," he answered for her.

She wrapped her arms around his neck and their mouths came together hard and fast in a kiss filled with the urgency of new lovers, giving him the approval he needed to set his desires free. He tangled one hand in her silky hair, angling her head and opening her mouth wider for him to take—and holy hell did he take. He kissed her with reckless abandon, tasting every dip and curve of her mouth, sucking on her lower lip, then crashing their lips together again in a deep, passionate kiss. Her hands slid into his hair, down his neck, and over his back, sending shocks of heat straight to his groin. His free hand blazed south, traveling over her bare leg, beneath her dress, to the curve of her hip. Lord, she felt good, soft and luscious and so damn tempting that he groaned with need as he lowered her to her back. She went with him willingly, pulling him down on top of her and arching up to meet his eager arousal.

"You feel so good," he said between kisses.

The air left her lungs in a hot rush as he nibbled on her neck and sucked her earlobe into his mouth, earning him another needy moan. His hand slid up her sweet curves to her breast as he rained kisses over her shoulder.

His thumb brushed over her nipple, bringing it to a tantalizing peak. Her eyes were closed, her lips slightly parted, and her breasts heaved with each breath. She was stunning, lying beneath him in the moonlight.

"God you're beautiful."

"Kiss me," she whispered, pressing her hands to his lower back.

He sealed his lips over hers and ground his hips against hers, letting her feel the effect she had on him. The night air sizzled around them as they took and gave with equal measure. Every touch of her fingers sent bolts of heat through him. She clutched his ass as he lowered the strap of her dress, exposing her breast, covered only by a delicate lace bra.

He touched his forehead to hers in an effort to regain control and breathed in her heavenly scent. "I have to see more of you, Leese, feel more of you."

She tugged his shirt from his pants, and he leaned back, drinking in the hungry look in her eyes.

"Fair's fair," she said with a seductive grin.

Cole went up on his knees, making quick work of taking off his shirt. The second his chest was bare, her hands were on him, touching, groping, driving him out of his freaking mind. She rose off the bench and dragged her tongue over his nipple, tearing another groan from his lungs.

"Leese," he warned as she reached for his zipper.

The air between them pulsed with a life of its own.

"You're sure?" More than anything, he wanted to feel her naked beneath him, their bodies as close as two people could be, but they'd moved so fast that he needed her to slow down and think—hell, he should slow down and think, too, but he already knew what he wanted.

Her eyes darkened, and she spoke in a firm tone. "I'm twenty-seven years old, Cole. The rest of my life might be up in the air, but I know who I want, and I want you." Her eyes shifted to the dock. "You said no one would come by here, right?"

"No one will come near us, angel, but we can go inside if you prefer." He touched his lips to hers, and she closed her eyes with the tender kiss. "Or we can stop. I don't want you to have any regrets."

"I like the moonlight and the cool breeze on our skin." A devilish grin curled her lips. "And unless you really suck at what we're about to do, I can't imagine regretting one single second with you."

"Oh, I'll suck all right. And lick, nip, bite—whatever you want, angel, and in all the best ways."

Their mouths crashed together in a fiery kiss as they fought to strip away their clothing. Shoes *clunk*ed to the deck and clothing flew through the air, their lips parting long enough only to draw her dress over her head. Finally naked, both panting for air, Cole lowered her down to the cushion beneath him and took a moment to rake his eyes over every lush curve to the damp curls between her legs. She reached for him and he came down over her, feeling her thighs open to accommodate his hips and powerful thighs as he took her in another deep kiss. She rocked her hips, urging him on. He drew back and gazed into her eyes as he laced his fingers with hers and brought them to his lips, pressing a kiss to the back of each before placing them beside her.

His mouth explored her heated skin from her lips to her jaw and down to the hollow of her neck, where he lingered with openmouthed kisses. He kissed the length of her collarbone to the center of her breastbone, then dragged his tongue between her breasts. She arched up to meet his mouth, and when she reached for him, he laced his fingers with hers again to hold them in place as he pressed his lips to the tip of her nipple.

"Oh God. *Cole*," she said with a shaky breath, her hips rising against his eager erection.

He sucked on the taut peak, pressing the sensitive nub against the roof of his mouth. He released one of her hands and slid his palm down her waist, over her hip, holding her there against the cushions as he rubbed his erection against her, feeling her wetness on his balls and earning himself a symphony of sexy, wanton moans. Their laced fingers rested beside her head, her fingernails digging into the back of his hand.

"Cole, I need more," she begged.

Her thighs pressed against his hips as he moved down her body, tasting every inch of heated flesh, laving the underside of each breast, kissing her ribs, her stomach, the sweet center of her navel, as she writhed and begged beneath him. He wasn't about to hurry. Touching Leesa, hearing her sexy pleas, smelling her desire, was too intoxicating to rush. He kissed her inner thighs and teased her damp center as he brought his mouth to her. She gasped a breath, rocking her hips to meet every swipe of his tongue. She tasted sweet and hot and so damn good he wanted to bed down for the winter right there, giving her pleasure, feeling her body tremble against his touch.

"Oh...*God*." Her hands clutched at his shoulders, her nails digging into his skin as her thighs tightened and she shattered against his mouth. "Cole—"

He stayed there, enjoying every last pulse, until the last of her climax shuddered through her. Only then did he move up and claim her with a possessive kiss. He held her until her breathing calmed and their kisses turned tender.

"Condom," he whispered against her lips. He scanned the deck for his pants. Spotting them a few feet away, he groaned, not wanting to leave her for even a moment. The thought of what she'd been through and how recent the end of her last relationship was slipped into his mind. He didn't want to rush her. Lord knew she was worth waiting for. "Leesa, are you sure you want to go further? We can wait."

She pressed her hand to his cheek, her green eyes as warm as a caress. "I want this, Cole. I want you."

He retrieved his pants, dug a condom out of his wallet, and tore it open with his teeth. She helped him roll it on, then lowered herself to the cushion, her hands reaching for him, knees widening as he perched above her, searching her eyes to make certain she was still on the same page.

She smiled up at him. "I'm okay. Promise."

As their bodies joined, their mouths came together again. They moved slowly at first, finding their groove.

"So tight," he said between kisses. "So good."

The feel of her softness pressed against him, her legs

wrapped around his waist, and her hot, eager mouth meeting every thrust of his tongue with an effort all her own was too much. He had to slow their rhythm to regain control. It had been too long since he'd been intimate with a woman. Between work and family, dating had fallen by the wayside, and now all he wanted was to pleasure Leesa over and over until she could barely move. He wanted this moment to last a lifetime. The thought startled him, but as they kissed and groped, their bodies slick with sweat, their hands roving over hot skin, memorizing, touching, clutching every inch they could reach, he knew it was true.

And when he gazed down at the woman beneath him, so trusting, so lost in him—*in them*—and her eyes finally came open, they were pools of emotion, just as he was sure his were, too. He angled his hips, driving in deeper and quickening his pace, needing to see her come apart for him again. She came hard, her hips bucking off the bench, her fingers digging into his skin, and his name sailing off her lips like a plea.

Her body shivered and shook as she gasped for air, and he sealed his lips over hers, breathing for her. The last of the climax rolled through her, and her body went soft. They kissed as cool air danced over their heated flesh. A sensation of oneness came over him, the line between them blurred.

"Feel that?" he whispered.

"I feel everything," she said.

He sealed his lips over hers again, unable to hold back for another moment. He drove in hard, burying himself deep time and time again as he took her up, up, up, and higher still. When her eyes slammed shut and her body tightened like a vise around his hard length, he didn't just follow her over the edge—he leaped, hard and fast and with every ounce of his heart.

Chapter Ten

THEY LAY IN the moonlight for a long time, their bodies wrapped around each other, talking about everything and nothing—until Leesa's stomach growled so loud she curled up against him in embarrassment.

"I think that's a sign," he said as he retrieved a blanket from beneath one of the benches and draped it over her. "I'm going to uh…" He eyed the condom lying on the deck.

"Okay."

He kissed her sweetly before disappearing inside the boat. She wasn't sure if they had lain together for ten minutes or a hundred, but in that time she never once felt embarrassed or uncomfortable, and regret wasn't even on her emotional radar. If anything, she was surprised by how relaxed she felt with him. Even with Chris she had always jumped up after sex to wash up and put on clothes. But the way Cole had worshipped her body, he'd made her feel beautiful and desired.

He'd seemed equally comfortable with her, but then again, guys were usually much more comfortable naked than women were, weren't they? She could count the number of men she'd slept with on one hand, but it was enough to realize that none of them seemed to worry about being seen naked.

She shifted on the cushion, knowing she'd be the best kind of sore tomorrow. She was surprised at how much she'd wanted to make love with him. Sex had never felt as good as it did with Cole. With Chris she'd never even had an orgasm without helping herself out. She smiled to herself and closed her eyes. If she concentrated, she could still feel the weight of Cole on her, hear his seductive murmurings in her ears. Surely this couldn't be real. Men like Cole Braden didn't exist and remain single, did they? In a quiet little town like Peaceful Harbor? She felt like she'd been plunked down in Handsome Town, USA, where Bradens were hot and loyalty ran deep.

"That's one hell of a wicked smile you have going on there."

Her eyes flew open and she swallowed a laugh. *If you only knew.*

Cole stood shirtless, in a pair of jeans. More than six feet of hard muscle, with big hands, a talented mouth, and she didn't dare think of the thick rod between his legs and the pleasures it had brought her. And those eyes. She'd never met a man with more expressive eyes. They were always focused and alert. Even midorgasm his gaze was penetrating and intense, and somehow full of warmth, too.

He reached for her hand and drew her against him. His body was warm and hard, and his embrace felt safe. He kissed her, and she'd already come to anticipate the slant of his lips, the slide of his hand beneath her hair, and that sexy half-moan, half-groan thing he did that was so darn masculine it made her body prickle with desire from head to toe.

When he drew back, she went up on her toes and pressed her lips to his again.

"You need to patent your mouth," she said.

He laughed and tugged her impossibly closer. "Yeah?"

"Oh yeah," she said. "Insure it, too. I've never tasted such mind-blowing lips, and we won't even get into the torment of that tongue of yours."

He kissed her again. "I like you, Annalise Avalon. A whole hell of a lot."

"That's a good thing, considering you just got to know every inch of me quite intimately."

"Speaking of which. We should get cleaned up. I heard your belly growl before you took advantage of me, and I'd hate for you to think you could use me just for sex."

"Oh, you would, would you?" She laughed at his tease and followed him down a few steps inside the boat. Her breath caught at the elegant finishes. The floor looked like it was made of fine wood, the couches were off-white, with navy and tan accent pillows complementing the decor. There were photographs of Cole's family on the wall, a small dining table, and a complete kitchen off to her left.

"This is like an apartment," she said, mystified. "I had no idea it was so luxurious."

"It's just an illusion." He held her hand and led her to a bedroom, with a wide, inviting bed and a bathroom that looked fancy enough to be in a hotel, even if a little tight.

"Wow, Cole. I have a feeling you're way out of my league." She ran her hand over the sparkling sink.

"Out of your league? Because I have a boat?" He arched a brow, amusement dancing in his eyes.

"Yacht, you mean." Her eyes skimmed over the plush blanket and expensive-looking pillows, over to a two-tiered shelf filled with medical and boating books.

"Boat." He wrapped his arms around her waist from behind and nuzzled against her neck. "You're not going to get all weird on me, are you? This was my grandfather's boat. He sold it a decade before he passed away, and when I had enough money, I tracked it down to a guy on Cape Cod and bought it. I had it refitted out there by a buddy of mine, Pete Lacroux. To me it's the boat my grandfather used to take us out on. The boat I learned to fish on. Nothing fancy." He shrugged, and she turned in his arms.

"You just went from me worrying that you had some hidden pretentious side to exposing the most wonderful, sentimental thing a person could do."

"Nah. I told you, there's always bad with the good. I upgraded the engine and the interior. I didn't go all-out. I mean, it could have been much more elegant. If I didn't like nice things, I probably would have had it refitted to exactly replicate the way my grandfather had it."

She smiled at his confession. "If that's all you've got that fits into the *bad* category, that's pretty darn good."

"Good enough to join you in the shower?" He raised his brows again, looking sexy and handsome and enticingly seductive.

"Not if you want to get out of here tonight." She pushed his chest playfully, sending him out the bathroom door as she blew him a kiss.

In the privacy of the bathroom, Leesa leaned on the sink and stared at her reflection. Had she really just given herself over to this man on their first date? She'd waited three weeks before sleeping with Chris, and with the men before him she'd had a three-date rule. She always went out with a man three times before sleeping with him, because by the third date she usually knew for sure if she wanted to see him again or not. But *one date? One!* Surely this put her into the *easy* category.

But God…Could any woman resist Cole? He was romantic and charming, and…There were no words to describe what she thought of him. Only to describe what she felt when she was with him—that everything was finally *right*.

She turned on the shower and stepped beneath the warm spray. As she soaped up and rinsed off, she let her hands linger over the swell of her hips, thinking of how much Cole seemed to enjoy them. He was always placing a hand on her hip. She didn't feel easy or like a slut. She felt…*happy*.

She used a fluffy towel to dry off and pressed it to her nose, inhaling deeply. If *right* had a smell, then Cole, this towel, and this boat where they'd just made love was it. She knew she should be careful with her emotions, but how could she when she felt so good?

She realized she'd left her clothes up on the deck. Great, now she had to walk out in a towel. She covered herself up and opened the bathroom door. Her clothes were folded neatly in a pile on the bed. Her sandals were on the floor. Warmed by his thoughtfulness, she dressed and hung up her towel, then went in search of the man who was chipping away at the walls she'd put up around herself.

She heard his voice before she saw him pacing on the deck, his phone pressed to his ear. His hand rubbed at the back of his neck. Her hands itched to massage the tension out of him, but she remained where she was, giving him privacy for his phone conversation.

He turned, a smile spreading across his face when he caught sight of her.

"Hey, Rush. I've got to run. The last thing you need to worry about is my schedule. Okay." He paused, closing the distance between him and Leesa, his hand outstretched. "See ya, buddy."

His hand slid around her waist as he put his phone in his pocket. "I'm sorry. Work stuff."

"That's okay. I should probably let you get back to—"

"There's nothing I want to get back to besides dinner with you." He pressed his lips to hers, and her body melted at the contact.

"My friend Rush Remington was just letting me know about a patient he's sending in to see me Monday." He put on his shirt and shoes and helped Leesa onto the dock. "Rush is an Olympic skier, and his friend's daughter is an Olympic contender in gymnastics. She injured her back, and he wants me to evaluate her."

"Oh, that's terrible. Sports injuries are bad enough, but I'd imagine that at that level, it's everything." As they left the dock and headed back toward town, she wondered how long they'd been down at his boat. She wasn't tired, but the streets weren't busy and the marina was near deserted, telling her they must have been there quite a while. She couldn't get over the fact that she'd so quickly taken their relationship to a more serious level in the span of a few short hours.

"It is, but I don't want to talk about work." He draped his arm over her shoulder and kissed her again.

His eyes took in their surroundings. His strong jaw was darker now as stubble appeared, giving him an edgier look. He glanced at her as they walked, and his smile softened his appearance again.

"You're bound to burn a hole through me if you stare too long."

"I'm just trying to figure out why I did this. How you got through the carefully erected box that I've lived in for what feels like forever."

He stopped at the corner and faced her head-on, his eyes serious. "Do you regret that we were close?"

"No." *Regret* wasn't the right word. She was glad they'd been close, and she felt good about being with him now, which was also strange for her. She was very aware of *how* comfortable she was with him.

"But don't you find this just a little weird?" She suddenly had a thought. Maybe he did this all the time. Maybe this wouldn't feel weird for him—or anyone else for that matter. People slept together on first dates all the time, didn't they? Or did they? She'd never worried about what other people did with their sex lives, but she wondered if she was a step behind after being out of the dating scene for so long.

"Which part?" he asked, stepping in so close that if she went up on her toes their lips would touch. "The fact that we were intimate on our first date, or the fact that I'm hoping tonight never ends and secretly trying to figure out how to get you to wake up in my arms tomorrow morning?"

"Cole," she whispered. How should a woman respond when a man said something so beautifully romantic that she wanted to wrap it up in a pretty ribbon and set it on a shelf to revisit a million times over her lifetime? *I want to go home with you, too, but I'm too scared of what tomorrow will bring? Or next week? Or next month? I should take tonight and run, preserve it forever, and let you move on to a woman without a tainted past?*

He lifted her chin with his index finger and smiled again. Did he know how his smile made her insides go squishy? Could he see it in her eyes? And if so, did it bother him or turn him on?

"I didn't mean to embarrass you."

It would be easy to go home with Cole, to wake up in his arms and pretend that if her past became the talk of the town, he really would stand up for her. But she couldn't expect anyone to do that, despite what he'd said. For her own safety she needed to preserve the strength and hard shell she'd developed before coming to Peaceful Harbor.

She went with silence and a smile instead of responding as they continued walking along the quiet road, passing Chelsea's Boutique, Jazzy Joe's Café, and a number of other dark, closed stores. A dog barked in the distance, and every so often a car drove past. As they neared the bar, she remembered the scene with Kenna, and her stomach clenched. She tried to tell herself that it wasn't jealousy she was feeling, but a normal emotion anyone would have if the guy they were out with was kissed by a woman.

Yeah, that's called jealousy.

She tried to distract herself from the unfamiliar emotion. "Tell me about your brothers. I know Nate owns the restaurant and Sam owns a rafting company. Is that right?"

"Yes," he said as they crossed another street and walked through the parking lot of Tap It. "He rents boats, but he also takes people out on wilderness excursions. It's pretty cool. When Ty's in town, he hangs with Sammy a lot."

"I've never been rafting. It sounds fun."

"Really? Never?" His brows furrowed.

"Towson isn't really a river town," she said. "We have the harbor nearby, but between school, then working full-time, there wasn't much time for other stuff. I had hoped to do some fun things once I was settled in my career, but then I was dating Chris, and...*life* got in the way."

"What else besides rafting did you hope to do?" He stopped

beneath a light by the front of the restaurant.

"Well, river rafting wasn't on my list, but it does sound fun. The things I wanted to do probably seem silly because they aren't very outlandish. There are things I haven't done since I was a little girl, like hiking up a mountain and having a picnic. And then there are things I've simply never done, like seeing an outdoor concert."

"I know they have outdoor concerts in Towson."

"Yes, but I've never been. Oh, and one day I'm going to learn to play the guitar."

"The guitar." He shook his head. "Seriously?"

"Yes!" She laughed. "See? My wish list is boring, isn't it?"

"Not at all. I happen to be a pretty good guitar player, and I'd be happy to teach you."

"Right. Of course you are. Is there anything you don't do?"

He laughed. "Yes. I don't lie, cheat, or steal."

She rolled her eyes and wondered when it would rain on the Cole parade.

"My mom made us all learn an instrument when we were younger, probably to keep us out of trouble. Anyway, I'm pretty good at the guitar. I'd be happy to teach you."

His *mom*. He'd had such a solid upbringing. Maybe there would be no raining on this parade after all. She'd seen the outcome of his parents' efforts in five of their six children, and she felt like the luckiest girl on earth.

"I'd like that. Is there anything you've always wanted to do but haven't accomplished?"

He tugged her in closer and said, "There are lots of things I have yet to accomplish." Lowering his lips to a breath away, he said, "I've never kissed you right here beneath the moonlight, in front of this restaurant, after making love to you on my boat."

He sealed his lips over hers in a sensual, dreamy kiss that left her breathless. "Now I have."

As they walked into the restaurant, Cole asked, "Do you have plans tomorrow?"

Her pulse tripped with hope. "I'm working at Mr. B's until seven."

"Can you pencil me in at seven thirty?"

There was nothing she'd rather do.

Chapter Eleven

MONDAYS WERE ALWAYS crazy at Cole's medical office, and fitting in Elsie Hood, the gymnast, meant rescheduling patients and bringing his last patient of the day in during his lunch break in order to free up that appointment for Elsie. He didn't mind long hours or taking extra time with patients; in fact, the time with patients was something he tried never to skimp on. But tonight he had a date with Leesa, and that changed everything. He checked his watch and hoped he'd make it out of work by six.

Shannon had called him earlier in the day to tell him how much she'd enjoyed getting to know Leesa—and to pry him for details about their date. He'd taken the opportunity to enlist her help with a surprise he'd planned for Leesa. He smiled to himself thinking about how he hadn't had to spill a single detail about their date. His sister said she'd heard his excitement in his voice.

Now, as he walked toward an exam room to meet his newest patient, just thinking about seeing Leesa again made his body thrum with desire.

Jon came out of another exam room in his white lab coat. He put a patient chart in the holder by the door and smirked at

Cole. "You'd better get that freshly fucked grin off your face before you go in there."

Cole scrubbed a hand over his mouth, trying to put on his game face. *Epic fail.* The contented grin was there to stay.

"I've never seen you like this," Jon said with amusement in his eyes.

"I've never felt like this."

"You seeing her again tonight?" Jon lifted his eyes as a nurse came out of another exam room. She pointed to the door, indicating that Jon had a patient waiting. He held up one finger to the nurse as Cole answered.

"I hope to. So you might as well get used to the look." Cole reached for the doorknob.

An hour later Cole had examined Elsie Hood, a confident, determined fifteen-year-old gymnast with the most obnoxious father and silent mother Cole had ever come across. He sat across from Ann and Martin Hood, no longer smiling or thinking of Leesa, but consumed by the well-being of his new patient.

Martin was a paper-thin, diminutive man who'd probably never played a sport in his life. He had a nasal voice, beady, ratlike eyes, and kept a firm grip on the arm of the chair where he sat between his wife and daughter, opposite Cole. "If the tests show this spondo…"

"Spondylolysis, which means a defect of the vertebra. In Elsie's case," Cole explained, "I think she has a pars fracture, or more specifically, a fracture in the pars interarticularis of the vertebral arch. But we need to get X-rays and a bone scan done to confirm the diagnosis."

Elsie had her mother's green eyes and flame-red hair. A spray of freckles peppered her nose and cheeks, and Cole noticed that she hadn't looked at her father the entire visit. Even when her father spoke to her, she kept her eyes on her mother, or Cole, or on her lap, which in Cole's mind confirmed his greatest concern. She was either fearful of her father or worried about disappointing him. He'd seen it a hundred times with young athletes with overbearing parents. They either homed in on their parents, holding eye contact too long, stiffening under their assessing gazes, or addressing them with a coldness that should never be present between a loving parent and their child. Cole had been lucky in that regard. His father hadn't taken sports nearly as seriously as he had. It had been his own determination and drive that had fueled his need to propel himself to all-star status, and having an overbearing coach had fed into his obsessive need to be the best. The right coach would have helped him learn to back off. God knew his parents had tried time and time again. But Cole had been a stubborn teenager, and as with medicine, he'd been determined to be the best and hadn't let on to his coach or his parents how badly he'd been injured until it was too late.

Now, as he took in the worried look in Elsie's eyes, he wondered if she'd been experiencing pain for longer than she'd let on. Each time he'd asked, her parents had answered for her. The tests would reveal the truth, and he hoped to hell he was wrong.

"And the treatment?" Ann asked.

"That will depend on what the tests reveal, but if Elsie has only recently been experiencing pain, and if it is indeed a pars fracture, then we'll try rest from exercise and anti-inflammatories for a few weeks. Many times with kids Elsie's age, that's enough to allow their bones to heal."

"Rest from exercise?" Martin snapped. "She's an *Olympic* contender. She can't take a few weeks off now."

Cole bit back his disdain for parents who put anything above their children's health and put on his most professional face. "Yes, Mr. Hood, I understand that she is an Olympic contender, which is a magnificent achievement." He smiled at Elsie and said, "You should be very proud of yourself, Elsie. Not many adults have the determination and drive that you show at such a young age."

"Thank you, Dr. Braden," she said with a proud smile.

Cole shifted his eyes as he spoke, to indicate that the conversation was meant to be inclusive of Elsie and both of her parents. "We will know more when we get the results, but it's important that you begin thinking about treatment options. If there is a fracture and it's not given appropriate time to heal, the fracture gap at the pars can widen, and if that happens, the vertebra shifts forward. That condition is called spondylolisthesis. Typically it's the fifth lumbar vertebra that shifts forward, on the part of the pelvic bone called the sacrum. And, of course, undiagnosed, this can lead to the vertebra pressing on a nerve, which will bring even more pain."

"What then?" Ann asked with fear in her voice.

Cole didn't want to go to the what-if stage with these parents even though he hoped a little fear might push Elsie's father to stop thinking about the Olympics and instead focus on his daughter's future health. He tempered his response just enough to ride the line between fear and reality.

"Hopefully we've caught this early enough that rest and anti-inflammatories, and if necessary, a brace for stabilization, can correct the issues and we won't have to think about the rest."

"A brace?" Martin moved forward in his chair and lowered his voice. "May I remind you again, Dr. Braden, that she is an

Olympic contender."

"Yes, thank you, but I can assure you, Mr. Hood, that I have not forgotten Elsie's achievement. I need for you and your family to clearly understand that if this is a pars fracture, and if it does not heal appropriately, bone to bone, it will never again be fully stable without surgery. Your daughter could experience a lifetime of discomfort if this isn't diagnosed and treated appropriately." Cole had seen both parents and patients who were afraid of treatment and failed to return for tests or follow-up visits. He turned to Elsie and asked again, "How long have you been experiencing pain?"

"Two weeks," Martin said before she could answer.

Cole's job as a physician was to treat the patient, and he rode a fine line trying not to overstep his boundaries when parents were involved. He respected those invisible lines and gave it one last shot.

"Two weeks? Is that right, Elsie? Please remind me what you were doing when you first noticed the pain."

Her eyes darted nervously between her parents and Cole. "It was after practice one night. I turned to pick something up and it really hurt."

The fact that she avoided responding to the timing of her symptoms was not lost on Cole, but he wouldn't push any further. He already knew that she had classic symptoms of a pars fracture—pain when bending back and rotating.

He ordered the appropriate tests and hoped they'd return to discuss treatment options on Friday, as agreed. His bigger worry was that Elsie hadn't been telling the truth about when her symptoms had begun and that they were dealing with a progressive rather than an early-stage injury.

After work he tried to push those worries aside as he showered and changed and drove over to Mr. B's to surprise Leesa.

LEESA'S SHIFT WAS over in ten minutes and she had no idea how she'd made it through with her sanity intact. She'd been up half the night again, thinking about Cole, and when she was wide-awake at five o'clock, she'd accidentally woken up Tegan with the smell of coffee from the coffeemaker. While she felt guilty for waking her, at least chatting with Tegan had allowed Leesa to focus on something other than the man who had infiltrated her every thought. She'd confessed that they'd slept together, and since it was so out of character for Leesa, Tegan had taken the opportunity to tease her about having sex on her first date until Leesa was laughing so hard she had tears streaming down her cheeks. It felt good to experience happy tears instead of sad ones. *Really, really good.* It seemed everything about Peaceful Harbor was good for Leesa. Or maybe she was rationalizing because of her mounting feelings for Cole.

When she'd gone out for her morning run, she'd found a greeting card from Cole on her car. It was one of those cute, old-fashioned-looking cards that had a black-and-white picture of a little girl and boy on the front. The little girl was holding a bouquet of flowers and the boy was kissing her cheek. He'd written *Me and You* and drawn arrows pointing to the children. Inside the card he'd written *If only I'd known you back then. We have a lot of time to catch up on and memories to make. Cole.*

She'd been so touched by his romantic gesture that she'd taken off for her morning run with the intention of passing his house, hoping to see him. But by the time his beach house had come into focus, she'd felt that showing up unannounced *again* was a clingy thing to do—and she'd turned around and headed back the way she'd come. Now she stood behind the bar with Ace while he mixed her customers' drinks. She noticed the tightening of his jaw and brow and the way his breathing changed when he walked to the other side of the bar. Ever since learning about his amputation, Leesa had been thinking about the young girl from her Girl Power group who had lost her leg below the knee.

The other kids had been curious about her prosthesis, and the little girl had explained how she'd lost her leg, how long it had taken to get used to walking again, and eventually running. She'd told them how she'd experienced phantom limb pain, and her mother had later explained to Leesa that phantom limb pain was psychological, caused by the brain attempting to move the absent limb, sending out abnormal neural patterns, which are experienced as shooting pain. She further explained that a few weeks of mirror therapy, where the little girl had sat with a mirror facing the remaining leg while she moved it as she watched its reflection in the mirror, so that it appeared both the good and the amputated leg were moving, had retrained her brain and alleviated her pain.

Leesa watched Ace now and wondered if he was experiencing the same sort of thing.

Ace set the drink he was mixing aside and crossed his thick arms over his chest. He leaned his hip against the bar and narrowed his eyes in what Leesa imagined was the stern look he'd aimed at his children when they were younger.

"You know, when my kids have something to say to me, they just blurt it out. They learned that somewhere along the way." He smiled, and it softened the sternness in his eyes. "Do you want to talk about something?"

Yes. She opened her mouth to ask about his leg, but at the last second she chickened out. "No. I was just waiting for the drinks."

"Uh-huh." He unfolded his arms and turned to finish preparing the drinks. With his back to Leesa, he said, "That was a big win you landed at the auction the other night."

Embarrassment swept through her. "Cole asked me to bid for him."

"Ah, so you were just helping him out?" He glanced over his shoulder at her with an arched brow.

"Yes." She sighed and admitted, "Sort of. At first, I guess."

He set the drink on the bar and smiled. "Good. My boy needs to get out and have some fun."

She didn't know how to respond to that, and thankfully, they were interrupted when Shannon walked into the restaurant. She was a whirlwind of energy, waving as she approached in a cute skirt and flowing cotton top.

"Hi, Leesa." Shannon kissed her father's cheek. "Hi, Daddy."

"Hi, sweetie. I didn't expect to see you today."

"I had to run an errand for Cole, so I thought I'd stop by on my way back." Shannon's eyes filled with delight. She tucked her brown hair behind her ear and nudged Leesa's arm with her elbow. "I heard you guys had a lovely date last night."

Leesa felt her cheeks flame up. "We, um. Yes, we had a great time." She set the drinks on a tray and said, "I'd better get these to the customers before my shift is over." She felt their eyes burning a path to her as she served the drinks. What on earth could Cole have said to Shannon? She was dying to check her phone to see if he'd texted, but that would have to wait until after her shift was over.

When her shift ended, she went into the back room to clock out. Ace walked into the kitchen area a few minutes later with that pained look on his face again. She took her things from the locker as he lowered himself carefully to a chair. She sat in the chair beside Ace, and after awkwardly starting to ask, then stopping enough times that she felt ridiculous, she finally said, "I heard that you were in the military."

"Yes, that's right."

She noticed that he took his weight off his leg by resting his left foot on the table stand.

"I'm sorry to hear about your accident."

He crossed his arms again, and she wondered if it was a defensive barrier or a habit. She was so used to looking for nonverbal cues from her years of teaching that she couldn't stop herself from noticing the slightest of things.

"Thank you, but in every profession there are risks. As you've found out firsthand." He lowered his chin, and his gaze softened. "I'm sorry about what you went through back in Towson, but I'm glad it brought you here. We like having you as part of the Mr. B family."

His kind compliment made her heart squeeze. "Thank you. Like you said, every profession…" She watched him watching her and finally found the courage to ask what she really wanted to know. "Ace, does your prosthesis hurt you?"

His smile faded to a tight-lipped line. "No, ma'am. It does not."

The formality of his words spoke louder than the words themselves. "I'm sorry. I noticed that sometimes you look a little uncomfortable, and I knew a girl once who had phantom limb pain and she used mirror therapy. I just thought…" *I'd make an ass of myself.*

130

Ace leaned forward, his jaw tight, his eyes soft. Leesa held her breath, feeling that she'd crossed a line from which there might be no retreat.

"You have a very tender heart, Annalise. May I call you Annalise?"

"Yes," she managed with her heart thundering against her ribs. She didn't know if she was going to be fired or told to butt out, but she probably deserved both for sticking her nose into his business.

"You went through a traumatic time and you didn't come out unscathed. Agreed?"

Unable to find her voice, she nodded.

"I'd bet that not a day goes by when you wish you could escape the hurt that accusation caused you." He held her gaze, and she couldn't turn away.

Another silent nod, and he dropped his eyes for a beat. He lifted those warm, intelligent eyes again, and his gaze turned serious.

"Sometimes it hurts to lose things, to leave them behind. We can't really forget them, so they linger. A twinge here, a sharp reminder there. The things we gain from the loss puts perspective on that pain. We can try to bury the pain, mask it, ignore it." He shrugged, and an easy smile lifted his lips, flashing a hint of Cole, which made her stomach tighten for a whole different reason. "You might not understand this yet, but sometimes that pain is necessary in order to move forward. There are times when those painful reminders drive us to be stronger."

She knew there was a message in his words that was bigger than phantom limb pain, but she was still holding her breath, waiting for him to fire her, and she couldn't process any hidden meanings. It wasn't until he patted her hand and said, "We can run from our past, but we can't really move forward until we accept it. Pain and all," that she realized he was talking about her. And his wisdom, the warmth of his gaze, the solid strength of his hand, made her long for her father.

He rose to his feet. "I appreciate your concern."

Cole walked through the kitchen doors, his eyes moving quickly between the two of them, and her heart skipped a beat.

"Did I interrupt something?" Cole asked. He pointed his thumb over his shoulder. "Shannon said I'd find you in here."

"I'm going to assume you mean Leesa and not me." Ace patted Cole's back on his way out the door. He hesitated and looked at Leesa again. "Annalise. Thank you for the chat. I'll see you tomorrow for your shift?"

"Yes. Thank you."

He nodded and disappeared out the doors, which swung closed behind him. Cole leaned in for a kiss. "Hi. Everything okay?"

"Mm-hm."

"Did you get my texts?"

She shook her head to clear her mind. "I haven't had a chance to check my phone."

"No wonder you didn't answer." He reached for her hand and she took it absentmindedly. "Ready for your first guitar lesson?"

"My first...?" Her mind was still stuck on what his father had said. *We can run from our past, but we can't really move forward until we accept it. Pain and all.*

She wondered if she'd ever get to the point of not feeling like she had to look over her shoulder. If she could ever use her given name again in public. She'd picked up on the way Ace had used her new name in front of Cole, and it magnified just how much of herself she'd left behind. She had the distinct feeling that he'd been trying to tell her that she had no reason to hide who she was, but she sure didn't feel that way.

She followed Cole out the door, realizing that she wanted the freedom to use her given name more than she cared to admit. Her father had never called her *Leesa*. She was always Annalise.

Elegant and strong, like a river. That's my Annalise. That's my girl, he'd said.

She'd thought she could leave it all behind and start over, but as *Leesa* rather than *Annalise,* she felt like a felon running from something she'd done. A fake, borrowing someone else's career, someone else's name—and wishing she had someone else's past.

Chapter Twelve

LEESA WAS QUIET on the drive to Rough Riders, and Cole took that time to try to settle his own mind, which was still wrestling with Elsie Hood, her overbearing father, and her meek mother. He hoped her parents wouldn't abandon the tests or the treatment. At her age, treatment would certainly lead to proper healing, but if her parents insisted that she continue to train, Elsie faced a painful future—he knew that even before seeing the test results.

Knowing there wasn't much he could do without coming across too aggressively, he tried to push those thoughts away and parked amid a sea of cars. Rough Riders was a local hangout for teenagers. Even when they weren't taking the boats out, they were hanging out around the river. The river had a different vibe than the harbor. It was cooler, because of the shade from the trees that lined both sides, and Sammy was so effervescent that people had always flocked to him. He didn't let customers take boats out after sunset, but Cole had spoken to him earlier in the day and had made arrangements for his and Leesa's date, and Shannon had taken care of the rest of his surprise.

He opened Leesa's door and gathered her in his arms, kissing her softly. "You okay tonight? I hope it was okay that I showed up and stole you away."

"I'm glad you did." Her words were honest, but there was a shadow in her eyes that worried him.

"Do you want to talk before we go down to the boat?"

Her eyes widened. "We're going in a boat? I thought you were teaching me to play the guitar."

"I am, but you've never been on the river, so I thought we'd take the boat down a ways, have a picnic, play a little guitar..." He kissed her again, and her lips curved up in a sweet smile.

"Cole, you took all my hopes and wrapped them into one evening?"

He kissed her again, and the darkness in her eyes slipped away. "Surely not *all* your hopes, but I love to see you smile."

They headed down a path toward the boathouse. Canoes and kayaks were lined up at the water's edge, and rowboats were tied to the dock. Teens and twentysomethings were sitting on beach blankets and hanging around by the boathouse. A young couple sat on the dock with their toes dangling in the water.

Inside the boathouse Sam was hanging up life jackets and talking with a group of wet and smiling teens who looked like they'd just come in from a boat ride. He glanced at Cole and Leesa.

"Hey, bro," Sam said. "Leesa, good to see you again. Your boat's all set. Grab some life preservers and you can take off."

"Thanks, Sammy." Cole helped Leesa put on her life preserver.

"This must look attractive," she said softly.

"You could wear a Hefty bag and you'd look hot." He winked as he put on his own life preserver. "If it's any consolation, I hate wearing them, too, but Sam insists."

"I don't mind. I know how to swim, though, so I'm not too

worried about falling in, unless you're taking me over rapids." Her eyes widened. "Oh my God, you're not, are you?"

"It's too dangerous for that in the evening, but if you're into it, we can go some other time." He helped her into the boat, untied it from the dock, then climbed in himself and paddled them out into the river.

"Into it? Um…" Her eyes were as wide as hard-boiled eggs, which made him laugh. She scanned the riverbank as she asked, "Is there a place downriver to have a picnic?"

Cole didn't want to spoil the surprise he'd set up and realized he shouldn't have said anything. "You'll see." He paddled away from Rough Riders, the lights of the boathouse fading into the distance as the river wound like a snake past the wooded banks. The smell of wet earth and evening rolled in, and a peaceful feeling settled over Cole, shifting his work-related worries aside and allowing him to enjoy the beauty of their surroundings and the luxury of Leesa's company.

"This is just what I needed tonight, thank you," she said, turning sideways on her seat and pulling her knees up to her chest. She rested her cheek on her knees and watched him row.

"Me too."

"Did you have a rough day with patients?" she asked.

"Not rough. Typical." He didn't want to burden her with the particulars.

"You saw that gymnast today, right? How did that go? Can you help her?" She lifted her head, and a serious look came over her.

He liked that she'd remembered. "I hope so. I sent her for X-rays and a bone scan. I'll know more after we get those results back." A lantern hanging from a tree appeared in the distance, the spot where Shannon had set up the picnic for them, and he rowed toward the shore. "I don't want to bore you with my work."

"Bore me? I miss my students so much, I feel like I'm starved for conversations beyond the best-tasting beer and lunch orders. Don't get me wrong, I love working at Mr. B's. I love your parents, the customers, everything about it, but I actually miss helping the kids I worked with. That probably sounds weird, but hearing about your day is nice. I love that you help people. I know teaching English is a world away from medicine, but helping others is helping others."

He let the boat float toward shore as he rolled up the bottoms of his jeans. Leesa followed suit, rolling up her pants, too.

"I can only imagine how that feels. You *can* get a job as a teacher here in Peaceful Harbor, can't you? You weren't charged, so there shouldn't be anything on your permanent record." A pain in his gut accompanied the words. He hated that she even had to consider such things, and if he felt a pang, what was she feeling?

He stepped from the boat into the cool water and helped Leesa to shore, then tugged the boat up at the water's edge.

"Getting a job as a teacher means telling a new employer what happened, and even though I wasn't charged, references come into play. I'm sure my boss would give me an excellent reference, but she'd probably still have to mention what happened. I assume she would, anyway, and it's embarrassing even though I wasn't charged. Not to mention that it would open up a whole world of gossip that you don't need in your life." She looked at the lantern hanging on the tree and raised a hand to touch it. "This is beautiful."

"It's battery operated." He reached for their shoes, and after they put them on, he laced their fingers together and said, "I wish you'd stop worrying about what I do or don't need. I'm a big boy, and I can assure you that I can make those decisions for myself." He caressed her cheek and kissed her softly. "Trust me, Leese."

After what she'd experienced with her ex-boyfriend, Cole didn't blame her for being wary of his confidence, but that didn't mean that he wouldn't remind her every chance he got that he wasn't her ex, and that his words always came from his heart. In an effort to get her mind off of her past, he changed the subject as they started up the hill.

"Shannon helped me get things set up since I had to work."

"So that's what the look she gave me earlier was about. She's sweet, and she really loves you guys. It shows when she talks about her family."

They followed a narrow path up the mountain, where Shannon had hung lanterns every few feet to light their way.

"She's a great person. I'm glad you've had a chance to meet her. She's leaving soon to go back to Colorado, and then I think it'll be a while before she's back again."

"Is this my mountain climb?" she asked as he held branches to the side for her to pass.

"It is. I hope I didn't assume too much. This is where I used to come when I wanted to get away, and the summer before I left for college I brought Ty and Shannon here, so they'd have a place to disappear if they wanted to." He remembered that summer, and the excitement in Shannon's eyes. It was the type of excitement that only a younger sister could bestow on a brother she looked up to. He'd been proud to see it in her eyes. Ty, on the other hand, had been only about eleven years old, and he'd always found mountains *cool*. To him it was just another fun adventure.

"I can't imagine wanting to disappear from a family like yours. Everyone's so supportive."

"Yeah." A soft laugh escaped his lips. "Along with that ever-present support comes the presence of family twenty-four-seven. Sometimes I needed a little solitude."

The woods smelled like pine and dampness, and as they came to the ridge of the mountain, a picnic blanket surrounded by more lanterns came into view. His guitar sat at an angle at the edge of the blanket.

Leesa gasped with delight, and her beautiful green eyes widened with excitement. He'd never tire of seeing her smile.

"You and Shannon did this? For us?"

"We did. I got everything ready last night and ordered dinner for tonight. She picked it up and set it all up. She made it happen, so she should really get the credit." He kissed her again as they left the trail and sank down to the blanket.

"Don't sell yourself short. You thought of this. It's..." Her eyes warmed. "No one has ever done anything like this for me. Thank you."

He leaned over and tugged her into another kiss. "You're worth so much more, Leese. This is just the beginning."

She didn't do anything more than smile, but the look in her eyes gave her emotions away.

He opened the picnic basket and took out a bottle of wine and two wineglasses. Leesa peered into the basket, her eyes skimming over the containers of fruit, the carefully wrapped fresh baguette, jar of olive tapenade, and containers of cheese, and finally came to rest on the dishes.

"You brought real plates and glasses?" She sat back as he handed her a wineglass, then filled it and one for himself.

"Sure, why not?" He held up his glass and toasted. "To our

second date."

"Gosh, it feels like we've known each other a lot longer than we have, doesn't it?"

"Most definitely."

They drank their wine and talked about the view of the river and how pretty the setting sun was in the distance. Cole picked up his guitar and strummed out a tune, but he couldn't stop thinking about what she'd said about missing her students. He wanted to help her get her life back, and if he were honest with himself, he'd admit that he'd also like to get her to stick around Peaceful Harbor.

"Leesa, I'm close with the principal of our middle school, and I'm sure there are tons of kids who could use a good tutor. Maybe you should give the idea some thought."

LEESA DIDN'T KNOW how to respond. Cole made no bones about his feelings for her, and she knew her references would be fine, but that wasn't what she feared the most. "I don't think I'm ready to face those challenges yet. I still feel like I'm looking over my shoulder at every turn, and I have a job waiting for me back in Baltimore."

"Baltimore," he said more to himself than to her. His eyes filled with disappointment. "What exactly are you looking over your shoulder for?"

She finished her wine and set her glass aside. "For someone to *out* me in public, I guess. Like today, I was serving an older couple, and the husband kept staring at me. He finally said he thought I looked familiar, and my mind went directly to Towson. I thought he'd read about what happened online or something. He was looking at me so intently that even now my heart is racing just thinking about how nervous I was. I felt like I wanted to run."

She tried to smile but couldn't muster it as he reached for her hand and squeezed it.

"Please don't run." His eyes pleaded with her as he kissed her knuckles. "I already know that my life would never be the same without you."

She lowered her eyes, feeling her throat thicken and her heart swell. "I'm not running, and it turned out that the customer thought I looked like Naomi Watts, of all people. He was complimenting me and I was totally freaking out." *And still am.*

"I understand that fear, and I wish there was some way to stop it from creeping up on you. Is there anything I can do to help?"

She shook her head. "There's nothing anyone can do, and I don't want to ruin our wonderful picnic with my past. But I thought you should know the truth. I do worry about it, every minute of every day. Every time I'm in public I feel like I'm watching everyone for signs of recognition."

"I don't know if that will ever change for you, but maybe you just need to bite the bullet at some point and get back into doing what you love."

She tried to laugh it off. "That's so much easier said than done. It's not in the least bit funny, but when I think of where I was—at a solid place in my career, well respected by parents, my peers—and then in one afternoon the rug was pulled out from under me. It's kind of crazy that things can happen that quickly."

"I'm sure it doesn't help to know this, but if I had been

there, I would have stood by your side, fought for your reputation, and done everything within my power to make sure you never felt like you had to hide. Look at us, Leese. Good things can happen that quickly, too." He began strumming the guitar again and humming the tune to Jason Mraz's "I Won't Give Up."

Leesa couldn't stop emotions from clogging her throat as he sang about her eyes, and learning about who he was. She pressed her lips tightly together to stave off the tears as he sang about how he'd always be there for her—and he barely even knew her. She was no match for her emotions, which had given her whiplash over the past week. She wiped a lone tear as it rolled down her cheek.

He set the guitar aside and gathered her in his arms again, which had quickly become her favorite place to be.

"You barely know me," she said, even though she felt like he knew her better than any man ever had, besides her father. "You only know of my past."

"That's where you're wrong." He lifted her chin and gazed into her eyes. "I know you've got a big enough heart to not hold a grudge against the boy who set into motion an event that changed your whole life. I know you have a best friend who cares enough for you to warn me not to hurt you."

"Tegan?"

"Yeah." He smiled. "The night of the auction. She pulled me aside when I first arrived and said I was free to date you, but if I hurt you, she'd 'kill me.'"

"But we weren't even seeing each other then." She made a mental note to have a talk with Tegan.

He held a palm up toward the sky. "Take it up with her. Leesa, people don't protect those who don't deserve it. Not like that. You're right. I don't know everything there is to know about you, but I want to. I know you lost the one man who knew you best, and I can only imagine what that feels like. I want to be there for you and to get to know you just as well. I want you to feel safe and secure in our relationship. Most of all, I want you to never feel alone again."

"How have you stayed single all this time?" She couldn't imagine anyone dating him and *not* wanting to stay with him forever.

He laughed at that.

"I'm serious. You're handsome. You're romantic. You're too good to be true in lots of ways."

"I told you there was good with the bad. I'm a workaholic. I go in early, and before meeting you, I worked late every night. And I'm sure I'll be working late nights again. That's just who I am. Hopefully less so, now that we're together, but..." He shrugged.

"Those are hardly reasons for a town of pretty beach girls not to vie for your attention."

He dropped his eyes in a shy way that tugged at her heart. "They do. I don't mean that in a bragging way, but I get my fair share of offers." He handed her the guitar and moved behind her, wrapping his arms around hers and helping her hold it properly as he spoke. "I can't explain why no one has made me feel the way I do when I'm with you."

She liked the feel of his chest against her back, his arms circling her, and his big hands guiding hers onto the neck of the guitar and around the base.

"There are things about the heart no research in the world will ever figure out." He kissed her cheek. "Maybe you were destined to experience that awful accusation and I was fated to be on call the night Tegan injured her ankle."

"That's a depressing thought."

He arched a brow.

"Not the meeting you part," she explained. "That I could have been working so hard and all that time the accusation was looming in my future."

He placed his fingers over hers and helped her strum the guitar. "Yes, if you think of it that way, it is. But what if there's more to it? What if our destiny has nothing to do with the difficult things we go through and everything to do with the effect of our actions on other people?"

She chewed on that while Cole explained about frets and tuning pegs and feeling, rather than reading, music. And she wondered, what if she was looking at the whole mess too selfishly? Was there such a thing? She worried about Andy often, but her mind always came back to the devastating effects his actions had on her life.

"Do you believe that?" she finally asked.

"I don't know what I believe. I'd like to think that everything bad, everything you went through, has some sort of silver lining. For example, if Kenna hadn't wanted a different lifestyle, I might never have met you. Selfishly, the upside of what happened to you is that I was able to meet this amazing woman, who I might never have had a chance to meet otherwise. I have to think there's a reason things happen, because the idea of you enduring all that you have and losing everything you've worked so hard to achieve kills me. If there's no good to come of it, and bad things just…*happen*, well, isn't that worse?"

Leesa stilled his hands and leaned back against his chest. She closed her eyes for a moment, feeling the steady beat of his heart.

"I think you're my silver lining, too," she said. "This whole thing scares me. How fast we're moving, how much I'm feeling. My past looming, like it's going to come out of the shadows at every turn."

She turned to him, letting the guitar slide to the blanket. She didn't want to tell him that ever since hearing his father's thoughts on the past, she'd been wondering if she should try to gain some closure. Maybe go back to Towson and at least try to get Andy to admit that he'd lied, which she had to believe would help them both on some level. A heavy conscience was no good for someone trying to heal—emotionally or physically. Instead she pressed her lips to his and let the depth of his kiss, the exploration of his hands, and the intensity of their emotions transport her away to a dreamy state where nothing else existed.

Chapter Thirteen

LEESA LAY IN Cole's arms, listening to the sounds of the sea as they sailed in through his bedroom window. Once they'd started kissing, she hadn't wanted to stop, and when he'd invited her to come back to his place, she hadn't hesitated to accept. It was still dark out, and she should probably get up, go back to Tegan's, and try to sleep for a few hours, but she didn't want to move. Not when Cole was holding her so lovingly against his warm, naked body and she was happy for the first time in ages. Too happy to care about how tired she'd be in the morning.

Cole's house was exactly how she'd imagined it would be, open and understated, with more reading materials than anyone could ever dream of—from medical journals and novels to magazines featuring sports, boats, and news. The furniture was clearly high-end, but it wasn't flashy or ornate. It had the subdued elegance of masculinity that came from dark wood and warm colors. Hardwood floors were home to large planters, and every bookshelf was littered with family photographs between rows of books.

Her eyes skipped across his dark wooden dresser, where bottles of cologne were placed next to his watches—two with dark bands, one with gray, which she'd noticed when they'd first come into the bedroom. There was an oversized chair built for two by the French doors that led out to the deck off the bedroom, and she wondered how many women had cuddled up in it beside him like she wanted to. As she lay there thinking these things, drinking in his private oasis, her mind traveled to his family. How strange it was that Cole would be so monogamy minded while his brother Sam, he'd said, was anything but. She wondered if that had something to do with their birth order or if it were something more.

Her thoughts moved to his parents. She'd noticed how they were always catching each other's eye, smiling, touching every chance they got. Cole obviously had loving role models, as she'd had with her father. She'd been working so hard since she'd lost her father that she hadn't realized how alone she'd felt. And since being here, she hadn't felt lonely at all.

Cole stirred beside her, tightening his grip around her middle and nuzzling against her. She could get used to this, falling asleep draped in Cole, drenched in his open, giving self. He'd been so happy that she'd agreed to stay over, and still, somewhere deep inside her, his father's words bounced around, unsettling her reverie. *We can run from our past, but we can't really move forward until we accept it. Pain and all.* Would she ever be able to accept it? Put it to rest? Move forward without fear? Was it fair to be with Cole if she couldn't?

The breeze picked up Cole's scent, and Leesa closed her eyes and breathed him in. When she opened her eyes, she gazed at Cole's sleeping face. There was kindness there, even while he slept, in the soft lines of his lips and the lack of grooves across his forehead that angry people sported even when relaxed. For the millionth time in too few days she thanked her lucky stars that she'd taken Tegan up on her offer and come to Peaceful Harbor. She'd been at her wit's end in Towson, struggling to figure out the right thing to do: take the job in Baltimore and try to make a go of it despite what had gone down, change careers but remain in Towson, or move away altogether. Every day she spent with Cole she felt herself inching in the direction of making this move permanent—and in the next moment she'd second-guess herself. They were in the early stages of their relationship. The honeymoon stage, everyone called it. Could this kind of happiness last? More importantly, could it *ever* erase the lingering fear of her past ruining it all?

She closed her eyes again, this time pushing those uncomfortable thoughts away and focusing on the feel of Cole's nakedness against her. The hair on his legs tickled her skin. His chest was pressed firmly against her side, every breath bringing a whisper of hot air across her bare breasts. His muscled forearm rested over her ribs, brushing along the underside of her breasts. One of his feet was tucked beneath hers, and the eager press of his arousal, which never seemed to go fully flaccid, warmed her outer thigh. Her nipples tightened with the memory of his tongue sweeping over them, the gentle suck of his mouth that had nearly made her come before they'd even made love. Breathing harder now, she felt herself go damp between her legs. Lord, what this man did to her was sinful. *Sinfully delicious.*

"Can't sleep?" Cole pushed up on one elbow, his eyes heavy with sleep, his hair askew from her fingers fisting it earlier when they'd made love, and a sexy smile graced his luscious lips.

"I didn't mean to wake you," she said, touching his whiskers. "I love your scruff."

He turned and kissed her palm, trailing his tongue over the center and causing her pulse to quicken.

"Yeah? Maybe I won't shave in the morning." He pressed his lips to hers, and she moaned with pleasure, her body aching for more of him. "I'm glad you stayed over."

"Me too."

Her fingers trailed along his back as he pressed against her. His erection was firm and enticing against her leg. Lust simmered deep inside her as his hand skimmed her hip and tickled across her thigh to the heat between her legs. He sealed his lips over hers as he dipped his fingers inside her, pulling another needy moan from her lungs. He knew just how to touch her, which was so different from the way Chris had been. Chris had seemed to fumble through their intimacy, looking for guidance, approval, while Cole was confident, virile, and eager. She reached for his hard length, stroking its wide shaft to the curve of the sensitive head and using the bead of dampness to moisten the slide of her palm.

He groaned, tugging on her lower lip as he drew back, his eyes dark as night.

"Jesus, what you do to me every time you touch me." He sealed his teeth over her shoulder and bit down just hard enough to send shocks of want between her legs as he expertly sank his fingers deeper inside her and stroked over the spot that made her eyes slam shut and her hips buck off the mattress.

"Cole—" She gasped as the orgasm rocked through her, tightening her inner muscles around his fingers as he took her in a demanding kiss, keeping her at the peak for so long she could barely breathe.

"Ohmygod," she said as she tore her lips away. "I can't...I can't breathe." His fingers began their talented movements again, his thumb gliding over her sensitive clit, and she gripped his wrist, holding him still.

"Too much?" He kissed her again, and her hips rocked against his hand.

She groaned at her body's betrayal.

He dragged his tongue over her lower lip. "Want me to stop?"

"No," she said breathlessly.

"Thank fucking God." He sealed his lips over hers again, resting his powerful thigh over hers and trapping her against the mattress as he brought her right up to the edge again.

Her nails dug into the backs of his biceps as she tried to lift her hips, to take his fingers deeper instead of allowing him to continue the exquisite torture he was bestowing on her.

"Does my girl want to come?" he taunted.

"Yes. Hell, yes!"

She didn't have to ask twice. In a few perfectly placed strokes, she was crying out his name, rocking off the mattress, and mauling his mouth. She needed more of him, *all* of him. As the last of her orgasm vibrated through her, she pushed him onto his back and straddled his hips. He cupped her breasts, leaning up beneath her to love her nipples with his mouth and hands.

"God, I love your mouth." She buried her hands in his hair, holding his mouth to her breast as he took her up, up, up again with nothing more than his mouth on her breast and the friction of his cock against her wet flesh. She rocked along his hard length.

"You're killing me," he growled. "I need to make love to you. I need to be buried deep inside you and feel you tight and wet around me. I need to feel you come."

She shook her head and slid down his body, lying between his legs. She stroked his cock, licking the tip, teasing him, enjoying the feeling of knowing her confident, always-in-charge man was hers for the taking. Finally, she lowered her mouth over him, tasting herself, then the overpowering taste of maleness. Of Cole. She stroked and sucked, feeling him swell impossibly bigger in her grasp. He pumped his hips with every stroke, groaning and making her even wetter with his sexy sounds. When she lowered her mouth to his balls, he fisted his hands in the sheets.

"Fuck. Fuck, Leese," he said between gritted teeth. "You're gonna make me come."

She didn't relent. Instead she moved slowly over his erection, holding it straight up in front of her mouth. With her eyes set on his, she licked him from base to tip. He groaned as she swirled her tongue over the swollen crown.

"See? I can inflict torture just as well as you can." She stroked him with her hand and moaned just to feel his cock twitch. Oh, how she loved knowing she turned him on so much.

"Leese, you're playing with fire."

"I like it hot," she said seductively, taking him in deep and earning another heady groan.

"I want to make love to you." He eyed the open box of condoms on the bedside table.

She crawled over him in what she hoped was a sexy, catlike move, and retrieved one. After she'd sheathed him, he lifted her easily, and she felt every inch of him fill her as he lowered her until she was fully seated.

"Come here, angel." He gathered her against him and kissed her passionately as she gyrated her hips. He rocked in time to her efforts, and her breathing hitched with the immense pleasure rolling through her.

"So…good," she said between kisses.

Cole moaned in agreement. His hands clutched her hips, guiding her, quickening her efforts. Lust coiled low in her belly, circling her waist and climbing her spine, spreading like sharp pricks in her nipples, and finally—*Lord, finally*—she shattered around him. Cole thrust in deep, clutching her hips, keeping her tight against him as he found his release. She collapsed atop him, their bodies slick with sweat, each gulping for breath. He gathered her hair over one shoulder and pressed a kiss to her heated skin.

"You do me in, Annalise Avalon. You totally, completely destroy me." He lifted her chin, and the look in his eyes was overwhelmingly alive with emotion. He swallowed hard, as if he were trying to push past the strength of his feelings.

Without another word, he swept her beneath him, cocooning her body within the powerful confines of his. He brushed his thumb over her lips and searched her eyes. She wondered if he saw how full her heart was.

"You're feeling it, too, aren't you?" He pressed a tender kiss to her lips.

"Am I that transparent?"

"Like a window," he teased. "I feel it more than see it. The look in your eyes is still cautious, but the way you're holding me…"

She realized she'd wrapped her right leg around his, and her hands were splayed on his back, holding him tightly to her. She trapped her lower lip between her teeth to stifle her guilty smile.

"Don't tell anyone," she whispered, only half teasing.

He moved to her side and gathered her in close. Just as she began to doze off, he whispered, "I want to tell the world."

Chapter Fourteen

THE NEXT FEW days Cole and Leesa spent every minute they could together. They took walks on the beach, had dinner by candlelight, and Cole taught her how to strum a few chords on the guitar, but that usually led to them kissing, which led to touching and much, much more. He tried to get over to Mr. B's during his lunch hour, when he had one, so they could steal a few minutes together during her breaks, and thankfully, she'd been spending the nights with him, too. She'd become less cautious with him, but the haunted look in her eyes when they were out remained.

It was Friday afternoon, and he and Leesa were planning to take his boat out overnight. He hoped that being away from people would help her relax. On the water, there was no one to worry about but the two of them.

He was reviewing charts in his office when his cell phone rang. Hoping it was Leesa, he smiled as he picked it up, and that smile turned to a stiff line when Mackenna's name appeared on the screen. If there was one person savvy enough to dig up dirt on Leesa out of spite, it was Kenna. It was time, once and for all, to deal with her.

"Kenna," he said flatly when he answered the call.

"That's hardly a kind greeting to the woman you dated for two years."

He sighed. Was she really going to push this, even after the other night?

"Can we please stop this game playing?" he asked. "Why are you suddenly interested in me again after all these years?"

"It's not sudden, Cole. I've never stopped being interested in you. But I knew I had to get things out of my system before you'd even consider seeing me again. And I have." Her tone softened, and he'd be lying if he didn't admit that the tightening in his gut did, too. He felt bad for her and her delusions. There was no way in hell he'd want to go out with her again, whether he was seeing Leesa or not. But he'd probably always have a soft spot for Kenna, a sense of feeling sorry for her, really, because she was obviously searching for something that had gone unfulfilled. Although that soft spot was no longer in his heart and would never be again.

"Kenna, there's nothing left between us. I'm sorry."

She sighed loudly. "You're still hung up on my wanting an open relationship? Cole, we both needed that time to get the wildness out of our systems."

Maybe she was right. He'd thought about that over the years. Even thought she'd done him a favor. And now that he was with Leesa, he knew she had. Leesa filled him with emotions that Mackenna never had, and more than that, to Leesa he wasn't an afterthought. Even if she wasn't ready to admit it yet, he knew he was quickly becoming her everything, just as she'd become his.

"Cole? Don't you agree?" Kenna asked, bringing his mind back to the conversation.

"Yes, maybe you're right. We were young and we probably

needed that time to grow up." *But while I was growing up, you were proving who you* really *were.* He had a feeling she'd never let this go, and he had no choice but to bring it all out in the open. "That's not what solidified the end of our relationship. It was what you did to Beth."

Silence filled the airwaves.

"You found out about that?" Her voice was thin, shaky.

"Yes. Beth and I were the reason you and I met, remember?" He paused. She remained silent. "Kenna, family is everything to me, and the fact that you'd hurt your sister like that tells me who you really are."

"Who I really am? I was a kid, Cole." She raised her voice, and he pictured her eyes narrow and angry, as they'd been the other night.

He looked out the window, reminding himself that they needed to have this conversation to finally put an end to her hope.

"Age is a poor excuse, Kenna. And it's just that, an excuse." He checked his watch. "I have patients to see. Can we just move on from this? Please? I don't want to have to worry every time we run into each other."

"No, I guess you wouldn't, would you? You've always been too wrapped up in yourself, your schooling, and now your work to deal with anything or anyone else."

"Kenna, I'm not going there with you." He knew she'd been jealous of the time he'd spent studying, and maybe he hadn't given her enough attention back then, but that was a long time ago, and he didn't regret focusing on his studies.

"Why, Cole? Because your only excuse was that you were young and stupid, too?"

Cole rose to his feet, pacing in front of the window, looking over the town where he'd grown up, the only place he'd ever wanted to settle down. But no longer did he think of Kenna when he walked through the streets, or while he sat on the beach at night, like he had the summer they'd broken up. He knew she'd never understand what he was about to say, because to Kenna, college was about fun and sowing her wild oats, while to Cole it was about achieving the grades to get into medical school and pursue his career. But he'd never been a liar, and he wasn't about to start now.

"No, Kenna. Not because I was young and stupid. I'm sorry if I hurt you, or didn't give you the attention you deserved, but I was at school to learn. To study and make it into medical school. The rest...well, I was perfectly content with just one girlfriend. I didn't *need* more the way you did. Now, I hope we can put this behind us and move on. I have patients to see."

As he ended the call, he had a twisting feeling in his gut that this wouldn't be the last he heard from her. He couldn't worry about that now, though. He had Elsie Hood's follow-up appointment to tend to. And then a blissful weekend with Leesa.

Cole sat across from Martin, Ann, and Elsie with one goal on his mind—getting Elsie proper treatment for her pars fracture, which the test results verified. When the Hoods had entered his office, they'd brought with them tension so thick Cole could cut it with a scalpel. Elsie sat between her parents, fidgeting with the fray on the edge of her shorts, her eyes trained on Cole's desk. Her father sat pin straight, rigid, as if he were preparing for a debate. Ann clutched the arm of the chair in her left hand. Her right hand rested on the arm of Elsie's chair.

It was times like these that Cole wondered what it must feel like to be a parent, torn between doing the right thing for a child's well-being and coming between that child and her dreams.

He and his siblings had been involved in every sport growing up, from football and baseball for the boys, to gymnastics and swimming for Shannon. Tempe hadn't been into aggressive sports, but their mother had insisted that she choose something. She'd chosen golf and sailing. Cole was well aware of the hours and commitment it took from the family for typical sports, and he knew serious athletes practiced upward of three hours a day, some as much as seven days a week. Hell, he'd been one of those. And for Elsie, he'd learned during the initial exam, much of that practice meant leaving home at four thirty in the morning to get to the gym before school.

Elsie's chance at this year's Olympic tryouts wasn't just about Elsie and her success. This was about the hours and lifestyle her parents had given up in order for her to succeed, and Cole had a feeling that wasn't going to be put aside easily.

"Thank you for coming back to discuss the findings. The tests confirmed that Elsie has a subacute pars fracture of the lumbar spine, bilateral at the fifth lumbar level. This means that there is a fracture on both sides of the lumbar vertebra."

"Subacute?" Ann furrowed her brow and reached for her daughter's hand.

Cole was thankful that one of the two parents thought to help their daughter through the diagnosis. He paused for a moment while she gave her daughter's hand a comforting squeeze.

"Subacute. This means that the fracture occurred roughly six weeks to several months ago."

Elsie kept her eyes trained on his desk, her free hand now

fisted tight.

"Elsie?" Worry filled her mother's eyes.

Elsie remained quiet.

"Elsie, do you remember having pain prior to a few weeks ago?" Cole knew she must, even if it had felt only like a pulled muscle. This type of fracture could not go unnoticed for so long. What he didn't know was whether Elsie had complained and her father had disregarded her or pushed her through the pain, or if this was Elsie's battle, *supported* by her father. Her mother seemed too surprised by the suggestion for it to be a feigned reaction.

"I don't remember." She finally lifted hopeful eyes and asked, "But you can fix it, right, Dr. Braden?"

He smiled to put her at ease and because, yes, he believed they could heal her injury with the right treatment. "Yes, Elsie. At your age, your spine is still growing, and bone-to-bone healing is not only possible, but if treated correctly, you should be able to compete again next year."

"Next year?" Martin snapped. His beady eyes narrowed. "Olympic trials are in two months."

Cole nodded. "Yes, I'm aware." He folded his hands on the desk and leaned forward. "Mr. Hood, your daughter's injury is not a pulled muscle. It can't be fixed with a week of downtime. Bones need time to heal, and with a fracture of this type, at this stage, they need to be stabilized during the healing process. I can't, in good conscience, recommend anything less than a thoracolumbosacral orthosis, or TLSO, in combination with anti-inflammatories, and of course, limited activity."

"We came to you because we were told that you had other treatment options available. You came highly recommended by other athletes," Martin said with an accusing tone and a stare to match. "Isn't there a surgery you can do that would fix this quicker?"

Cole reined in his irritation at this man's complete disregard for his professional opinion. "Mr. Hood, back surgery is serious business and not something we recommend unless we see that less-aggressive treatments aren't effective first. In addition, recovery from back surgery is not any easier than what I'm recommending." He turned his attention to Elsie, wanting to help her understand the treatment as much as her parents. "Elsie is a teenager. Her body is still growing, and healing naturally is always a better option for patients Elsie's age. I realize that this puts a hitch in her plans, but once healed, after she demonstrates full range of motion, strength, and is symptom free, she should be able to return to competing."

"Dr. Braden, how long do you think that might take?" Elsie asked.

"It's hard to say, Elsie. Anywhere from two to several months."

Her eyes filled with tears. "If I *had* felt something weeks earlier and I had come in, would that have made a difference?" She must have felt her father's dark stare shift to her, because while her eyes remained trained on Cole, she said, "I'm not saying I did, but if I *had?*"

"It's always best to tend to injuries when they first occur," Cole explained. He didn't want her to feel guilty about something that he could guess was probably directed by her overbearing father, but she was an athlete, and she needed to understand the ramifications of not tending to future injuries in a timely manner.

"The important thing is that you're here now and your injury is treatable."

Martin rose from his chair. Fear filled Elsie's eyes as her mother rose beside her while she remained sitting.

"Thank you, Dr. Braden. We'll take this under consideration," her father said.

Cole came around the desk. "Mr. Hood, I've already spoken to our orthotist, and he can see Elsie today to have her fitted for a brace and to discuss—"

"That won't be necessary," Martin said. "We'll go home and discuss treatment options among ourselves, and then we'll be seeking a second opinion. Thank you for your time."

"Mr. Hood, if not treated properly, your daughter could experience life-long pain. I hope you'll give my suggestion serious consideration. There will be other competitions."

"Dad," Elsie said, her eyes darting between Cole and her father.

Martin looked at his daughter, his wife, then at Cole, and said, "Thank you for your time," and left the room.

"Come on, honey," Ann said with a hand on Elsie's shoulder.

Elsie hesitated with a frightened look on her face. "Dr. Braden, are you pretty sure I'll hurt like this forever if I don't do this treatment?"

Cole hated to say it, but he owed her the truth. "Unfortunately, if you continue practicing with your injury, I'm afraid the pain will get worse, Elsie." He lifted his eyes to Ann. "I'm sure your parents will help you make the right decision."

She looked up at her mother. "Mom?"

"Thank you, Dr. Braden." Ann held her hand out to shake Cole's hand, and when he did, hers trembled. "I'll speak with my husband."

Some patients moved in and out of Cole's office like a gentle breeze, smooth and easy. As he watched the Hoods walk away, he felt the power of a gale-force wind follow them out.

LEESA SAT IN the parking lot of Jazzy Joe's Café with her heart in her throat and her cell phone pressed to her ear as she listened to her friend and previous coworker, Lena Bail, tell her about Andy. Leesa was meeting Tempe in a few minutes to discuss the Girl Power group. She'd thought Lena was calling her to chat, but boy was she wrong. She knew from the tone of her voice during their brief catch-up on how Leesa was doing in Peaceful Harbor that Lena's call was not a social one.

"Annalise, I'm worried about Andy."

Leesa held her breath, both soaking in the comfort of hearing her given name said so naturally and from the sound of her friend's voice and rattled by the thought that Andy wasn't doing well.

"We're not supposed to talk about the case." Leesa's stomach knotted. As much as she wanted to know what was going on with Andy, she also didn't want to do anything that would get her into trouble again.

"I know. We're not talking about the case. We're just two friends, and I happen to need your guidance."

"Lena."

Her friend sighed. "Okay, fine. Let me just ask your professional opinion, because everyone around here is fucking tiptoeing around this kid and his hard-ass father, and I'm really worried about him."

Leesa hated the gruffness of Andy's father and the demeaning way he'd spoken to him, but she'd been unable to intervene beyond the occasional, *I'm sorry, Mr. Darren, but we really have to get back to Andy's studying now,* to get him to leave the room. A fact that he'd tried to use to his advantage during the investigation.

Just the thought of the investigation made her feel sick to her stomach. But Lena was a fellow teacher. A pure professional, from her slacks and heels to her smart bob cut and the way she handled her students, with equal amounts of empathy and authority, sprinkled with guidance. They'd become fast friends, and Lena had been there for her throughout her ordeal. This was the least she could do in return.

Leesa looked around the parking lot, as if someone might hear her talking about Andy through the closed windows of her car. *Ridiculous.*

"Okay, but we never had this conversation."

"Of course not," Lena agreed. "He's not communicating *at all.* I mean, the boy doesn't crack a smile, doesn't look at his cell phone, doesn't interact with other kids. He sits there stone-cold and silent."

"Oh, Lena. That's horrible."

"I know. Andy's always been a pretty involved kid. Opinionated, you know. Annalise, I'm worried that he's gotten even worse than he was right after the accident. Remember how closed off he was?"

Leesa inhaled a jagged breath. "Yeah."

"I just…I feel like I shouldn't ignore this. Like I should say something to someone, but I know everyone else sees it, too, and no one is doing anything. And Lord knows what that jackass father of his would say if I tried to talk to him about it."

She paused, and Leesa knew Lena was thinking the same thing she was—that Andy's lies were eating him up from the inside out.

A tap on Leesa's car window startled her. She turned to see Tempe's smiling face, her hand waving happily. Leesa forced a smile and waved as she said to Lena, "I'm meeting someone and she's just shown up. Can I think about this and get back to you?"

Tempe pointed to the café and indicated that she'd wait inside. Leesa nodded as she ended the call with Lena, suggesting that Lena think about the best route before doing anything. "You know his father won't be open to suggestions, especially from you since you were supportive of me the whole time that mess was going on."

"I know. That's why I was hoping you had some insight of a better way to handle it. I tried talking to the guidance counselor, but she pretty much said they'd done all they could do. I'll let you go, but I feel like I'm sitting on a time bomb. We read all about kids doing awful things because of depression these days. I don't want Andy to become a statistic. Hey, Annalise, I miss you."

"Yeah, I miss you, too. I'm glad you called, even if you made me feel like I want to throw up."

"Sorry! I just didn't know who else would care enough to try to help. Everyone here is on Team Annalise, so they don't have much sympathy for Andy, and I know you do. Are you really okay? Have you made any decisions about the job in Baltimore, or has Tegan convinced you to move there?"

"No, I haven't made any decisions yet, but the people here are really nice, and..." She knew Tempe was waiting for her, and she had to make this quick, so instead of gushing about Cole and about her frustrating, ever-present worries, she said, "Things are good. We'll catch up soon, and, Lena? Thanks for caring about Andy. He's just a kid, and he has sucky parents."

Thoughts of Andy refused to be thwarted as Leesa walked into Jazzy Joe's.

"Welcome to Joe's!" Joe called out.

She waved to him and spotted Tempe sitting in a booth. She tried to recapture her enthusiasm about their chat, but it was tainted by worries of Andy. She stepped up to the counter to get a cup of coffee, then joined Tempe at the booth.

Leesa slid into the seat across from her. "Hi. I'm so sorry about that. A friend from back home called right when I pulled into the parking lot."

Tempe waved a dismissive hand. "No worries. You must miss your friends there." She smiled as she looked over Leesa's blue top and flowered miniskirt. "We must shop at the same places." She looked down at her own skirt, the same type as Leesa's, but a different color. "We could be sisters with our blond hair."

"You're right. Most of your family is dark, too. My mom was blond, but my dad had brown hair, like this." She lifted her hair and leaned forward, showing Tempe the dark roots at the base of her skull. "It's like God gave me a little reminder of him beneath the blonde."

"I have the same thing." Tempe lifted her hair and showed Leesa. "But, of course, my dark-haired siblings don't have light roots. So unfair." She laughed. "I heard you and Cole are spending tonight on the boat."

"You heard that already? We just decided last night."

"Braden grapevine. I was at the pub when Cole called to tell our dad that he wasn't able to help with the boat until Sunday." Tempe sipped her coffee.

"I hope your dad's okay with Cole going. We can go some

other weekend." She had forgotten that he was helping his father with the boat when Cole had suggested the getaway.

Tempe's eyes widened. "Are you kidding? Dad's thrilled. He said he's never seen Cole so happy, or so distracted. Your boyfriend is a bit of a workaholic."

Boyfriend? She let that word flit around in her happy little heart for a few seconds before answering. Tempe had used the word so easily, it made Leesa feel like she'd seen their connection as strongly as Leesa felt it, and *that* was a great feeling.

"I know," she finally answered. "I actually like that about him. I think I used to bore my ex, because I'm pretty much of a homebody. I've always been more of a reader than a partier. Last night Cole read through patient charts while I caught up on the latest Jill Shalvis novel. My dirty little secret. Loved it."

"I love her, too!" Tempe wrinkled her nose. "Shannon reads her, too, and so does my mom. So, I won't pry too much or anything, but you and Cole...? You guys are really getting along."

She couldn't stifle the grin that snuck across her cheeks. "To be honest, I have no idea how he's stayed single for so long. He's such an amazing man. He's warm and loving and smart and funny, and—" She covered her face with her hand and laughed. "And your *brother!* Sorry."

"Oh, please. Don't be. I want him to be happy." Tempe leaned forward, wrapping her hands around her coffee cup. "So, Girl Power. I'm really excited about this. I wrote down some suggestions." She reached into her purse and withdrew a notebook.

Leesa realized that since spending time with Cole, she'd stopped carrying her notebook with her and hadn't felt the need to write her feelings down. The realization brought relief, but that relief was not stronger than the churning in her stomach over starting a Girl Power group.

She set her hand over the top of Tempe's. "Wait. I've been thinking about this." *Even more so since Lena called.* "You know that even if we plan this, it might not happen, right? I'm still not sure I'm staying in the area."

"So you really *are* considering moving back? I just thought, with what's going on with you and Cole…"

"Well, yes. I mean, I…" She tried to pull her thoughts together, but they were all over the map. She loved Peaceful Harbor, and she didn't want to even think about leaving Cole, but her life was back in Towson. Although what life did she have left back there? If she went back, she had to work someplace else. But after Lena's call, she felt even more like she had unfinished business there. Tempe was looking at her expectantly, waiting for a response. She took a deep breath and confided in Tempe, because she felt like she could, and she was sick of the thoughts pinging around in her head.

"I honestly don't know where I'll end up. I thought I could just start over, but I'm living in fear of someone finding out."

Tempe's blue eyes warmed. "Aw, Leesa, I understand completely. But don't you think that'll change after some time passes?"

"I hope so. I can't imagine living like this forever." She sipped her coffee, trying to ignore the incessant nagging in the recesses of her mind about what Lena had told her and what Ace had said to her. And then there was Cole, who was stealing her heart one day at a time. That was the best feeling in the world, but the timing was awful, because her past could ruin his present.

"Is there anything I can do?"

"I wish there were a magic switch somewhere. But there's not, and even though I didn't do anything wrong, I still worry. Just the idea of having to explain myself here is frightening." She sank back against the booth. "I'm sorry. When my friend called, she said Andy wasn't doing well, and I'm afraid it's really got me sidetracked. If I'm having this hard of a time miles away from Towson, I can only imagine how hard it is for him, knowing he caused my world to fall apart. And it sounds like where I felt like I was tainted, the people who believed in me are looking down at him for what he did. And that makes me feel horrible, because he's just a kid."

"Have you thought about talking with him? That might help you both." Tempe smiled at Joe as he wiped down a nearby table. "And then maybe you can figure out if you'd like to stay here and really try to start over."

"I think about it all the time. I'm not supposed to talk to Andy, though." The empathy in Tempe's eyes drew more of the truth from Leesa, and it felt good to talk about the things that felt like they were burrowing a hole in her. "Cole suggested that I apply for a teaching position here, but all it would take is one person saying the wrong thing and then the whole town would know what happened in Towson. And as much as I'd be mortified, he'd be put in the position of having to defend our relationship. I've been *that* girlfriend before, and it wasn't fun."

"God, I hate that one kid could change your life like that. I can't imagine not doing music therapy. I'd miss it every minute of the day." She reached across the table and touched Leesa's hand. "I'm sure you have friends there who love and support you, but know you have them here, too. My whole family is here for you."

"I do miss it, and your family has been so kind. Thank

you."

Tempe opened the notebook and spun it around for Leesa to see what she'd written. "We're probably not going to figure this all out over coffee, but I hope it helps to talk about it. I think time and something else to focus on will help." She lifted her eyes and smiled. "Something besides my brother."

"Are you trying to make me blush? Because you're doing a good job of it." Leesa glanced down at the notebook just as the front doors of the café opened and Mackenna walked in. Leesa used her hand to shield her face from her.

"You can't hide from her. That only gives her more power." Tempe pushed Leesa's hand down. "Besides, you're who Cole's with. Own it, woman. No one else in this town has been able to for years."

Leesa whispered, "She kissed him at Tap It the other night. She knew I was there with him, too. I don't want to get into anything with her. It's not my battle."

"There's no battle to be had." Tempe pointed to the notebook. "Let's focus on this. You might be surprised at how inspiration can quiet rocky thoughts."

They concentrated on Tempe's notes, and before Leesa knew it, two hours had passed. Mackenna had left without Leesa even noticing, and they had a complete to-do list to get a future Girl Power group up and running. She wondered if she could get so entrenched in the Girl Power program that her past would simply go away, too.

"Thank you, Tempe. You really took my mind off of things, and this is a great plan if I do decide to move here permanently." She handed the notebook back to Tempe.

"Keep it." Tempe pushed the notebook across the table. "This way we can keep all the notes in one place. You might think of more ideas, and I have a ton of notebooks." They threw away their coffee cups and headed outside. "I'm really glad we got to know each other better, Leesa. If you ever need a friend to talk to or anything, I'm here."

"Thank you. I didn't mean to be such a downer at first."

"You weren't. It's nice to talk about real things sometimes. I work with a lot of kids, so it's rare that I get to actually have coffee and chat with people outside of my family." She leaned in close and said, "We homebodies have to stick together."

They hugged goodbye, and Leesa watched her drive away. Could she move away from the place she'd lived all her life and start over? Could she leave the house she'd grown up in, the house that held so many memories of her father, or would that feel like too big of a betrayal? What would he want her to do?

As she climbed into her car and checked her cell for messages, she pondered that thought. She'd missed a text from Cole. *Sorry I'm going to be a little late. Two more patients to see. Pick you up at eight?*

She worried that he'd be too tired to go on the boat trip after a long day of patients and quickly typed a response.

Aren't you tired? Want to go another time and hang out at your place tonight? I don't mind.

His response was immediate. *Never too tired to spend time with you.*

How many nights had Chris put off seeing her because he'd been too tired? Even at the beginning of their relationship, they'd seen each other only twice a week or so. She'd always understood, but of course part of her had wondered why he didn't think it would be nicer to spend the time relaxing together. Cole never made her feel like she was an imposition or an obligation. He was always truly happy to see her. She saw it in his eyes every time they were together, and now she wondered why she'd thought anything less had ever been okay.

She thought about Cole's father and the things he'd said. And although Ace had been just as pleasant to her as always, she still worried that she'd overstepped her bounds when she'd asked about his leg. But she wondered, with all the doubt that she carried around these days, if that was just in her mind. She didn't feel like her judgment was the sharpest lately. She thought about what Lena had told her, and her worries about Andy came rushing back. Was she overthinking or overstepping her bounds with Andy, too? She tried to convince herself that Andy wasn't her student anymore and she had no reason to worry about him. That he was her past, not her present. But it wasn't the teacher in her worrying about him. It was the human being in her. The empathy and internal conflict she couldn't escape.

She read Cole's text again—*Never too tired for you.*

She wanted this—to be with Cole, to be happy. She wanted to feel the emotions that sent her heart soaring and her mind reeling. The tingling from head to toe and warming in the best places in between that she had every time she thought of him. She wanted to let herself feel those things for Cole so badly she ached. *I deserve to be happy. The situation with Andy has already stolen enough of my happiness.*

For the hundredth time, she told herself to slow things down with Cole until she put her past to rest, not to let him risk his reputation on her.

And for the hundredth time, as she sent her response to Cole—*Eight sounds perfect*—she ignored the suggestion.

Chapter Fifteen

COLE REACHED FOR Leesa's hand as they sailed away from the harbor, and the lights of the marina faded into the distance like diamonds in the night.

She smiled up at him from where she sat and asked, "How did things go with the gymnast's parents?"

He loved that she didn't feel jealous over his work or by the hours he sometimes had to put in. He'd always believed that one day he'd find a special woman who was his equal in every way. Someone who was equally dedicated to career, family, a significant other, and to themselves, the way he believed a person had to be in order to be truly happy. He'd grown his career, he was there for his family, and he was proud of the man he'd become. He knew that when he found that special woman, their happiness would blossom to another level. And each time he and Leesa were together, he felt their bond deepen and solidify.

"They're talking over the treatment plan. I hope they'll come back next week ready to proceed, but sometimes with young athletes, the parents hold all the cards. You never know."

As they sailed into the darkness, she joined him at the helm. Her skirt swayed over her legs in the night breeze, and her eyes smiled back at him. He was falling fast for Leesa, and surprisingly, he wasn't scared by the emotions that kept him up at night and pulled him through his long days. He felt like he'd been waiting for her his whole life.

"And how's Dr. Braden going to feel if their family makes the wrong decision?" she asked.

He touched his forehead to hers and pulled her in against him. Her question, her concern over him, could come only from someone as caring as her.

"Honestly? I'm not sure. Part of me wanted to shake some sense into her father. That's his baby girl. His daughter. She's just a kid, and the idea of her continuing with her rigorous training schedule and injuring herself further scares the crap out of me." He pressed his lips to hers and brushed his thumb along her cheek. "But that's not something I can control." He'd long ago learned that those types of decisions were out of his hands. He and Jon had spent many evenings helping each other through the torturous web of emotions that came with being a physician that cared.

"That doesn't mean it's easy to turn those worries off," she said. "Do you want to talk about it? Your feelings about it, I mean. I know patient confidentiality needs to be respected."

"I'm okay," he said out of habit.

"You know what I think?" She ran her finger down the center of his chest. "I think you're so used to shutting off this part of yourself that you're not even sure if you're okay with it or not."

"I thought you were a teacher, not a psychologist." He kissed her again, thinking about what she'd said. "I guess you're right. I'm used to keeping my feelings about work to myself, or sharing them with Jon when we're at the breaking point. I've never had anyone else to share those feelings with." He ran his fingers through the ends of her hair. "I've never been with anyone like you before."

"You're always willing to talk to me about my feelings and about my past. I want you to feel the same freedom with me."

"You're right. Let's anchor and we'll break out that bottle of wine I brought and talk."

As Cole anchored the boat and settled it for the evening, Leesa went down below to retrieve a blanket and the wine. They cuddled up on the bench beneath the starry sky with their wine.

They talked about his meeting and the frustrations that grew out of seeing such a clear and easy path to a patient's recovery not being followed because of roadblocks such as overbearing parents or, with adult patients, fear of treatment or worries over needing time off from work to recuperate. As he spoke, he felt weight lift from his shoulders, and with that lifting came a modicum of guilt.

"I didn't realize how much I've been keeping inside, but I also don't want you to be a dumping ground for my irritation about work," he admitted.

"I don't feel like you're dumping on me at all. When you're in a relationship, you can't just share the good things, or when something bad happens, there's no foundation, no building blocks of smaller frustrations to learn and grow from. There's not enough strength to support it."

"Is that what happened with you and Chris?" he asked. He'd wondered what their relationship had been like. He couldn't imagine a day without Leesa, and the thought of a man dating her for almost two years without making her his own with a ring and a wedding date was incomprehensible enough, but to leave her during such a traumatic time in her life? That was unforgivable.

"I had a long time to think about that when I was in Towson. We had it pretty easy, without any real hardships to speak of, and even though we were both teachers, we basically lived separate lives. It was easy, convenient. We didn't talk about work, and after being with you, I realize that we didn't talk about much, really. It sounds like a shallow relationship, but when we were dating, it didn't feel that way. We started as friends, and I don't think I ever realized that there was no passion between us. One night he asked me out, and we were friends, so I said yes. After that it became comfortable, and I know this sounds bad, but I didn't have any point of reference to fall back on. I had never felt passionate about a man before the way I do with you. Remember, there was just me and my dad, so I never saw my father shower a woman with affection. Well, besides me, I guess, but that was a father-daughter relationship, not a lover. And when my friends would talk about their stomachs quivering or their heads spinning over guys, I just figured that I didn't have that with Chris because we were friends first."

She gazed into his eyes and knew that even if she had felt passion for Chris, it wouldn't have been anything like what she felt with Cole.

"I never knew that anything could feel as powerful and all consuming as this does until us, either." He pulled her in closer. "I'm not used to sharing the details of my workdays, so if you ever feel like I'm shutting you out, please tell me. I never want to do anything that makes you feel unimportant, because, Leesa, you've already become the most important part of my life."

She looked at him through her thick eyelashes with so much love that he felt his insides go soft.

"If ever there was a perfect moment, it is right here, right now." Cole kissed her. She tasted of sweet wine and hot desire. The blood from his head rushed south. It was always like this with Leesa when they were close. He intended to talk, but the minute their mouths came together, he wanted to touch, to taste, to devour her.

She kissed him hungrily, and he broke the kiss just long enough to set their wineglasses to the side. When he gathered her in his arms again, an invitation beckoned in the smoldering depths of her eyes. Every time he saw that look, his heart turned over in his chest, and he knew that feeling would grow only more intense with every minute they spent together.

"I feel like we have years to make up for," he said before snaking his hand around to the back of her head and taking her in another deep kiss that opened the cap on his desire and sent it surging forth. Her hand fell to his thigh, squeezing as it inched higher.

His tongue swept over the seam of her lips as she opened to him. He traced the swell of her lower lip, over the sweet bow of her, earning a sexy sigh before claiming her mouth again. The way she clung to him, kissing him like she never wanted to stop, taking his breaths as her own and arching against him, spurred him on. He loved knowing what his kisses did to this overly cautious woman. His hands slid beneath her skirt, and he lifted her onto his lap. She straddled him effortlessly, gazing into his eyes, so beautiful in the moonlight, a rosy blush on her cheeks, her eyes heavy with desire.

"Leese," he said as she ground against his arousal. "I'm falling hard for you. So hard." He rocked his hips to emphasize his point, earning a sweet giggle as her head fell back and she opened up to him.

He fumbled with the buttons on her shirt, getting frustrated because his thick fingers were no match for the tiny buttons. He tore them open, sending the buttons pebbling against the deck. They both laughed, their eyes connected, and in the next breath, carnal need took over. He pushed her blouse off and tossed her bra to the deck, filling his palms with her luscious breasts and lowering his mouth to them. He sucked hard, and she cried out, digging her nails into his shoulders as he moaned with pleasure.

"I love your breasts, your body. You're incredible," he said as he lavished her other breast with the same attention.

Her hands slid down his biceps, squeezing as he sucked harder and grazed his teeth over her taut nipple. She dropped one hand to his lap, stroking him through his slacks. He tangled a hand in her hair and brought their mouths together again in a demanding kiss as she worked his zipper and set his erection free. She sucked his tongue into her mouth, driving him out of his fucking mind, then pulled abruptly back, her eyes dark as a river.

Without a word she slid from his lap to the deck and hooked her hands in the waistband of his pants, tugging them down. He lifted his hips, helping her take them down past his knees. She licked her palm, and her eyes locked on him in an erotic dance of seduction. She wrapped that hand around his cock and squeezed before stroking him slow and tight. His head fell back as she lowered her mouth to him, and he had to look. Had to see her. The sight of her lips wrapped around him, her hand stroking him, just about pulled him over the edge. He couldn't help fisting his hands in her silky hair and guiding her efforts as she licked and sucked and blew his fucking mind.

"Leese. Stop. I'm going to come."

She grinned, her lips curling around his shaft, her eyes filled with wickedness. She held his stare as she quickened her efforts, taking him so deep the sensitive tip of his rigid length bumped the back of her throat. Seeing her love him with her hand and mouth, her breasts bare, her hair framing her beautiful face, stole the last shred of his control.

"Leese," he warned.

She brought her other hand into play, perfecting her actions as she stroked his balls, squeezing just hard enough to make him come unglued. His hips bucked and—*holy fucking hell*—she didn't slow, didn't pause, just drank in everything he had to give. When the last of his orgasm pulsed through him, she swirled her tongue over his glistening head and then licked his shaft clean.

He sank down to his knees in front of her, gazing into her lust-laden eyes.

"You own me," he whispered as he laid her gently on her back and loved her in the same eager way she'd loved him. Bringing her pleasure over and over again, tasting her desire, feeling it in the intensity of her release, until they were both too spent to move. And there beneath the moonlight, with the sounds of the sea surrounding them and the scents of their lovemaking hovering in the air, Cole felt his heart become hers. It wasn't fast and hard or shocking and scary. It was an effortless filling of his soul, a lifting of his emotions, and a complete and utter surrender.

Chapter Sixteen

SATURDAY BROUGHT BRIGHT skies and a shift in the energy between Cole and Leesa. She'd felt things changing between them over the past week, but out on the water all alone, without the world breathing down her back or the threat of a stranger saying something that would dredge up her past, she was finally able to take a step back and see their relationship more clearly. Feel it more deeply. She was falling in love with him, and he was falling in love with her. She'd never fallen in love with Chris, and she had no measure of love beyond that which she felt for her father and closest friends.

This was stronger. Bolder. More present in every movement, every glance, every thought. And it thrilled her and scared the daylights out of her at once.

They were anchored far from the marina, having sailed for much of the morning. They'd just finished lunch and were lying on the deck in their bathing suits. The sun beat down on Cole's bare chest, bringing his sculpted physique to a delicious bronze color. He propped himself up on one elbow, casting a shadow over her face, and she opened her eyes and smiled at him.

"Hey there," she said as he came in for a kiss. God, how she loved his kisses. Each and every one was so much more than a peck or a hello or goodbye. Every kiss, even the tender ones, was filled with emotions that were new and exciting, fulfilling and tantalizing. She felt restraint in his kiss the same way she felt it in her own body, because they both knew that when they kissed, it was an easy tumble into an entanglement of their naked bodies. Being intimate with Cole was like nothing she'd ever experienced before. He filled all the places she'd never known were lonely. Not just her heart, but her mind and certainly her soul. This scared her, because he was willing to risk so much for her. He was at the pinnacle of his career in a small town, where everyone loved him, and she worried that he didn't realize how an accusation could change a person's life. How being associated with her could change his. She hadn't realized how a sentence, a handful of words, could change a person's life either, until she'd gone through it herself.

"Your lips are smiling, but your eyes speak of trouble, my beautiful girlfriend. Care to share your thoughts?"

"How can you be so in tune to me every minute of the day?" She lifted onto her elbow, matching his position and tracing her fingers over the muscle in his arm.

He placed his hand on her hip and clutched her heated skin. His hand was big and strong, and that simple touch made her want to forget her worries, wrap her arms around his neck, and kiss him until the world disappeared again.

"Leese? Talk to me, angel."

She blinked away the fantasy—*for now*—and knew she owed him the truth, even though she felt like she'd said it a hundred times already. Somehow that wasn't enough. It wasn't just his career on the line. It was his heart—and hers.

"I've been thinking about how it feels to be out here with you. It's magical. Like nothing else exists."

He tightened his grip on her hip. "And that causes you to look worried?" He moved closer, bringing their thighs together and making it difficult for her to think.

"Yes," she managed, feeling him getting hard against her. She should just shut up, because telling him the truth would ruin the moment, and she was loving the moment.

"I didn't know magical was bad. Want me to whip up a squall, or maybe a tidal wave, so you don't have to enjoy the serenity of the sunshine and the sea on a Saturday afternoon, alone with a guy who adores you?"

She dropped onto her back and sighed. "I feel like you're putting your life on hold for me. You should be working, or—"

"Lying with the woman who made me realize that I was biding my time until I met her?" He brushed her hair from her shoulder and pressed his lips to the spot he'd bared. "Leese, I want to be here. I told you I work a lot of hours, and you've seen that that's true, but this…being with you, this is what I want. You're what's been missing in my life. Is it wrong to want to enjoy us on a Saturday instead of working?"

"Cole." She didn't even really know why she was pushing him away, but she couldn't stop herself.

"Leesa?"

"You shouldn't put the other parts of your life on hold for me." She shifted her eyes away, and he drew her chin toward him, forcing her to look at him.

"I'm not putting anything on hold. I'm just starting to live my life. There's a difference." His tone was serious, and his eyes pinned her in place, making her heart race.

"Don't you see, Cole? Out here I'm fine. There's no one here to worry about, just you and me."

"Again, I'm not seeing the issue." He sat up and rested his

forearms on his knees.

She sat up beside him, feeling her heart swell and a fissure form. "The issue is that when we're alone, everything is amazing, but back there." She pointed toward the harbor. "Back there, my past hovers over every step I take."

He folded her into his arms, his eyes dark and serious again. "I told you I can handle that. There's nothing I wouldn't do for you."

"I believe you. *That's* the problem." She drew in a deep breath. "I can't let you put your career at risk when I'm carrying so much baggage." She pulled from his arms so she could see his face more clearly, and she pressed her hands to his cheeks. "I'm falling in love with you, and you don't put someone you care about in harm's way."

"Do you know what it does to me to hear you say that? To know you're falling as deeply for me as I am for you?" He smiled, and it made her worries deepen.

"I know, but I can't..."

"What are you saying? You want to break up with me because of what *might* happen?"

She heard hurt in his voice. "No. I don't want to break up with you at all. But I think I need to go back to Towson and try to, I don't know, find some closure. I can't get Andy out of my head, and if he needs help and doesn't get it, I'll never forgive myself if something happens to him."

Cole's arms circled her again. "Angel, you had me so worried. I'll go with you."

She shook her head. "I thought about this all morning as every breath we took brought us closer together. God, Cole. Another week and I'd be ready to marry you."

"Again, not seeing an issue here. I'd marry you tomorrow—

and I don't give a rat's ass if we've only known each other for a few days." He gazed into her eyes and she felt her resolve slipping away. "Leesa, don't try to tear us apart because of some sense of responsibility. We can figure this out together."

"I'm not tearing us apart. Or at least I don't mean to. But I don't even know if I should, or can, pick up my life and move here."

He pressed his lips to hers, and she soaked in his strength. In the moment, as their lives seemed to fall into sync so quickly, she knew without a shadow of a doubt what she had to do.

"I have to go back, Cole. I need closure, a resolution beyond the charges being dropped."

"What more do you hope to accomplish? I'm not sure I understand what you're seeking. Do *you* even know what you're looking for?" He stood and paced, looking devastatingly handsome and hurt, and that made her ache more than she already was at the prospect of leaving.

"To be honest, no. I don't know what will give me the closure I need. But I know I can't live like this. Do you know that every time I hear you say my name I long to *become* Leesa? A waitress without a past?"

"Angel." He gathered her close again.

She couldn't stop the tears from slipping down her cheeks. "I miss *me*, Cole. I miss hearing my name, and I miss teaching. I miss my students. I miss the way they looked up to me, knowing that I was helping them. I miss the girls from the Girl Power group. I miss my life."

She was sure on some level that probably felt like a dismissal of their feelings, but she couldn't stop the truth from pouring out. "I miss the freedom of walking around in public without fearing that someone will say, 'Aren't you that teacher who…?'"

She couldn't bring herself to finish the sentence.

He held her close and wiped her tears with the pads of his thumbs. "I understand. I'm so sorry. What can I do? How can I keep that fear from taking over?"

She shook her head. "You can't. I'm not sure anyone can. This is something I need to do. I ran from my past. I packed up a few things and left my life upended back in Towson with the hopes of…God, I don't even know what I thought when I came here. That a few weeks away would make everyone forget? Or that I could become someone else? I sure as hell never expected to find you." She lifted her eyes to his, and tears streamed down her cheeks, unstoppable, unwanted, taking a piece of her heart with each warm slide.

He pressed his hands to her cheeks, and she half expected him to tell her good riddance, because she was such a mess. That thought brought more tears, and she pulled from his grasp and buried her face against his chest. "I'm sorry," she whispered.

"You don't have to be sorry. When will you go? How long will you be gone?" He held her so tight that she knew this was killing him as much as it was hurting her.

"I don't know. As long as it takes, I guess. I need to talk to your parents to see when they can do without me at Mr. B's. God, I feel so bad for doing this to them, to you." She slammed her eyes closed against the truth. "To us."

Chapter Seventeen

COLE WATCHED LEESA talking with his father on the dock. They'd come back to the marina after she'd cried all her tears and she'd tried to reassure him that this wasn't goodbye. Although he knew she couldn't stand behind that because even she didn't know what she was looking for back in Towson. She'd lived there her whole life. All of her memories of her father, her childhood, and her college years were tied up in the town where one act of betrayal had turned her life upside down. What if she went back and, as he hoped she would, she found everything she was looking for and then decided to stay? He couldn't blame her for that. If anyone understood the significance of memories and family, he did.

The truth was, he'd been fooling himself these last few days. She'd been honest from the start, never committing to remaining in Peaceful Harbor. He'd known that Leesa was unsettled, but he hadn't realized the extent of her turmoil. She obviously wasn't used to anyone having her back or taking care of her the way he wanted to. He got that, especially since her asshole ex had left her right when she'd needed him most. But he wasn't that guy, and he would do whatever it took to prove that to her. What worried him most wasn't whether someone would bring up her past and they'd have to deal with it. Hell, if it were up to him, he'd call a town meeting, get it out in the open, and deal with it once and for all. Of course, that would be possible only if there were such things as town meetings. But life wasn't that simple. Life was full of what-ifs and hidden obstacles, like what Elsie was facing with her family. What worried him most was the idea of Leesa going back to her accuser's family and whoever else she felt she had to clear the air with without him standing beside her, supporting her in any way she needed and in all the ways she deserved.

He never realized that what they'd experienced out on their magical boat ride was the calm before the storm. When they'd arrived back at the marina, Leesa had gone directly to his father, who was working on the boat with his brothers. They'd taken a walk down the dock and were just now, forty minutes later, heading back. Cole had told Sam and Nate what was going on, and then he'd walked off the boat and had been pacing the dock ever since, trying to figure out how she'd ever find closure with something like this.

He felt Sam's and Nate's presence behind him before he heard them. Nate's hand landed on his shoulder, heavy and supportive. "You okay?"

He turned and faced his brothers' serious gazes. Nate had suffered far greater losses than what Cole was facing. His brother had sent his best friend on the assignment that had cost him his life. What kind of strength did it take to pull through that? Leesa's leaving tore him to shreds. And what was worse was that she wanted to handle it alone. She'd already had to handle enough alone. As much as he admired her strength, he hated not going with her, protecting her, being there for whatever she needed.

"Yeah. It's not me I'm worried about. She needs to do this. I get it. I just can't figure out what kind of closure she's going to find, and I'm worried about her." He glanced over his shoulder just as his father embraced Leesa, and he felt his heart swell with love for them both.

"If there's one thing I've learned, it's that finding peace has nothing to do with making sense of something. If you ask me," Nate said, "closure is different for everyone. Look at me and Jewel. Jewel needed to learn to let her younger brother and sisters grow up without micromanaging them, while I needed to figure out how to move past my part in Rick's death. If you had asked me how I was going to do it, I wouldn't have seen a way. I think Leesa probably doesn't know, either."

"I can't imagine that any of what you just said is going to help Cole." Sam's eyes narrowed as he crossed his thick arms over his chest. "How long's she going for?"

"I don't know," Cole said, realizing that she could be gone for weeks. She hadn't given him any indication of how long she was thinking of going or even whether she was coming back. "I assume as long as it takes. She's worried about the kid who accused her." Thinking about the unfairness of what she was going through and how she didn't deserve any of it, he said, "What I'd like to know is how does someone as good as Leesa get kicked in the ass and put through hell while people who cheat and lie never have to deal with shit."

"You know what Tempe would say," Sam said. "This is her 'test of fortitude.'"

"Spoken like a person who has never had to deal with some-thing as life changing as this." As soon as the words left his mouth Cole felt guilty, because Tempe helped people every day of her life. She saw the ugliest of cases from the hospital—young kids in hospice whom she tried to help manage their discomfort through music. She knew exactly how life changing this was for Leesa.

"I don't mean that. I'm just pissed." Cole ran a hand through his hair as he told his brothers the truth. "I feel useless. And like a total asshole because part of me wishes the kid were an adult so I could beat the shit out of him."

Sam scoffed. "That's normal, dude. I think Nate and I feel the same way."

"I just can't help but think that if she comes back, she'll come back in worse shape after being back in a town where her ex treated her like she didn't matter and the kid she helped betrayed her." He stopped pacing and said, "What I really want is to go with her and be right by her side as she does whatever she needs to."

"So do it," Sam suggested. "Jon'll cover your patients."

"I'm not worried about my patients. Leesa said she has to do this alone."

"Shit, all girls say that. But they don't mean it." Sam rubbed the scruff on his chin. "They need men to pull them through the hard stuff."

Cole shook his head. "Dude, you've got a lot to learn about women. There's a huge difference between a woman *needing* a man to take care of her issues and a woman determined enough to prove herself." And even though he knew Leesa was the latter, and he respected the hell out of her for it, that didn't mean part of him didn't wish she *needed* him to be right there with her.

LATER THAT AFTERNOON Tegan sat on the edge of Leesa's bed, watching her pack. "I can't believe you're going back. You seemed really happy here."

"I am happy here." She shoved a pair of jeans into her suitcase. "But despite needing to go figure this stuff out, I've mooched off of you for too long already."

"Hardly. What about Dr. Oh-So-Orgasmic Braden?" Tegan's words were teasing, but her tone was semiserious. "You know, it's dangerous to leave such a cute doc all alone. What if I break my ankle again? He might fall for a damsel in distress."

Leesa threw a pillow at her. "You'd never hit on him. Besides, his ex seems to be all up in his stuff right now. If anyone will see this as an opportunity, it's her."

"Doesn't that worry you?" Tegan asked.

She sat down beside her friend and sighed. "After having my entire life ripped out from under me by a twelve-year-old's rebellion, or heartbreak, or whatever the hell it was, I've learned that I can't control what other people do. Worrying about it won't stop it from happening. I'm worried about *Cole*, but not about him finding another woman. I don't even know if our being together is the right thing for *him*. It *feels* right to me. I mean, I never once felt for Chris what I feel for Cole after just a few days. We're both already in so deep, and I worry that his being with me just puts him in harm's way. I would never forgive myself if he had to deal with explaining my background to his patients or his friends, or…" She looked away, trying to stave off tears.

"Annalise Avalon, you're an incredibly talented, giving person, and Cole sees that. He told you that he'd support your relationship no matter what. Maybe you should just accept that and move forward."

"That's just it. I can't. I thought I could, but it turns out that pretending everything I went through never happened isn't easy. I want to go back and deal with it. I feel like I've left an open jar of snakes and they're creeping out all over the place, just waiting for the right moment to strike. I need to close that jar once and for all."

"If you *want* to go back, why do you look so sad?" Tegan reached for her hand.

"Because." Her eyes dampened despite her best efforts to keep her emotions in check. "I know I have to do this. For my own sanity and for any future I hope to have with Cole or anyone else. But that doesn't mean it's easy. I'm throwing myself to the wolves, and I don't know what to expect, or how long I'll be gone, or…" She swiped at her tears.

"Aw, Annalise," Tegan said as she hugged her. "I really think you should reconsider staying here, or let me or Cole go with you so you're not alone. Or just stay here," she repeated. "My vote is definitely stay here. No one is making you go."

Leesa wiped her tears and drew her shoulders back, gathering her courage yet again. "No one has to make me go, Teg. I could no sooner turn my back on Andy than I could look the other way for any of my students."

"That's really selfless of you, considering the kid slaughtered your life."

"No, it's actually *very* selfish of me. I'm doing this for *me*. I need to make sure he's okay because I have a feeling that's the only way *I* can be okay."

Later that evening, Leesa packed up her car and drove over to Cole's house. It was humid and the air felt heavy—or maybe that was just her heart.

She followed the sounds of his guitar down to the beach and

found him sitting by the water, strumming a melancholy tune.

"Hey," she said as she sank to the cool sand beside him.

He set the guitar down and pulled her in for a kiss. "Hi, angel. You know, before you came into my life, it had been ages since I'd played the guitar."

The comment was so far from what she'd expected to talk about that it took her a second to process it.

"Oh, well, you play so nicely. I'm glad you're playing again."

"I had forgotten how much emotion playing stirs up. I was inside the house, and even though you've only spent a few nights here, it felt empty without you around. Playing the guitar made me feel closer to you."

They sat in comfortable silence, as the waves rolled gently in, swishing loudly against the shore, then rolling gracefully back out. Cole laced their fingers together and brought hers to his lips, kissing the back of her hand as he'd done so many times before that she'd memorized the feel of his soft lips pressed to them and the minute scratching of his upper lip against her skin.

"I wish you'd let me go with you. I hate the thought of you going back alone."

His eyes were so serious and his voice was so tender that she felt herself wavering about leaving him at all. She wanted to get past whatever her mind was having trouble letting go of, even if she couldn't quite grasp what that was. She needed to try.

"I don't want you tangled up in my mess." She leaned her head on his shoulder. "Wouldn't it be easier for you to get involved with a normal girl who doesn't have eight hundred pounds of baggage on her back?"

He tipped her chin toward him and kissed her softly. "Angel, you're better than normal, whatever *normal* means. You're spectacular. And there's no creature, real or imagined, that could scare me away." He kissed her again, and she felt herself melting into their closeness. "Open your eyes," he whispered. "Look at me so I know you hear me."

She did.

"I don't want someone else. I feel like I've waited my whole life to meet you. When you're ready, I'll be here, whether it takes a day, a week, or a year."

She touched her forehead to his and closed her eyes again before asking, "You're not upset with me for wanting to go back?"

"I support whatever you need to feel safe. And if you think you'll find the answers there, then I support the trip."

He gathered her in close, and she wondered what she'd done to get lucky enough to have found such a supportive man. Listening to the steady beat of his heart, breathing in his now familiar scent, her throat thickened. Was she really going to leave him behind? Did she have the strength to get up and go? To drive the few hours to Towson and face what she'd run from? She knew she had to. Staying here and pretending everything was okay had seemed like an option, when really, it was only a bandage on a wound too deep to ignore.

"I'll miss you," she finally managed.

"I'll miss you, too." He kissed her again and held her gaze as he cupped her cheeks in his warm hands. "Whatever happens, know that I'm here, and my family is here. Tegan's here. We're all here for you, and…" He paused, searching her eyes as his brows drew together. The warmth in his eyes grew stormy. "Damn it, Leesa. I wish you'd let me be there with you. *For* you. It doesn't make you any less determined if you let me be there to support you, and saying 'I'm here for you' doesn't give you arms to walk into at the end of the day. It doesn't allow me to stand up for you if you need me to, or to give an icy stare to someone who looks at you the wrong way."

She nearly lost her resolve right then. She'd never been with a man who was willing to fight for her, and she didn't want to lose him. But she knew, even though her heart was swelling and aching in alternating beats, that she had to do this alone. The only way to keep a sob from breaking free was to try to tease herself out of the emotion.

"Aw, my alpha boyfriend wants to get all tough and protective."

"I'm serious, Leese. How am I supposed to get through each day knowing you're facing everything you fear most?" He caressed her cheek and slid his fingers into her hair, holding tight. "I don't want to suffocate you. Okay, maybe I do." He smiled.

"Your patients need you, and your partner doesn't need your extra caseload."

"Let me worry about that," he insisted.

She shook her head. "You think you can handle it, but you weren't there. You have no idea what it's like to face the types of looks I faced. As bad as it was that Chris left me, I can't really blame him. That's not something I want you to see, Cole. You know me as Leesa Avalon, a waitress with a past. Let me remain that person in your mind until I can be Annalise Avalon, a woman without any labels. Let me clear my name and then you can decide if this is what you want." As she said it, she realized that was *exactly* what she needed.

"Annalise. Leesa. You can be anyone you want to be. I just wish being here with me was enough."

"It *is* enough." She clutched his hand, but she knew her claim wasn't true. Now that her need had clarified itself in her mind, she needed that, too. Maybe even more, so that she was starting from a place of stability rather than a place of escape.

Cole must have sensed her lack of faith in her words, too, because he rose to his feet and reached for her hand. He gathered her in close, to the place she fit so well. The place that had somehow felt like home, and as they walked toward her car, he said the words that nearly brought her to her knees.

"Angel, when being here with me is enough, you won't need to leave."

Chapter Eighteen

LEESA STOOD ON the sleepy street where she'd grown up, looking at the small, bungalow-style home she and her father had shared. It was a funky little house with a roofline more typical of the Dutch style than of bungalows. A wide peak rose above the front door and the bay window to the right of it. The left side of the house was shrouded by bushes and a pine tree that shadowed her second-floor bedroom window. The other bedroom window sat high in the peak, not quite centered. She took in the neatly trimmed yard—maintained by a lawn service while she was away.

Away. Boy did that sound strange in her head. She hadn't even gone away to college, having attended Towson State. She'd never strayed far from her hometown until she'd felt pushed out. She opened the trunk of her car, retrieved her suitcases, and lugged them up the front walk, the familiar cracks in the sidewalk bringing with them a hint of familiarity.

She inhaled the scent of pine, mulch, and *home* and crinkled her nose. The scents smelled funny. Had she already gotten used to smelling the sea in every breath? Was the air here thicker, more polluted? Or was that just her heart tugging her back toward Cole?

She tried to brush off the thought as she pushed open the front door and stepped onto the worn and scuffed hardwood floors. The same floors she'd used as dance floors for her Barbies. The floors she used to curl up on in front of the fireplace while her father read to her. The floors she'd crossed in her first pair of high heels. The floors her father had taught her to dance on. Her heart squeezed at the memory. She had too many father-daughter memories to count. Half the time, while her friends were out testing their newfound hormones in high school, she'd been home playing games and watching old movies with her father. How could she leave this all behind?

Guilt threaded around her as she set her bags by the door and walked through the hall, trying to ignore the way the house felt like a shell, with no heartbeat keeping it alive. She walked through the living room, her eyes skirting over the wall of books surrounding the tiny fireplace. She hadn't changed much after her father had passed away, keeping the same furniture that was permanently molded to his middle-aged frame. She picked up a pillow and closed her eyes as she brought it to her nose, inhaling deeply. She didn't expect to still smell her father's scent. She could barely conjure up his voice any longer without listening to the sole voicemail she'd saved on her phone, but still, she tried. She inhaled two, three times, smelling nothing but old fabric.

Setting the rust-colored pillow back in place, she ran her finger along the bookshelves, eyeing the titles. Her father was an avid reader and had enjoyed reading everything from Stephen King to self-help books and anything in between. He wasn't a well-educated man, but he was brilliantly savvy and intelligent in ways that couldn't be learned in a classroom. As an insurance salesman for twenty years and a manager for six before he became too ill to work, he could negotiate with the best of them and his work ethic was unparalleled by most men. *Well, except Cole. He seemed to put as much into his work as he does into his family and…and me.*

She walked into the cozy kitchen, smiling at the table built for two, and retrieved a glass from the cabinet. She filled it with water and leaned against the counter as she drank it, thinking about her father. It wasn't his brilliance that she missed. It was his presence. Walking into the house and hearing him call out her name. *Annalise? That you, hon?* And his ever-present support. The ache of missing him clung to her, and her hands began to tremble. She set the glass on the counter with a *clunk* as tears sprang to her eyes. Her chest felt heavy, and her legs must have taken the cue, because as she lowered herself into a wooden chair, they simply gave out, and she landed with a *thump* on her butt.

She gave in to the ugly sobs that bubbled up from her chest. She cried for the father she wished she could have saved and for the life he'd lost at too young an age. She cried for the way she felt certain Andy's life had also been ruined, and she cried for the loss of Annalise Avalon, the woman her father had worked so hard to raise in all the right ways. She cried for the girl she'd tried to become in Peaceful Harbor, and she cried for the people she'd left behind there, too. She cried because as she sat in the house that had once made all her troubles disappear and all the answers become clear, it no longer held those powers.

Chapter Nineteen

MONDAY MORNING ARRIVED without Leesa in Cole's arms and with a full patient load at the office. It was officially the shittiest Monday of the year, and there had been plenty of not-so-pleasant ones. Somehow the not-so-pleasantness of patients who argued about treatments and complained about Cole running late for their appointments didn't compare to Leesa, alone in Towson, facing down demons she didn't deserve.

She'd called last night to let him know that she'd arrived safely, and he'd heard sadness in her tone despite the brave voice she was putting on. It had cut him to his core.

He lifted his eyes from the chart he was reviewing at the sound of a knock at his office door.

"Yeah, come in," he said. He was surprised to see his brother Sam open the door.

"Hey, dude. Sorry I didn't call, but...yeah. I wanted to see your ugly mug." Sam strutted in, wearing a pair of cargo shorts and a tank top, his tanned muscles on full display. Cole was sure his staff got a kick out of that. He'd heard the murmurings about his siblings. They were hard to miss when the single girls lit up like the sun whenever his brothers came by. He'd heard words like *stud* and *hot* too many times to count.

Cole pointed to a chair. "Take a load off. I have a patient in ten, but what's up?"

Sam rubbed his chin. The spark of mischief in his eyes dimmed to a concerned, assessing gaze.

"Did Mom get ahold of you yet?" Sam leaned forward, resting his forearms on his thighs, his hands rubbing in the way he did when he was trying to figure out how to say something.

"No. What's up? She usually doesn't call during patient hours unless it's an emergency." Cole closed the file and shoved it to the side to focus on Sam.

"She's pulling together another goodbye dinner for Shannon, and Ty's coming back for it. It's in two weeks. Saturday night, at Mom and Dad's."

"You came all the way here to tell me that?" He cocked a brow.

Sammy's lips curved up. "Nah. I came to make sure you weren't crying into a hanky or hiding under your desk." He laughed. Cole shook his head. "What? You go all gaga over a woman for the first time in forever and she left you high and dry. Someone's gotta watch out for the master at hiding his emotions, Dr. Braden."

Cole walked around his desk and sat beside Sam. "I suck at hiding my feelings where she's concerned, but I'm fine. I'm a big boy, and she's a big girl." He scrubbed a hand down his face, hoping Sam would buy the lie. "But that doesn't mean I don't want to pound the shit out of something or someone for the position she's in."

"That's what I'm talking about." Sammy patted him on the back as another knock sounded at the door.

"Come in," Cole said.

Faith, a physician assistant who had worked for Cole for the last year and a half, peeked around the door, and her eyes stole to Sammy. Her dark hair was piled on her head in a tight bun, and she held the edge of the door in a death grip. She was usually professional and confident, except when Sam came around—then she became meek and nervous.

"Excuse me. Um. Hi," she said to Sam, holding his gaze a beat longer than necessary, making Cole chuckle.

Sam lifted his hand in a wave. "Hi, Faith. It's nice to see you. I love your hair like that."

Her cheeks flamed as she tore her eyes away. "Um. Thank you. Um…"

Cole glared at Sam. He did shit like that just to make her blush. His glare was wasted, as Sam's eyes were still locked on the pretty, flustered brunette.

"Faith, is there something you needed?" Cole asked.

"Oh. Yes, sorry. Mr. Hood showed up early, and he's waiting to speak with you."

"Okay. I'll be out in a sec. Thanks." He didn't bother to wonder why she'd come to tell him instead of the front desk staff calling him. Whenever one of his handsome siblings was in the office, one of the single girls always popped in with some excuse to get a peek.

She closed the door behind her, and Cole nudged Sam with his knee.

"Cut that shit out. She works for me, remember?"

Sam snickered. "It's not like I'm sleeping with her. I think she's cute as hell when she's embarrassed, but don't worry. She's way too *good girl* for me."

"Yeah, let's let her stay that way. She's the best PA we've got." Cole rose to his feet, and Sam followed. "Listen, I appreciate you coming by, but I'm fine, really. I talked with Leesa last night and again this morning. She's heading over to talk to her old boss today. She's a smart woman, Sammy. She's doing the right thing for her, even if it sucks for me." He nodded toward the door. "Now get outta here so I can talk to my patient's father and get him to do the right thing."

Sam pointed at him. "Drinks tonight at Tap It. Me and Nate'll be there, and if you're not there by eight, I'm going to find you and drag your ass there."

Even though drinks were the last thing on his mind, Cole knew that when Sam was determined, there was no fighting him, so he agreed. "You mean you're actually giving up a night with a random chick to hang with your brothers?"

Sammy winked. "Hey, you're the one who taught me that family has to come first. Besides, the thought of you crying at home makes my stomach turn."

Cole took a quick step toward his smirking younger brother.

Sam sidestepped the feigned grab and said, "See ya tonight, bro," before disappearing out the door.

A few minutes later Mr. Hood had replaced Sam in the chair across from Cole's desk. His beady eyes held a look of determination that Cole had seen many times and almost always led to a poor choice for his patients. The churning in Cole's gut told him that this was not a good day to face the man who stood between him and his patient. Especially when he'd prescribed a treatment plan that would certainly lead to her full recovery. It didn't bode well for Elsie that she wasn't present for this meeting. Usually when a patient was going to forgo treatments, they simply canceled their appointment or didn't show up at all, but there were a handful who sought his approval. It was approval he never gave, but at least with those who came to see him, he had one last shot at changing their minds.

"Dr. Braden, by now you understand the difficult position I'm in as a parent. My daughter has worked for years for all that she has achieved, and she has a chance to reach a level of success doing what she loves most. A level of success that very few people can claim."

"Yes, I can appreciate why this seems like a difficult decision for your family. Please understand, Mr. Hood, that from a medical perspective this decision isn't just a matter of Elsie missing her chance at competing in the upcoming Olympics. This is a choice between a resolution to the pain that your daughter has clearly been experiencing for longer than she's indicated and a future that will likely include further injury, which could lead to missing the Olympic competition anyway and a lifetime of underlying pain."

For the first time since they'd met, Cole saw a hint of emotion other than vehemence in the man's eyes. He placed his hands on the arms of the chair and let out a long sigh that sounded a lot like defeat. Unfortunately, as his fingers curled around the edges of the chair, Cole worried that was just wishful thinking on his part.

"Mr. Hood, you drove two hours to see me instead of seeing a doctor in your hometown. You must have trusted that I'd have your daughter's best interests at heart."

"You came highly recommended," he offered weakly.

"I appreciate that." Clearly if Elsie's father approved treatment, she had Rush Remington to thank for it. "As I said, then you must have trusted my capabilities to come all this way."

"Yes. I do, despite how it might look." He lifted hooded eyes to Cole. "How do I say to my teenage daughter, who has worked her butt off for years—literally years—giving up time with friends, sleepover, dances, summer vacations...? How do I say, you did a great job, and I'm proud as hell of you, but now we're pulling the rug out from under your dreams?"

Cole wanted to get up and hug the man for showing that he wasn't the robotic, angry man he'd come across as. Instead, he clasped his hands on the desk and smiled at the troubled man, appreciating the position he was in. He drew upon all he'd heard from his father over the years and hoped his words would help.

"I think you start with, 'I love you and I'm proud of you,' and you end with something about how when she was born, you promised to protect her *and* support her, and that as her father, or as her parents, that's exactly what you're doing. And you reassure her that this treatment will hopefully allow her to one day fulfill those dreams."

Mr. Hood's jaw tightened as he sat silently looking at Cole. Cole waited patiently for his words to find their path to either pissing the man off or soothing his worries. He could take either, though he hoped for the latter. In the silence, Cole searched his face for clues, but the man wasn't giving anything away.

"Do you have children, Dr. Braden?"

Cole smiled at the thought, and it brought his mind to Leesa. He fought the urge to look at his watch and see how much time had passed since their call, or whip out his phone and check for a text, and focused on getting Elsie the best treatment he could. "No, sir. Not yet."

Mr. Hood steepled his hands beneath his chin. His brows drew together as his eyes dropped to Cole's desk, lingering there as the minutes ticked away. When he finally rose to his feet, his narrow shoulders weren't pulled quite so tightly as they had been when he'd arrived, and when he extended a hand to Cole, gone was the angry grip.

"Thank you. Being a parent is the hardest job in the world. Being a good parent is even more difficult. I only hope I'm doing the right thing."

Hoping he'd choose to get his daughter proper treatment and not wanting to push him, Cole said, "I'm sure you will."

Mr. Hood nodded, and as he opened the office door, he turned and said, "I'll make the appointment with the orthotist on my way out."

LEESA SILENCED HER vibrating phone for the fourth time in as many hours. She cut the engine, parking in front of the middle school where she'd poured her heart and soul into every class. Cole had called her at the crack of dawn, offering again to come to Towson, and as much as it hurt to do it, she'd turned him down. He had sent two text messages before she'd left the house. They probably weren't meant to soften her resolve, but hell if they didn't have that effect at first. She still felt the need to handle this on her own. She'd never had to rely on a man before, and she wasn't about to start now. Her father would roll over in his grave if he thought she'd allowed herself to fall apart at a twelve-year-old boy's bad judgment. She was stronger than that. She had to be. And on the off chance she wasn't, she sure as hell didn't want Cole to witness her weakness.

She thought of those text messages now as she stared at the redbrick building, gathering the courage to walk inside.

I have faith in you. Go reclaim your name! You can do it!

She knew it must have killed him to send a text instead of being there to tell her in person. She also knew Cole wouldn't have sent the supportive texts if he didn't believe she could do it *and* didn't sincerely want that closure for her, even if it might mean that she would remain in Towson long-term. If his tone last night hadn't choreographed his sadness and discomfort over her leaving, his actions had. She'd noticed that he was good at brushing things off with others, but with her he was an open book. One look in his eyes told her everything she could ever want to know—from how much he adored her to the intensity of his passion.

He'd sent a selfie a few minutes after she'd responded to the texts and thanked him for understanding. He was smiling and giving her a thumbs-up. She'd laughed, despite the tightening of her chest. She held on to that image, soaking in his support.

Tegan had texted before she'd even showered. The first text told her to kick ass and the second told her to come back to Peaceful Harbor if she'd rather not kick ass. She glanced down at her phone now, thinking one of the two were texting again, and was surprised to see Tempe's name on the screen. She opened the message and a long text bubble appeared.

I heard you went back to Towson. Proud of your strength. Want me to come down? I don't mind. I know this is going to be hard for you.

Another text bubble appeared as she was reading.

Let me know. BTW this is Tempe in case you don't have my number in your phone yet.

Goose bumps raced up her arms. She'd never been embraced by people so completely and seamlessly, and Cole's family accepted her despite this mess that she carried around like a ball and chain. She glanced up at the building, using the support of Tempe, Tegan, and Cole to fuel her courage for the meeting she would have with the principal, Darlene Sentry, in a few minutes.

She started to send a reply to Tempe and hesitated. What could she say? Thanks for the kudos? Thanks for the friendship? Sorry I took off and left your brother's head and heart spinning? The truth in that thought gripped her, sending her stomach into a tizzy. Every time she thought of Cole it was like a double-edged sword. She wanted to be his, to accept his love and support and disappear into him forever, but her past felt like a ticking time bomb.

She had to do this.

She typed a quick response to Tempe—*Thank you! Your support means the world to me, but I'm sure you can understand my needing to do this alone. Hug Cole for me?* She deleted the last sentence before sending it off. She had no idea how long she'd be here, and she didn't know Tempe well enough to send something like that, regardless of how close she felt to her. She stepped from the car, and with her heart racing and adrenaline pushing blood through her ears so loudly that she could barely think, she headed for the building.

She inhaled the familiar scent of *school*. It was the same at every school she'd ever been in, the smell of hard work, too many hormones, and knowledge waiting to be learned. She used to revel in that pungent smell. Now, as she pressed the button and the buzzer sounded, unlocking the front door, nothing felt right. The smell and sights were the same, and the halls were wide and empty. Erin Walsh, the perky brunette who had manned the front desk for the past several years, was working at her computer behind the glass doors that separated her from the entrance, but somehow the school felt as foreign as everything had after she'd lost her father.

She pulled open the doors to the office, and Erin lifted her eyes from her computer.

"Annalise!" She came around the reception desk and threw her arms around Leesa. "Ohmygod! I've missed you. How are you? Wow, you look tan and beautiful." Erin was a bundle of energy and positivity.

She took Leesa's hand and dragged her behind the desk, lowering her voice even though there didn't seem to be anyone else around. The door to the nurse's office was closed, and she couldn't see far enough down the hall to Darlene's office or the teachers' lounge. "How are you?"

Leesa was reeling from her friendly greeting. Erin had cried when Leesa was put on leave during the investigation, but she'd worried that over time, between rumors and speculation, Erin would have a different view of her. She was beyond relieved that time had not changed things for the worse. But just because exuberant Erin didn't hesitate to welcome her into her arms again didn't mean that others would do the same.

"I'm doing well, thanks, and I'm sorry to surprise you like this. I thought Dar would have told you I was coming in to meet with her."

Erin shook her head. "Dar is crazy busy these days. I'm not surprised she forgot to mention it. Let me buzz her and let her know you're here." She picked up the phone and called Darlene. Leesa took a few deep breaths, mentally preparing to see her old boss again. She'd been supportive of Leesa during the investigation, and when the accusation had been found to be false, Darlene had offered Leesa her old job back. Of course, strong advice came along with the offer—*Don't put yourself in any situation where you're alone with a student again. Don't tutor kids outside of school.* But Leesa had been quick to refuse that opportunity. She'd felt like every kid would look at her differently, and she knew she'd look at them differently, despite how much she enjoyed teaching.

Funny, she'd forgotten that feeling until just now.

Darlene had been quick to find her the job at the school in Baltimore, and she'd encouraged Leesa to take it. But the uneasy feeling of being accused and of being looked at sideways lingered, whether it was all in her head or not.

Erin hung up the phone and said, "Dar said to go on back." She stood and hugged Leesa again and said quietly, "It's so good to see you again, and I'm happy that all that stuff didn't take a toll on you permanently. You look amazing!"

As Leesa walked down the hall, closing in on Darlene's office, she wondered how she was pulling off *amazing* when she felt like a nest of bees was swarming in her stomach.

Chris stepped out of the lounge, nearly barreling into her. "Annalise. You're back in town?"

She was surprised at the bile rising in her throat for the man she once believed would always be there for her. Well, she was no longer the naive woman she'd once been. *Holy shit. I'm not* Annalise *anymore.*

She realized she had become someone else entirely. A woman who was pulling her shoulders back, lifting her chin up high. A woman who hadn't fallen to ground zero after the accusations but had been strong enough to run—and sure, that might have been a weak move, but it was also a show of strength. *An act of courage*, just as Cole had said.

She looked Chris in his beautiful eyes, remembering how they had once affected her, seemed honest and caring. But then he'd shown his true colors, and *he'd* been weak. She gave a curt nod. "Chris."

"How are you?" He raked his eyes down her body, and then his gaze darted down the hall, as if he wanted to make sure no one saw them talking. He lowered his voice and said, "We should get together and talk. Want to come over for a drink?" He stepped in closer and placed his hand on her forearm. His touch felt wrong.

She shifted out of his reach. "I really don't have time—" That wasn't true. She had all the time in the world. She was here to clear her name, reclaim herself, not to hide behind a thinly veiled excuse. She held her chin up high again and said, "You made your choice about me weeks ago, Chris. I don't think we have anything to talk about."

She turned on her heel, her chest filling with pride and a smile forming across her face as she made a beeline for Darlene's office.

Chapter Twenty

DARLENE'S OFFICE FELT smaller than Leesa had remembered, but that might have been the suffocating feeling of being back where her nightmare began. Darlene's lips curved in a welcoming smile, and her dark eyes warmed as she came around the desk and opened her arms to Leesa.

"Annalise, it's so nice to see you. I was surprised to get your call. I thought you wanted to take the next few weeks to make your decision."

"Thanks for making time for me, Dar."

"Of course. Always." Darlene waved to the couch beside the door. "Let's sit."

She had always taken her meetings with Leesa on the couch rather than sitting behind the desk, and it usually put Leesa at ease. Today it felt strange, like Darlene was trying too hard. Or, Leesa realized, like she no longer fit into the environment, despite the momentary bout of courage she'd found when she'd walked away from Chris.

"Tell me how you are. What have you been doing these last few weeks? Relaxing, I hope." She angled her body toward Leesa, her arm outstretched along the back of the couch, the epitome of an old friend sincerely interested in hearing about

Leesa's life.

Why, then, did Leesa feel like the room held no oxygen and the walls were closing in around her? Was she just used to the openness of her job at Mr. B's, or was this something more? Her inability to break free from her stifling past?

She couldn't weed through her thoughts quickly enough to make heads or tails of them. Forcing her voice from her lungs, she said, "I'm still trying to decide what I want to do."

Darlene placed her hand on Leesa's and her gaze softened. "There's no rush. The job in Baltimore is waiting for you. They have coverage for now. And, Annalise? Make no mistake, they want you to take it."

Her throat felt like it was closing up.

"You were one of the best teachers we had, and all that stuff that happened is water under the bridge. No one thinks any differently about you."

The truth spilled from her lips, unbidden. "I do."

Darlene tilted her head in question.

"Oh, Dar. I don't know who I am anymore, or where I belong. What happened to me *did* change me, whether you can see it or not. I can feel it in here." She pressed her hand over her heart.

"I'm sure it did in some ways, but, Annalise, that was a scorned kid rebelling. You could have been anyone. You just happened to be the teacher in his line of fire. A crush gone wrong. You can't let that take you away from everything you worked so hard to achieve."

Leesa wanted to believe her, but her heart was racing just being back in these offices. Would it be this way in any school? Would she ever have the confidence to tutor again one-on-one, or would she always feel the need to have a witness to her actions?

The questions came in rapid-fire. Questions she hadn't given enough weight to before this moment. She was so wrapped up in what other people thought of her that she hadn't slowed down enough to think about what *she* thought of herself.

She dropped her eyes to try to gather her thoughts.

"Annalise, talk to me. Please. I know what you went through was terrible. The whole investigation, the questions…" She paused, then added in a softer tone, "*Chris.*"

Leesa rolled her eyes and sighed. "He's not even a consideration. He probably did me a favor."

"You say that now, but we all know it hurt when he broke things off. No one here was happy with him for how he handled things." Darlene's lips curved up in a smile. "Just think, if you take the job in Baltimore, it opens up a whole new pool of single men, too."

She didn't need a pool of single men. She had Cole. What she needed was a clear head, and she had absolutely no idea how to get it.

"I need a little more time to make that decision, but there was something else I wanted to talk to you about. Andy."

"Annalise." Darlene's tone turned serious. "Lena told me about her concerns. We've discussed it."

"Then you can understand why I want to talk to him." She folded her hands in her lap to keep them from trembling.

Darlene's eyes widened. "You want to…? Annalise, what are you thinking? Not only would his father not allow that, but why open that can of worms again?"

"Don't you think that if I'm this torn up, then the kid who lied is even more so? How can he possibly move past that?"

"He can go to therapy like everyone else. He stole your life,

Annalise."

"He's a kid. He had no idea of the ramifications making those accusations would carry. I'm sure of it." She had to be. Otherwise, what did that say about her ability to read people, to differentiate between a malicious person and someone who'd simply made a bad decision? She'd seen malicious. Kenna kissing Cole was a malicious act to try to hurt her and win him back.

That thought made her gut ache. What would Kenna do when she found out Leesa was gone? Probably pull out all the stops to win Cole back.

She swallowed against the thought. She trusted Cole, but the thought of Kenna anywhere near him made her feel sick to her stomach.

She was getting sidetracked, and she couldn't afford to be sidetracked. She had to take care of herself before she could offer Cole any more of herself than she already had. She had to be healed, whole, confident. She didn't want to be a noose around his neck, a tether to a troubled past he didn't deserve to have to deal with. She listened to Darlene tell her again that she absolutely should not go speak with Andy, and right then and there she knew she wasn't going to heed her warning.

She needed to clear her name and find herself again more than she needed anything else.

Including Cole.

Chapter Twenty-One

"HEY, MAN, CONGRATULATIONS." Cole pressed the cell phone to his ear as he stepped from the car in front of Tap It. He'd called Rush to thank him for referring Elsie Hood.

"Are you kidding?" Rush said. "I only refer to the best."

"We'll have to plan a get together soon." Cole leaned against his car, thinking about Leesa. Rush and his siblings had all gotten engaged or married in the past few years, just as Cole's cousins in Colorado had. Nate and Jewel were on their way to a happy future, and Cole, the one who had always been more of a one-woman man than any of them, felt like he was on the cusp of losing the only woman he wanted a future with.

"Great. I can't wait to see you again, man," Rush said. "It's been too long."

He hadn't seen Rush since his wedding a few months ago, and he looked forward to seeing his old friend again. They shot the shit for a few more minutes, catching up on family members. After ending the call, Cole called Leesa. When it went to voicemail, he hoped she was out with her friends, having a good time, and left a message.

"Hey, angel. I, uh…" He laughed softly, realizing he didn't have a purpose for his call. "I miss you and just wanted to hear your voice. I'm meeting my brothers for a drink. Call me later, or text me? Hope things are going okay."

As he walked into the bar, he fought the urge to climb into his car and drive to Towson. He'd promised to give her the space she needed to deal with this on her own—or at least he'd promised to try. Although he knew himself, and he had no intention of waiting a week, a month, or a year. Yes, he'd wait that long for her if that's what it took for her to come back, but he wasn't about to wait that long to see her again. He'd already looked up her Towson address. He'd give her twenty-four hours to deal with this on her terms. If he could last that long.

"Finally." Sam greeted him loudly from a table near the back of the bar, where he was sitting with Nate, Jewel, Tempe, and Shannon.

Cole placed a hand on each of his sisters' shoulders. "I didn't know you two and Jewel were going to be here."

"You think we'd leave you guys to have all the fun without us?" Shannon said with a bright smile. "Tempe tried to beg off, but Jewel and I dragged her butt out anyway."

"Hey, how are you doing?" Tempe asked as he took the seat beside Sam.

"Fine. Sorry I'm late. Schedule ran late, and I called Rush from the parking lot."

"His wedding was so fun," Shannon said as Nate flagged down their waiter and ordered a pitcher of beer. "You're next, Nate."

Nate grinned and reached for Jewel's hand. "I'm ready, but my girlfriend isn't. She's the one you need to work on."

Jewel rolled her eyes. "Seriously, you guys? Let us be in this amazing stage of bliss for a while. After marriage comes babies and real life. You have to remember, I practically raised my little brother and sisters. I want to enjoy Nate for a while." She gazed into Nate's eyes with so much love that it practically reached out and embraced him. "I can still hardly believe we're a couple."

"Oh, we're a couple, all right," Nate said with a smirk. "Any other guy even tries to come between us and I'll—"

She silenced him with a kiss. "Not a chance. I'm yours, married or not."

Cole sipped his beer, trying to ignore the way watching Nate and Jewel made him miss Leesa even more.

"So, Cole, I was thinking," Sam said. "If Leesa isn't back this weekend, maybe you and I can take a rafting trip Saturday night? Come back Sunday?"

"I don't want to think about her not coming back for a night, much less through the weekend," Cole admitted.

Shannon patted his back. "You fell hard and fast, didn't you?"

Cole smiled but didn't answer. Yes, he'd fallen hard and fast, but he wasn't sure how much that mattered if Leesa decided to stay in Towson. He had a practice here that he had worked hard to build. His life was here. His family.

"Sometimes things just take a while to work themselves out," Jewel said. "Look at me and Nate. Years passed between—" She winced. "Oh, gosh, it won't be years for you guys. I just meant…"

"Don't sweat it, Jewel."

Sam narrowed his eyes at Cole. "It's not like you to sit back and let things happen *to* you, Cole. What gives?"

"I'm trying to give her the space to do what she needs to do. I've waited a long time to find someone I care about. I'm not about to suffocate her and push her away." His blood simmered at his inability to take control of the situation, and his frustration came out in a harsh tone. "Don't you think I tried to go with her? I tried like hell, but she's determined to do this on her own, and I get that. I do, but damn…" He shifted his eyes away from his siblings. "Can we not talk about this, please? I thought y'all were going to take my mind off this shit, not pound it into me."

"Yes, of course," Tempe said, glaring at Sam.

"Sorry, Cole. We didn't mean to pressure you," Shannon added.

"I did." Sam's voice was dead calm. "Just like you'd pressure me if the tables were turned."

"What?" Cole snapped. "You've never cared this deeply about a woman in your life."

"Neither have you," Sam challenged. "Until now."

Cole rose to his feet. He wasn't about to sit here and be pushed by his brother when he already felt locked in a corner. "In case you haven't noticed, Sam, I can deal with my own shit. I've got work to do. I'll catch up with you guys another time."

"That's it, Cole," Sam said, rising to his feet. "Bury your feelings in the lives of your patients, because that's worked out well for you so far."

Cole closed the distance between them, and Nate rose to his feet, his eyes darting between the two men. "You have a hair up your ass, Sammy? Because I'm not sure why you're pushing all my buttons in the middle of Nate's restaurant."

Nate put a hand on Cole's shoulder, and Cole shrugged him off.

"Hey, listen," Nate said in a stern voice. "Whatever bullshit you two have going on, take it outside."

"Sorry. I'm outta here." Cole stalked out the front door and right into Kenna. *Fuck*. Could this night get any worse?

"Cole. I didn't expect to see you here, but I'm glad I did."

She touched his arm, and he shrugged her off and headed down the stairs.

"Cole!"

He turned, trying to contain the anger clawing for release. "What do you want?"

She came down the steps, and her tone softened. "You really love her, don't you?"

"Yes, Kenna. I really do, and I'm in no mood—"

"Cole, it's okay. I'm happy for you. You deserve to be happy. Tell your girlfriend I'm sorry I kissed you. That was low, and I'm trying to turn over a new leaf. I just temporarily forgot how."

He huffed out a relieved breath, feeling like he was caught in a spider's web. He didn't trust Kenna, and it must have been written in his expression, because a sheepish look came over her face.

"I…" She looked away, and Cole swore her eyes were damp. "I know I've been a bitch. I never should have kissed you. Or bid on you. Or…"

He didn't have it in him to try to run through the things she *shouldn't* have done. He flat-out didn't care anymore. He had one focus, and that was Leesa.

"Cole, I owe your girlfriend an apology, and—"

"No. Don't go anywhere near her." He didn't mean to snap, but he was a hairbreadth from losing it, despite the sorrowful look in her eyes. "Look, Kenna, thank you. If you mean those things, thank you. But please don't say anything to Leesa. She doesn't need to feel threatened, or…"

He saw Sam come through the doors of the restaurant with

Nate on his heels and turned toward his car.

"Okay, okay. But I mean it. I *am* happy for you." Kenna headed toward the restaurant.

Cole fished for his keys, trying to ignore the murmurings between her and his brothers.

"Hey, asshole." Sam's deep voice was as calm as a summer's day.

Cole turned a dark stare to Sam and saw Nate on his heels. Cole fisted his hands at his sides. He'd never been a violent guy, but at just barely two years younger than him, Sam had always pushed Cole in ways none of his other siblings dared to.

"Sammy, I'm really not in the mood for games."

Sam held his hands up in surrender. "Neither am I. Dude, she's got you all tied up in knots. Don't you remember seeing this"—he motioned to Cole's fisted hands, the tightness in his jaw, and if he could, Cole knew he'd point out the burning in his gut, too—"in him?" Sam said, pointing to Nate, who stood with his legs planted hip distance apart, arms crossed, shoulder to shoulder between Cole and Sam, clearly ready to jump between them if need be.

Nate's eyes narrowed further at Sam.

"Cole, think about it. Nate stepped up to the plate with Jewel, even with all the shit he had hanging over his head, and you're going to bury yourself in medical cases?"

"It's different," Cole insisted.

"How so?" Sam crossed his arms and cocked a brow. "Enlighten me."

"She may not come back, Sam," he seethed. "Jewel was here. Nate was here. They had history. Leesa and I have *days*. Her history is back in Towson." *And it fucking sucks.*

"So?" Sam shrugged.

"So?" Cole shook his head. "Sam, she's either going to come back or she's not. If I go there and beg her to come back, she'll feel pressured in ways she shouldn't have to deal with while she's got so much other shit going on in her life. I'm trying to do the right thing."

"You always do the right thing," Sam said, stepping into Cole's personal space. Nate's thick arms unfolded and he stepped in just as close, breathing down his brothers' backs.

"You're *Cole Braden*. The eldest. The guy who always does the right thing. The guy whose shadow we've all walked in." Sam searched his eyes, and Cole was sure he saw fire in them. "Don't you ever get sick of being *that* guy? Don't you want to bust free? Say 'fuck it all' and do the thing that *feels* right instead of the thing that *is* right?"

"Dude," Nate said. "I hate to say it, but he's got a point. You always do the right thing."

"That's who I am," Cole said. "I don't know why it bothers you two so much. Tempe does the right thing all the time and you don't give her shit."

"No, because we want her to be that way. She's a chick. You're a dude. You need to cut loose, kick some ass." Sam laughed.

"I'm a doctor." He held up his hands. "These hands are made for healing, not fighting—although if you pull that shit again, I'll happily pound your ass into the pavement." He was breathing a little easier now, knowing that Sam was giving him shit because he cared and not because he suddenly decided to be a dick.

"Come back in and have a drink with us," Sam urged. "Don't pull the 'sit all night at the office' shit you do to avoid having a life."

"I'm not avoiding having a life," Cole muttered. "Sam, you're into the pickup scenes at night. I get it. You and Ty are made for that shit, but I'm not. I'm—"

"Ready for your real life to begin. I get it." Sam draped an arm over Cole's shoulder, turning him back toward the restaurant. "But your real life is in Towson, and we're here, so suck it up, tell me you'll think about what I said, and come back inside for a few beers. I promise I won't give you shit anymore. I just needed you to hear me for once, and you've got the thickest head around."

"That's not the only *thickest* thing I have in this family," Cole joked despite the frustration still simmering in his gut.

Sam gave him a shove as the three men headed back inside, and for the first time since college, Cole considered doing something other than the *right* thing.

LEESA LAY IN bed going over the things Darlene had said to her about the job in Baltimore and about Andy, but the only place her mind wanted to wander was back to Peaceful Harbor. To the man who'd never once flinched when she'd revealed the ugliness of what had happened here in Towson. The man who'd looked like he wanted to have more than a word with Chris over how and why he'd ended their relationship. The man who, when he held her, made her feel safe and happy and more complete than she ever had before. She picked up her cell phone and listened to his message again. She pictured his warm brown eyes, his cheeks, shadowed with manliness even when clean-shaven. After listening to the message, she reread the text he'd sent earlier.

Miss you so much. Are you sure you don't want me to come there?

It had taken all of her resolve to give him the same answer she'd given him last night and again this morning, that she had to do this alone. Now, as she closed her eyes and tried to will herself to sleep, she wondered why in the hell she'd wanted to do this alone. She'd expected to come back to Towson, have a talk with her boss, and then go talk with Andy. And then…she had no fricking idea what would happen.

She hadn't thought beyond hoping she'd feel better. Of course, she was assuming Andy would come clean about lying, so he could feel better, too. She hated that her feeling better relied on someone else's judgment. She wasn't someone who needed others in order to feel good about herself, and yet she felt like she was drowning and Andy held the only life raft in sight. She knew that was not the case. She was a professional, wrongly accused and found innocent.

Knowing that didn't negate the fact that the house where she grew up felt strange and empty, or that apparently she had changed so much that she'd felt uncomfortable in her own skin when she was in her old school despite how welcoming the staff was.

Was this how she was destined to feel forever, like she didn't know where she belonged or who she was supposed to be, untrusting of the professional relationships with students she'd once placed in such high regard? Or like everywhere she went she'd worry about all this shit cropping up and ruining whatever foundation she'd built?

She bolted upright in bed, her heart pounding hard, and stared out the window. Her mind spun, thinking about everything and nothing at once. Had she made a mistake by leaving Towson in the first place? Should she have stayed and dealt with the sideways glances, taken the job in Baltimore, and tried to move on despite the silent hell that followed her around?

Where would that have gotten her?

Would it have heightened her lingering worry that every time she was alone with a student, she could be accused of something unsavory? Or would it have had the opposite effect and strengthened her confidence?

Or...would it have landed her exactly where she was now?

She glanced down at her phone. If she'd stayed, she wouldn't have met Cole. She wouldn't have known what it was like to be loved so completely, or to be embraced by his family so wholly and without judgment. Being with Cole was like living in a fairy tale, only her fairy tale had hidden monsters lurking in the shadows.

She threw her body back down to the mattress with a loud groan, thinking about tomorrow. She was having lunch with Lena and then she was going to return the library books she'd found last night that she'd forgotten to return before leaving town. Her mind had been so scattered when she'd fled to Peaceful Harbor, it was a wonder she'd made it there in one piece.

But she had. And she hadn't felt scattered when she was there. She'd been nervous about all she'd gone through rearing its ugly head, but she hadn't felt scattered.

But hadn't she always landed on her feet? When she lost her father, when she was under investigation, when Chris broke up with her. She hadn't been weak. She didn't need anyone to save her or to make her whole. Why, now, did she need Andy to say those words to her? Why had he suddenly become the key to her confidence, and in turn, her future?

What the hell was wrong with her?

She didn't have the answers, but she knew that no matter what it took, she could handle it.

Now, if she could only sleep, she'd be in better shape to face the day tomorrow. She closed her eyes, knowing that even if she could resolve all the rest, there was one thought rattling around in her head that she knew she'd never quiet—and that was the thought that stayed with her as she drifted off to sleep.

Cole.

Chapter Twenty-Two

THE NEXT MORNING Leesa awoke with a sense of purpose rather than worry accompanying her every breath. She couldn't explain why she felt more confident or determined to set things right with Andy, but by the time she met Lena, she was sure she was doing the right thing. Lena, however, had other thoughts.

"You're insane. Crazy. You've left your good sense back in Peaceful Harbor or something." Lena's shoulder-length dark hair shielded one eye as she stared down Leesa. They were sitting in a booth at Panera Bread, and Lena was speaking loud enough that other customers were looking over.

"Shh." Leesa smiled at the onlookers. *Nothing to see here. Move on.* "Since when did you get so loud?"

"Since two minutes ago when you said you were going to do, oh, I don't know. Only the dumbest thing *ever*." She stabbed a forkful of lettuce from her salad and pointed it at her. "Annalise, you have a chance to get your career back. Dar is offering you a good job with a great team in Baltimore."

Maybe Dar and Lena were right. *Why risk everything for a kid who already stole her life once?* She'd thought about that for half the night, and by the time Cole had called her at seven this morning, she'd known the answer.

"I'm not sure if you'll understand this, because before all this happened, I don't think I would have if someone else were in the same predicament. But what happened *changed* me. I mean, really changed me, Lena. It made me unsure and untrusting. Knowing how easy it was for Andy to accuse me made me realize that any student, at any time, had the power to destroy my career. Or yours. Or any other teacher's."

Lena shook her head. "Already proven, and exactly why I'm telling you *not* to start the whole thing up again. Why open the door to trouble?"

"Don't you see? We're sitting ducks. I can't change that. We can't change that. But what happened to me is done. It's over, and I'm still paying the price. Emotionally, I mean. I know it's all me, in my head, whatever. I'm not pretending that it's something else. But I'm not going to sit back while Andy's life goes down the drain, too, when all it'll take is clearing his conscience to allow him to move forward. And I'm not going to lie; it'll do something for me, too. Getting him to admit he lied will do something to me *inside*."

"You'll feel vindicated," Lena said with a warm gaze. "It's the victim mentality. I totally understand where you're coming from, but if the kid didn't crack then, why would he crack now? And his father will tear you apart if he finds out."

Leesa sat back and sighed. "I'm already torn apart. I'm not afraid of his father, Lena. What else can he do? He can't accuse me of anything more than his son already has."

"I don't know, but aren't you worried that something will go wrong? And that whatever does go wrong will have an impact on the job they're offering you in Baltimore?"

"Yes. I'm afraid everything will go wrong." She tried to quell the fear filling her chest and stealing her confidence. "But I'm more scared of not doing it and of having to live the rest of my life wondering when someone's going to recognize me and out me to—" She stopped short of saying Cole's name, because she felt like he didn't belong here, in this conversation, around this ugliness. "Everyone in my new life."

New life. Did she have a new life? Had she made a decision to move? No, she surely hadn't. At least she didn't think she had, but she had definitely changed, and staying in Towson came with a slew of new realities she wasn't sure she cared for.

They talked until Leesa was so sick of debating the topic that she almost began to question her own motives. She knew Lena was just watching out for her, and she was probably right to be worried, but Leesa held on to the thread of hope that this wasn't going to be a mistake.

By the time she left Lena with promises to *think it over* and let her know if she decided to go through with it so Lena could *be there to pick up the pieces afterward*, she was trembling.

Instead of driving the three blocks to the library, she grabbed her books from the car and walked, hoping to work off the nervous energy that was making her stomach twist into knots. The street was busy with midday traffic, the sun was shining brightly, and Leesa's mind was reeling. She was so focused on talking with Andy, she tripped over the steps leading up to the library.

"Annalise?" Chris crouched beside her and helped her pick up her books. "Are you okay?"

No. "Yeah." She gazed into his kind eyes, and suddenly her throat tightened and she fought the urge to cry. *What the hell?* She sat on the steps with her books piled in her lap. "What are you doing here?"

"I have a meeting with Mrs. Long, the librarian. We're

discussing an after-school program." He sat beside her on the steps. "The real question is, what are you doing here? In Towson, not at the library. I thought if you were going to take the job in Baltimore, you would have already done it. I thought you were gone for good."

"Thought, or hoped?" She closed her eyes against her bitchiness. "I'm sorry. It's been a stressful day."

"I thought, not hoped, and it's been a stressful couple of months. I've worried about you." He held her gaze, his brown eyes full of empathy, without a hint of the lie she wanted to believe he was telling.

Chris was an honest man, and as she sat beside him feeling like the world was pressing down on her shoulders, she realized that his honesty was what had led him to break up with her, too.

"Yes, a stressful couple of months," she agreed. "But I'm on the upside now, trying to rebuild my life."

He shifted his eyes away, staring out at the street, his jaw clenching and unclenching. She knew he was thinking something over. Probably what he'd say next. She blew out a breath, readying herself for whatever it was. Sometimes honesty hurt. *Damn, did it ever.*

When he finally spoke, his tone was tender. "I'm truly sorry for everything. I should have stuck by you, but I was so worried about losing my job that I couldn't see straight. And you were so wrapped up in it all, not leaving the house much, closing yourself off from everyone who was trying to support you..."

"I...I was..." She looked away, the truth in his words cutting like a fresh wound. She didn't want to believe she'd pushed people away. Pushed him away? "I understand why you broke up with me."

"Do you?" He reached for her hand, and she let him take it, knowing that this was part of the cleansing of her past she needed to endure. "Annalise, I loved you. I still love you. But I think we both know that when all that happened, we were already over."

"Already over?" Where had she been in that decision?

His shoulders dropped and a look of disbelief filled his eyes. "Please don't pretend that you don't know what I'm talking about. I saw it in your eyes every time we were together."

"Saw what, Chris? That I was beaten down by the accusation? That I didn't know how to handle it? That being put on leave had torn my heart out?"

"After the accusation, yes, I saw all those things, but before it even happened, the way you looked at me…You weren't fulfilled when we were together. You weren't happy. You were *content*. I could never love you the way you wanted to be loved or the way you deserved to be loved." He squeezed her hand.

"How can you say that? I was—"

"You were gracious and loving and the most incredible woman I'll probably ever have the luck of being with. You accepted me for what I had to give. Two years is a long time. If all this hadn't happened, you might have even married me, and I'd have been the luckiest guy on earth. But when all that stuff went down, I knew I had to let you go. I wasn't strong enough to weather the storm, and trying to drag it out putting my career in jeopardy would have just led to resentment from both of us."

He released her hand, and an uneasy smile curved his thin lips. "You're the strongest woman I know, and it was a dick move to leave you when I did. I know that. But I knew you'd be fine." His lips pressed into a thin line. "I also knew that if my career had suffered because of my affiliation with you, I wouldn't have been fine. The truth is, you're much stronger than I am. More resilient in everything you do, and I'm sorry for the pain I caused you."

She wiped a tear from her cheek, trying to process what he'd said and realizing he was right. She *was* stronger than him. She always had been. In her heart, she must have known he wasn't the right man for her all along.

"Your father would be so proud of you." He pulled her into a hug, and her tears sprang free. "And he'd be ashamed of me."

Her heart ached for her father, and hearing Chris say that about him pulled more sobs from her chest. She opened her mouth to dispute the last of his words, but nothing came out. Her father had known Chris as Leesa's friend, but he'd never known him as her boyfriend. She didn't know if her father would have been ashamed of Chris or not. She only knew that he was right; her father would be proud of her.

She finally pushed from his arms and wiped her tears, swallowing past the lump that clogged her throat. "I'm making you late."

He smiled. "You always did."

A soft laugh escaped her lips, and salty tears slipped into her mouth. She wiped her face, shaking her head. She did have a habit of making him late, and he'd never complained.

"I think my father would have been angry at your timing, but I think he would have been proud of you for having the strength to walk away, because I might never have." Her heart sank with the admission. Now that she knew what real love felt like, how it consumed her thoughts, her body, mind, and soul, she realized that, if not for Chris's ability to walk away, she might have lost out on true love forever.

Chris nodded at the books in her lap. "Want me to return those for you?"

She handed them to him and pulled out her wallet, her tears finally subsiding.

"They're late." She handed him money to pay for the late fees and he pushed the money back toward her.

"I think I can handle a few bucks." He picked up his bag and said, "Are you taking over the Girl Power group again now that you're back? Louise would be thrilled if you did." Chris's younger cousin Louise was part of the group.

"Not right now. I'm still not sure if I'm back for good or not."

He arched a brow. "So you are thinking of moving away from Towson for good? You'd sell your dad's house?"

She shrugged. "Maybe. I haven't made up my mind yet."

"Damn. Peaceful Harbor must be an incredible place to steal you away from your father's house and the neighborhood where you grew up."

It wasn't the harbor that was pulling her in that direction. It was one amazing man, one incredible family, a host of new friends, and a chance at a very full heart.

COLE WALKED INTO Jon's office carrying a stack of patient files.

"I'm surprised you waited a whole day," Jon said with a laugh.

"To do what?" Cole set the files on Jon's desk, knowing his friend was already clued in to his plan.

Jon arched a brow. "When are you leaving and how long

will you be gone?"

Cole shrugged. "After work, and I have no idea. I don't even know if she plans to stay there or come back, but I tried to give her space to handle it on her own and I nearly drove to Towson last night instead of going to Nate's. Boy, was that a mistake. I should have gone to Towson."

"I saw Sam at Jazzy Joe's this morning. Sounds like it wasn't a mistake at all, but exactly the kick in the ass you needed." He reached for the files.

"I had all but decided to leave tonight before I even went into the restaurant. I didn't need Sam to—"

"I'm only giving you shit. But I do wish I'd have been there to see Sammy giving you hell." He chuckled and sifted through the files. "Elsie Hood? You said her father agreed to the treatment."

"He did. I want you to just eyeball her parents when they come in, quietly reassure her father. He had a hard time with the decision, and I want him to know, without a single doubt, that he did the right thing."

Jon shook his head. "You mollycoddle the hell out of your patients *and* their families. Let it go. He's a man. He'll deal with it."

Cole crossed his arms and narrowed his eyes.

"Fine. But I still think you're babying him."

"It's called good patient care. I want his daughter to get her treatment, and the more buy-in from her dad, the less guilty she'll feel for letting him down. And don't even get me started with that. I know there's a part of that guy that's not beyond a misplaced guilt-inducing word or two. Just do it for me."

"You're sure about this?"

"Sure I want Leesa in my life? Absolutely. Sure about leaving my patient load to you? No. It's a shitty thing to do."

"Don't worry," Jon said. "Paybacks are hell."

"Hopefully it'll be worth whatever payback you come up with."

Chapter Twenty-Three

LEESA SAT IN her car, parked at the end of Andy's street, where she'd spent the last hour willing herself to drive down the block. After seeing Chris, she'd gone home to have another good cry. She'd cried not only for the truth Chris had so graciously bestowed upon her, but for the relief that had swept through her at his understanding, his acceptance of who he was, and for knowing what she'd needed when she hadn't even known herself. She cried because there was a tiny sliver of light that had come out of this mess. And she cried because she knew that she couldn't be with Cole unless she could put this all behind her—and that was the part she hoped she was strong enough to do.

As the afternoon sun dipped behind the trees and the evening turned gray, she remained parked at the end of Andy's street. She simply couldn't get herself to start the car and drive. She remembered all the times she had driven down this street, excited to see what progress she and Andy could make. She'd spent countless hours with him, helping him not only with his schoolwork, but also in dealing with the emotional aspects of losing his mobility while his friends were out skateboarding, biking, and hanging out. Andy had taken root in her heart, the way any child she'd worked closely with had. She'd wanted him to do well and to get through his physical healing and schoolwork without being held back, but she'd always been careful to keep their relationship professional. She was still trying to figure out where she'd gone wrong. She'd never talked about girls or dating with Andy. She'd never talked about her personal life with him or led him to think they could be anything other than teacher and student. The shock of that terrible morning came rushing back. The surety that there had been some misunderstanding—that Darlene had somehow mistaken what Andy's father had said. She simply couldn't fathom the accusation, or any reason Andy would want to hurt her in that way.

She drew in a deep breath, accepting her new reality. It *had* happened, and she'd survived it.

That's what she needed to focus on. She didn't have cancer. She wasn't in jail for something she didn't do. She simply had to pull up her big-girl pants and start over.

And she needed to reclaim her reputation.

With that thought fueling her resolve, she cranked the engine and drove down the block toward Andy's house. Her heart was beating so fast she worried she'd be unable to walk, much less talk, when she got there. His father's black Buick was in the driveway, parked beside his mother's efficient Subaru wagon. The urge to keep going was stronger than the urge to breathe, but she forced herself not to chicken out and parked across the street from the modest Colonial.

She could think of a dozen things she could do right now to procrastinate, like calling Lena—who would conveniently talk her out of doing this—or Tegan, who would be so supportive Leesa was sure she'd break down and cry. She could call Cole, who she knew would lead her in whichever direction she asked him to, or she could even call Tempe, who would probably reassure her of her strength and fortitude.

She angled the rearview mirror until she could see her reflection. *I'm the only one I need right now. No one else can do this for me, like no one else could have endured the hurt after Dad died.* She lifted her chin, wondering what Andy and his family would see when she stood in their doorway. Would they see the woman in jeans and a blouse who had helped Andy through so much, or would they see a villain?

She fisted her keys in her hand and stepped from the car, immediately seeking the hood for stability. She stood there, breathing deeply, feeling like she was about to step into a lion's den at feeding time, but believing, truly believing, that after the initial shock and discord that was likely to play out took place, they'd talk things through and clear the air.

She heard voices coming from the backyard as she crossed the street. Okay. This would be easier, right? Not being confined inside their house?

She walked on shaky legs around the house, following the voices to the backyard, where she found Andy and his father sitting at a round table on their patio, dinner plates in front of them. Andy pushed food around his plate as his father spoke. One plate was set off to the side, a fork stuck in a piece of meat, resting on edge of the plate. Oh, man, she hadn't even considered that she might interrupt their family dinner.

She debated retreating before they could see her, but Andy looked up, his eyes landing directly on her. He looked smaller, frailer than he'd been just weeks earlier. He smiled for a second, maybe two, like he was happy to see her, before his father's gaze shifted to her and the man was on his feet, closing the distance between them. Andy was right behind him, pushing his wheelchair along the patio. Conflicting emotions swept through her. He looked so young, so fragile. How could she expect him to apologize?

Mr. Darren closed in on her, stealing her oxygen with a harsh glare and reminding her exactly why she'd come. Her hand dropped to her side, fidgeting nervously with the seam of her jeans. He stood a few inches from her, his dark eyes angry, his jaw tight.

"H-hello, Mr. Darren," she managed. "I'm sorry to interrupt."

"You shouldn't be here."

She shifted her eyes to Andy, despite her best efforts to remain focused on the man before her. Andy shifted in his chair behind his father.

"I was hoping to talk to Andy."

"He has nothing to say to you." His father moved into her line of sight.

She swallowed the fear threatening to bring her to her knees and forced her shaky voice from her lungs. "I just wanted to…"

"Dad," Andy said from behind him.

"Andy, you have nothing to say." His father stood between them, an immovable wall.

"I…I just wanted to see how Andy was doing," Leesa explained.

"He's fine, and he's been through enough—"

Andy tugged on his father's sleeve, and his father grabbed his hand. Andy struggled to free himself, and his father tightened his grip. In that moment she knew her presence was only making things worse for Andy.

"It's okay. I'll go." She'd been a fool to come here without a witness anyway. Anything could have happened, and then it would be her word against theirs again.

"Andy, settle down." His father released his hand and remained in front of his wheelchair.

She took one last look at Andy, and her stomach sank at what she saw there—regret, fear, and something else unsettling she couldn't pinpoint. She hesitated as she turned to leave. Her stomach tightened, her legs were weakening by the second with the reality that not only was she not going to clear her name, but that she'd been selfish enough to want that in the first place when Andy clearly had bigger issues than her to deal with.

She took a step away, the look in Andy's eyes searing into her mind.

Desperation. That's what that look was. She was sure she'd looked the same way the day she'd been accused and every day thereafter for a long time. The thought stopped her in her tracks.

She turned to face Andy. His father's face was red, the veins in his neck bulged, but the look in his eyes was no longer angry. It was pleading. Leesa forced herself to look beyond him to the boy she was sure needed to be set free, and she willed the words to come.

"I forgive you, Andy. Things are going to be okay."

She wasn't sure if she added the affirmation for his sake or for hers, but as she left the yard in a trembling mess of barely restrained tears, she hoped it was the truth—for both of them.

Tears blurred her vision as she drove away. Her heart going crazy, and she was breathing so hard she felt like her lungs were burning. But as she wiped the tears away, her vision cleared, and so did her mind. She felt as though a veil had been lifted from before her eyes, giving her clarity. She was never going to get what she thought she needed. Andy wasn't about to fess up to his lie. She rolled down her window and breathed in the cool night air, filling her lungs completely for what felt like the first time since she'd been accused. At a stoplight she noticed the message light on her cell phone. She picked it up with shaky fingers and scrolled through the texts.

Tegan: *I've called twice. Please call me back so I know you're alive and well.*

Tempe: *Are you okay? Remember, what happened wasn't your fault.*

Lena: *Sorry I told you not to talk to Andy, but...you know I love you. I don't want you to get hurt any more. Call me.*

Leesa's thoughts returned to Andy and the look in his eyes when his father silenced him. She didn't know why she'd put so much importance on him admitting that he'd lied. He was a kid who'd made a stupid mistake. She'd always known that, and he was obviously paying the worst price of all of them. He'd looked forlorn and distraught, and it had hurt to see him that way. But once she'd recognized the look in his eyes for what it was, she'd known. He was too mired down with guilt to even think straight. He might not have understood the levity of his accusations at the onset, but now he clearly did. She knew now that his words would have been the icing on the cake, but she didn't need icing on a cake. The help Andy needed would have to come from another source. His parents, therapists. The right people for the job. She'd needed to come back to forgive him, to set him free. And in doing so, she'd set herself free, too.

She didn't want to be back here where the accusation still seemed so fresh and her own home felt wrong. She didn't need to be here to keep the memories of her father, of her childhood, alive. They were part of her. They would always be part of her. And she knew now that even if someone, somehow, recognized her as Annalise Avalon, the teacher who was accused of touching a teenage boy, she was strong enough to hold her head up high and say, *Falsely accused*, and move on with confidence.

The light changed as she picked up the phone and hit Cole's speed-dial number and the speaker button. She couldn't wait to tell him she was coming back, and she hoped he still wanted her. As she turned down her street, her call went to voicemail. Fresh, happy tears slid down her cheeks as she left a message.

"Hi. It's me. I didn't get too far with Andy, but—" The phone slid from her hand at the sight of Cole stepping from his car. His dark eyes swept up the road. She threw the car into park as a smile tore across his cheeks and reached his gorgeous dark eyes. He came around the car as she pushed the door open and leaped into his arms.

He smelled heavenly, and when he sealed his lips over hers, he tasted like home, love, happiness. He tasted like her future.

"You're here," she said as their lips parted. "I told you not to come, and you're here."

"I missed you too much to wait another second. Are you okay?" He pressed his lips to hers again in another incredible kiss, and she melted against him.

"Andy didn't admit he lied."

"I'm sorry. I know you hoped for an apology."

"I did, but once I got there and saw how conflicted he was, I realized that wasn't what was important. I'll probably never get an apology, and that's okay. It turns out that's not what I needed after all. I told Andy that I forgive him, and even though I've never felt like I blamed him for what happened to me, somewhere deep inside I must have. I must have not only blamed him, but I must have been even angrier at him than I allowed myself to believe, because forgiving him set me free, too. I'll probably always worry about someone bringing up what happened, but—"

"Angel." He kissed her again, and the kiss said more than words ever could.

She wanted to tell him that he was what she needed—his faith in her, his arms around her—but when their lips parted, before she could get a word out, he said, "I love you. I love you for who you are, past and all. If you need to look over your shoulder, I'll look first. If you're scared, I'll keep you safe. Come home with me, Leesa. Move in with me. Build a life with me. Let me fight your battles with you. Let me love you in all the ways you deserve to be loved."

Chapter Twenty-Four

COLE LAY BESIDE Leesa with the breeze from the open window beside Leesa's bed brushing over their naked bodies. Leesa was draped across him, her thigh over his, her cheek against his chest, and she was fast asleep. The sun was just beginning to peek through the sheers, promising to smile down on them today. He threaded his fingers through her hair, marveling at the settled feeling inside of him. Normally, he'd pop out of bed for a run, or his mind would already be ticking through his patient load for the day or tests he needed to follow up on. Surprisingly, even as he drew those thoughts to the forefront of his mind, they didn't remain there. Thoughts of Leesa were too present to allow much else. He hadn't been sure what to expect when he'd driven to Towson yesterday, and if he were honest with himself, he wasn't exactly sure what he'd say to her when he finally saw her. He'd thought he'd made up his mind not to pressure her to come back to Peaceful Harbor.

But then he'd seen her car and his pulse had quickened.

And then he'd seen her face through the window, and his heart had leaped.

And when she was in his arms, he was powerless to restrain his love for her, and the words came effortlessly. By some grace of God, she'd agreed to move in with him. Afterward they'd made love, and she succumbed to the numb sleep of a satisfied lover. He watched her sleeping beside him and knew that if she'd said she needed to stay in Towson or move to Baltimore, he'd have given up his world to be with her.

Her hand moved sleepily over his chest, drawing him from his thoughts. She lifted sleepy eyes to his and smiled. "You really are here. It wasn't just the best dream ever."

He leaned in for a kiss, and she met him halfway. "I'm really here. I was so worried about you. How are you today? Any thoughts about the promises we made last night?"

She moved up so they were eye to eye and touched his scruffy cheek. Her brows knitted together. "Yeah, I have some thoughts."

His heartbeat kicked up, and as he turned his face to her hand and kissed her palm, he waited for her to say more.

"I like your promise to always be with me." She pressed her lips to his. "And I like my promise to move in with you." She kissed his cheek, and the worry that had toyed with him disappeared, replaced with desire as her hand dropped to his erection. "But there was one promise we didn't make."

He tried to think past the feel of her hand stroking over his hard length, but she knew just how to touch him, just how to whisper, to make his mind fuzzy and his body hot. "What...promise?"

She pressed a kiss to his chest and flicked her tongue over his nipple, sending shocks of lust straight to his cock.

"Leese..." Holy hell he wanted to be inside her.

"Mm, you like?" She kissed a path across his chest and teased his other nipple. Every flick of her tongue made his erection twitch in her hand. "Oh yeah," she whispered, "you like that."

In one swift move, he wrapped his arms around her and shifted her body beneath his, perching on his elbows above her smiling face. Her thighs fell open, and the tip of his arousal pressed against her wet center.

"The promise?" he panted out. "Tell me before my brain stops functioning. I'll promise you anything."

She lifted her hips and shifted south, pushing the wide crown into her heat.

"Leese," he warned. "We need a condom."

"I know," she said as she leaned up to kiss him. "I just wanted to feel *you* for a second."

"With how good you feel, if you sink down any deeper, you'll get us both in trouble."

She grinned, and he growled, which drew a sexy laugh from Leesa as he pulled out. She pressed on his hips, keeping him against her.

"Last night, before we made love, you said you were going to cut back on working long hours and not bring work home. I don't want you to change for me, Cole. I love who you are. I love how you care about your patients and that you read over their charts at night so you're prepared for the next day. You captured my heart while doing those things. It's who you are, and I respect that part of you. Please don't change."

He touched his forehead to hers and closed his eyes for a beat. How had he gotten lucky enough to find someone who accepted him for who he was? And would that lead him to lose her somewhere down the line? Would she feel neglected?

She must have seen the conflict in his eyes when he opened them, because she touched his cheek again in that soothing way she had and said, "And I promise you that if I ever feel like you're ignoring me, or like we need more couple time, I'll tell you before it becomes a problem."

He swallowed past the emotions threatening to claw through his chest.

"Leese, I don't want to start out wrong. I adore you, and I want you to know that with every ounce of your soul."

"I do. I promise."

"Okay. I promise, too. But when you eventually marry me, and we have a family, I'm changing my hours for good. Because when we have babies, I want to be right there with you every evening, every weekend, marveling at every milestone and every smile of the little people we bring into this world together."

She reached for a condom with a mischievous smile. "Perfect. But I think we'd better do a lot of practicing to make sure we get it right."

As he slid inside her, fully sheathed and so madly in love he'd do anything for her, Cole gazed into her eyes and saw all the emotions he felt reflected back at him. Their bodies joined together like they were made for each other, and when he was buried deep, they both stilled. He sealed his lips over hers, kissing her with all the surety he felt, all the passion that had been building since he'd first set eyes on her, and all the love that had grown in the days since. Her hands slid into his hair, and she clung to him, kissing him hungrily as he tucked his hands beneath her ass and lifted her hips. He moved slow and deep. Pulling nearly all the way out before pushing back in again, sliding over the sensitive places that made her gasp tiny bits of air. She tugged at his hair and he quickened his pace, heat coiling at the base of his spine. Their lips parted and her head fell back as she panted for breaths. He slid one hand between them, homing in on the one spot that he knew would send her over the edge.

She dug her nails into his scalp, rocking her hips to meet every thrust. He was ready to come from the sight of her flushed cheeks, the sheen of sweat between her breasts, and her slightly parted lips that just last night had been stretched around his cock.

"Oh God, Cole—" She bucked off the mattress as she came apart beneath him.

Her inner muscles tightened, pulsing waves of pleasure through Cole. He had to taste her, feel her energy as she fought for air. Their mouths crashed together in a clash of tongues and teeth, in a greedy, wet kiss. As heat shot through him and he gave in to his own intense release, she was right there with him, another orgasm engulfing her, and they spiraled over the edge together.

They lay together for a long while, bodies spent, hands clasped tightly together.

"Cole?" Leesa whispered into the early-morning silence.

"Mm?"

"Let's pack up my stuff and get out of here."

He opened his eyes and assessed her excited gaze. "Now?"

"After we shower, yes. I'm ready. I'm ready to be Leesa Avalon for real now."

He pushed up on one elbow and smiled, matching her beautiful smile. "So, I shouldn't call you Annalise?"

She sat up and pulled the sheet over her chest. "Only when you want to play a naughty role-playing game." She slid off the bed and said, "But then I get to call you something else, too."

"Like?" he challenged.

She shrugged, but the wicked glint in her eyes told him that she was about to rile him up.

"Sam?"

She shrieked and laughed as he leaped from the bed and chased her into the bathroom. He pinned her arms above her head against the bathroom wall and nibbled at her neck.

"You've got a thing for my brother?"

"No," she said with a dreamy sigh, craning her neck so he had better access. "I knew it was the only way to get you out of bed."

He trapped both of her hands above her head with one of his, and his other slid down her hip. He glared into her eyes and she pressed her hips against his growing erection.

"And into my shower." She went up on her toes and kissed him.

"Woman, I have a feeling you're going to try me every step of the way."

She wrapped one leg around his hips and said, "Oh, but what tantalizing steps they will be."

BY MIDAFTERNOON LEESA and Cole had boxed up most of the things she wanted to bring with her back to Peaceful Harbor. They'd planned to take whatever would fit in their cars, and they'd come back on the weekends to grab a few things until she was done.

"What about your furniture? We'll make arrangements for movers to bring whatever you want," Cole said as they carried boxes out to the car.

"You have such nice furniture already." She hadn't put any great thought into that yet. She set the box in the back of her car and watched Cole doing the same. His shirt clung to his muscles as he wiped sweat from his brow, but it was his easy smile that had her walking to his side and wrapping her arms around him.

"How about we just bring the hammock from the backyard. Do you think you and your brothers could finagle a way to hang it up?"

He pressed his lips to hers. "Anything you want, angel. If I haven't told you already, I want you to know that I'm really proud of you. You came here to do something that most people in your shoes never would have considered. You really are a courageous woman."

"Or really stupid. I'm not sure which."

He kissed her again. "Courageous. How did it go when you called Darlene to say you weren't taking the job?"

"Fine. I think she expected it. I just can't get the look on Andy's face out of my head. I know I did the right thing by forgiving him, but he looked so tortured."

"Tell me what you need. Do you want to try again to talk to him? I'll go with you if you do."

She gazed up and saw the sincerity in his eyes and knew he would. "No. I think I just have to realize that he put himself in that box. I did what I could to help him climb out, but really, it's not my place to do anything more."

They spent the next hour loading boxes and closing up the house for their return to Peaceful Harbor. Leesa and Cole were rolling up the hammock when she heard a car in the driveway.

"I'll see who that is." She came around the side of the house as Mr. Darren helped Andy out of the passenger's seat and into his wheelchair. Her heart nearly stopped. She'd just gotten to a good place. She didn't want to leave town on the heels of another argument.

If it weren't for Cole's comforting arm landing on her shoulder and his whisper in her ear, "It's okay, angel. I'm right here. I won't let anything happen," she might not have remembered how to breathe.

Cole walked ahead of her, placing himself between Mr. Darren and Leesa.

"Sir?" Cole's tone was firm and questioning.

Andy worked the wheels on his chair around Cole, and Cole reached down and stopped the chair by grabbing one of the arms. Leesa held her breath, having no idea why she was more nervous today than she'd been last night, but conflicting emotions warred within her again. The urge to run to Andy and make sure he was okay and the urge to run in the opposite direction tore at her.

"Hi, Andy. I'm Cole."

Andy blinked up at him without saying a word.

"We're not here to cause trouble," Mr. Darren finally said with a tight jaw and a stern look on his face. "My son has something to say to Annalise." He looked over Cole's shoulder and said, "And so do I."

Cole turned and reached for Leesa's hand. "Angel?"

She took his hand and stepped forward, forcing words from her lungs. "Hi, Andy."

Andy's eyes dampened. His fingers clung to the arms of the wheelchair so tightly that his knuckles turned white. "Ms. Avalon, I..." He looked down, then flipped his hair from his eyes with a quick flick of his chin and said, "I'm sorry for lying. Once I realized what happened, I wanted to tell the police I had lied, but—"

His father stepped to his side and placed a firm hand on Andy's shoulder. "But I didn't let him."

"You...? Why not?" Leesa couldn't believe her ears.

"Annalise, by the time he came to me and said he wasn't telling the truth, the harm had been done. The investigation was almost over, and your reputation had already been damaged." He looked down at the boy he'd been nothing but stern with, and the tight lines in his jaw and forehead softened. "He's a kid who made a very big mistake. He's already feeling like he's behind the rest of his peers with his injuries, and as his father, I didn't want him to have to battle the reputation of being the kid who lied and ruined your life, too."

Leesa's eyes filled with tears. "So you let everyone think I did something I didn't do."

His tone softened. "People in this town didn't buy the accusation, not when the police and school administration found no evidence of harm. It was wrong of me to hold him back, but I did it to help my son, not to hurt you. I'm terribly ashamed of my decision, but I hope, on some level, you can understand why I did it."

"Mr. Darren—"

Leesa squeezed Cole's hand to stop him from saying anything more. She needed to handle this, even if she wasn't quite sure how. "While I guess I can see why you chose to do that, to protect Andy, I have to ask. Do you realize what your actions were teaching him?"

"I told him," Andy said.

"Andy—"

"No, Dad. I need to say it. Ms. Avalon, I'm sorry for lying, and I'm sorry for not saying that sooner, but my dad's not a bad guy. I get that you think he's teaching me to lie to cover my butt, but I don't think that's the lesson I learned." He placed his hand over his father's and said, "By keeping up with the lie, I learned how bad it really was. It's been killing me, and I think that's why my dad finally let me tell you the truth. You're a cool teacher, and you didn't deserve to lose your job because I was mad. I know you said you forgive me, but last night I realized that I need more than that. I need you to know the truth and forgive my dad, because if you can't, I'm not sure I can, either."

Leesa crouched beside Andy's wheelchair, trying to reel in her emotions. The anger she felt toward Mr. Darren was no match for the pride she felt in Andy at that moment for the courage it took for him to come clean. She squeezed his hand, unable to find the words he needed to hear. She pushed to her feet and approached Mr. Darren.

"I don't have children, so I can't speak from a parental standpoint, but I know I would have done anything to help your son pass his classes and feel good about himself. You were willing to throw me to the wolves, to have my career, my life, torn to shreds in the very town where I grew up in order to protect your son." She shook her head. "That's a really horrible thing to do." Tears streamed down her cheeks.

"Yes, you're right. And I'm so very sorry," he said.

His eyes held so much grief and regret that it was hard for Leesa not to simply accept his apology, but she couldn't. She had to spell out her feelings to him. He needed to understand that words couldn't give her back what they'd stolen from her.

"'Sorry' can't fix what happened. An apology can't return my life to what it was. It can't erase the doubt from the minds of everyone around me, or give me back everything I worked so hard for, in the town where my father raised me." Fresh tears sprang from her eyes with thoughts of her father. She drew in a deep breath and held her chin up high, feeling a weight lifting from her shoulders. All it needed was a little harder shove for her to be able to breathe again. "But for Andy's sake, I forgive you. Maybe you're right. His life didn't need any more upending than he's already experienced. But that doesn't make what you did right. I just hope you'll both learn something from this." She reached for Cole's hand. "Luckily, things for me have turned out okay. And I hope for Andy's sake, things for him will, too. If you'll excuse me, I have a life to build."

Leesa walked back into her childhood home, her fingers laced with the man she loved, and finally—*Lord, finally*—she understood how things had gone so wrong.

Cole closed the door behind them, and she melted into his arms, happy that at least everything in her life finally felt right.

Chapter Twenty-Five

COLE AND HIS siblings, along with Leesa and Tegan, made quick work of moving Leesa's things into Cole's beach house the following weekend. Leesa listed her old furniture on Craigslist, and by the end of the following weekend, her childhood home was empty. She'd kept most of her father's books and all of his most treasured belongings, pictures, and other memorabilia from their lives, but her favorite thing was the hammock. Since there were no trees on the beach behind Cole's house, Cole, Sam, and Nate had constructed a wooden cradle and rigged the hammock up on that. It was, like everything Cole did, *perfect*. He'd cleared space for her in every room, including shelves in the living room for her father's books, and they'd even hung a few pictures of her and her father in the boat.

It's our life, not just mine. I want to feel your presence everywhere, he'd said.

It was Saturday afternoon, and Leesa sat on the stone wall in Cole's parents' backyard, watching Cole and his brothers toss a football. Ty, his youngest brother, had come back from his assignment for the get-together, and like the rest of Cole's family, he'd embraced Leesa without hesitation. He was big and strong, like the rest of the Braden men, and every bit as reckless as Cole was cautious. He wore his hair longer than the others, and the mischief in his eyes rivaled Sam's. Leesa saw a look that could only mean trouble pass between Sam, Ty, and Nate while Nate reached back to throw the football, and she held her breath. Ty tackled Cole when Cole caught the ball. Nate and Sam were quick to pile on top of them, and their laughter rang through the air like a celebration.

"They're still boys at heart," Ace said as he sat down beside her.

"They must have been quite a handful when they were growing up." Leesa tucked her hair behind her ear as a breeze swept off the water.

"Oh, yes. I hope that never changes." Ace turned a friendly smile in her direction. "So? You did it. You faced your past and moved forward."

"Yeah, I did. Thank you for the talk. It meant a lot to me," she said honestly. "And I'm sorry about overstepping my bounds." She still felt guilty for asking about his leg.

"Do you know that you picked up on the thing no one else did?" His gaze turned serious, and her stomach clenched.

"I'm sorry. I didn't mean—"

He patted her hand. "I called the docs at the VA hospital, and they put me in touch with a therapist out in Pleasant Hill. I start mirror therapy next week."

Leesa felt her eyes widen. "You do? So you're not upset with me?"

"I'm not a complaining man, Annalise, but when you brought up what you saw on my face, it made me wonder. What if my family saw it but never said anything?" He looked across the yard at Maisy and smiled. "I asked Maisy about it, and she reminded me that she'd asked about it for two years after the accident, and apparently I brushed her off so often that she stopped asking. You know, I think I lived with the discomfort for long enough that it became part of who I was."

"And now?"

He laughed softly, and it sounded so much like Cole's laugh that her eyes were drawn across the yard to the man she loved. Cole waved and blew a kiss. She waved back as Ace responded.

"Now it's time to accept my past and move forward."

"But you said the pain was a good thing, a motivator," she reminded him.

He pushed to his feet and reached for her hand, drawing her up beside him. "I think I've had enough reminders of what I left behind. Look at my beautiful family." His eyes moved from the boys to Shannon, Tempe, and Jewel, who were headed their way, and then to Leesa. "There is no better motivator than the people in this yard."

"Dad, Mom wants you to start the grill," Tempe said as the girls joined them.

Leesa watched Ace walk away. "You guys are so lucky. Your dad is wonderful."

"Yeah, we are," Shannon said. "But your father must have been pretty incredible, too. Look how you turned out."

"Thanks, he was." She handed the notebook she'd been carrying to Tempe. "I've added my ideas for the Girl Power group. And I was thinking, I really enjoy working at Mr. B's, but I also miss teaching, so I thought maybe I'd also start doing some tutoring on the side."

"Please can you help Krissy? Her creative writing is not nearly as strong as her creative dancing," Jewel said.

"Yeah, I'd like that." She watched Cole and his brothers

heading toward them.

"You're really ready?" Tempe asked as she leafed through the notebook.

"I am." She reached for Cole's hand as he came to her side.

"Hi, angel. You doing okay?" Cole asked.

"Yeah, perfect. I was just telling Tempe that I'm ready to think about starting the Girl Power group."

"And she's offered to help Krissy with her schoolwork," Jewel added.

Cole tugged her in closer. "Both excellent ideas." As he lowered his lips to hers, Shannon sighed. Cole shifted his eyes to his sister.

"Go ahead, kiss your woman," Shannon said with a wide grin. "I cannot wait until I have someone who looks at me the way you and Nate look at Leesa and Jewel."

"Well, you're not going to find him in the Colorado Mountains." Ty ran a hand through his shiny dark hair. His long bangs fell right back in front of his eyes. "I've been on nearly every mountain across the world, and I'm telling you, you won't find love on any of them. Sorry, sis." He draped an arm around Shannon and smiled at Leesa and Cole. "Besides, you got years before you're as old as Cole."

"Hey," Cole said.

Leesa laughed.

"I didn't know love had an age requirement," Jewel said as she snuggled up to Nate.

"I'm kidding." Ty gave Shannon's shoulder a squeeze, then released her. "Seriously, though, sis. Why the hurry?"

"I'm not in a hurry." Shannon gazed at their parents, hugging by the grill across the yard. "It just seems nice."

"Well, I'm not in a hurry. I've got too many things I want

to do before I settle down." Tempe tucked the notebook beneath her arm and waved to their parents, who were walking hand in hand on their way to join them.

"I'm with Tempe and Ty." Sam tossed the football in the air and caught it. "So many women, so little time."

"You guys have it all wrong." Cole smiled at Leesa. "One perfect woman, never enough time."

Sam and Ty scoffed. Tempe and Shannon *aww*ed, and Nate and Jewel nodded in agreement, while all Leesa could do was wonder how she'd gone from a woman scorned to a woman loved. But when Cole dropped to his knee and took her hand in his, that thought disappeared completely.

"Cole?" Leesa's eyes widened when he reached into his pocket and pulled out a jewelry box. *Ohmygod!*

"Leesa with two e's, you stole my heart from the moment you took my coffee and muffin." He smiled, and her heart was beating so fast it took all her focus to remain standing. "And every day since, you've made me the happiest man on earth."

"Cole—" The whisper slipped from her lips as his brothers and sisters smiled and looked on. Her hands flew to her mouth, and tears dampened her eyes.

Cole shifted a knowing gaze to Sam, then a loving gaze back to Leesa. "I'm not the kind of guy to wait around and let things happen *to* me. I love you, Leesa, and I would be honored if you'd let me love you for the rest of our lives, as husband and wife."

Her limbs were trembling so badly she was afraid to move her hands from her mouth for fear of losing her footing, so she nodded—hard—over and over, as Cole rose to his feet and gathered her in his arms.

"Is that a yes?" He guided her trembling arms around his

neck. "I need to hear it, angel."

"Yes. Oh my goodness, yes. Yes. Yes." Every word came out as a whisper, accompanied by fresh tears. Their mouths came together in a mind-numbing, forever-bonding kiss, while his family congratulated them, laughing and clapping and filling the air with their joy.

Cole set her feet back down on the ground and slid the solitaire diamond ring onto her finger. "I love you."

Leesa pressed her palms to the cheeks she loved so much and gazed into the eyes of the man she knew she'd love for the rest of her life. In that moment she knew that what he called her didn't matter. She could be *Annalise, Leesa,* or *hey you.* The person she was, the woman she'd become, was the woman Cole loved. And she couldn't wait to be called the best name of all—*Mrs. Cole Braden.*

Ready for more Bradens?

Get ready to fall in love with Sam Braden!

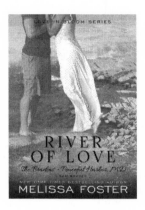

A MAN COULD take a wedding for only so long before he drank too much booze or left with a warm, willing woman to wash away all that purity. Sam Braden stood with a drink in one hand and a greedy itch in the other, debating doing both.

"I'll take the redhead if you want the brunette." Ty, his youngest brother, lifted his chin in the direction of the bar. In addition to being a world-renowned mountain climber and photographer, Ty was also Sam's carousing partner. "Unless you're double-dipping tonight, in which case I'll go for one of the Staley sisters."

Sam scoffed. *Been there, done them.*

He spotted two blondes slinking across the dance floor toward them. He'd hooked up with the one who was currently eye-fucking him last month, and the redhead Ty had been ogling moments ago had joined them in their hot, sweaty romp. His gaze shifted to the sexy brunette standing by the bar looking like she wanted to jump over it and hide behind it but she couldn't quite figure out how. *Faith Hayes.* He'd been trying *not* to look at Faith all night, but he was losing that battle. Faith worked in Sam's brother Cole's medical practice. She was sweet, and good, and smart, and... Sam should not be thinking about laying her on the bar and doing dirty things to her gorgeous body.

No. He definitely should not.

Every time he looked at her, every time he thought of her— *which was every damn day*—that feeling of wanting more than a few quick hookups resurfaced. He not only wanted to lay her down on the bar, but he wanted to take her home. That was bizarre, too, since as a rule Sam never took any woman to his cabin. But half his *visits* with Cole at his office were merely made-up opportunities to get a glimpse of Faith. He didn't fully understand his fascination with her, considering he usually preferred the kind of woman who wanted to jump *him* and damn well knew how, but there was no denying the stirring inside him every time she was near. He forced himself to look away and focused on the dance floor, where Cole, their eldest brother, danced with his new wife, Leesa, and just beyond, their younger brother Nate and his fiancée, Jewel, were gazing into each other's eyes. Weren't they always? Sam used to get hives just thinking about being tied down—*unless, of course, it was to a bed.* But he couldn't deny how happy his brothers seemed since they'd fallen in love, and lately he'd begun feeling as if he were missing out on something.

The tall blonde sidled up to Sam, blocking his view of Faith and blinking flirtatiously, while her friend joined Ty. "You boys look lonely."

"Ladies," Sam said smoothly, bringing his attention back to the pretty girls who definitely knew how to use their bodies for the good of mankind.

"Care to dance?" she asked, and like a puppy with a bone, Sam followed her out to the dance floor.

Music and dancing ranked right up there with white-water rafting in Sam's book. As the owner of Rough Riders, a rafting and adventure company, he rarely slowed down, but a strong beat calmed his internal restlessness. And Sam was always a little restless.

The blonde moved sensuously in his arms, reminding him of all the reasons a woman should win out over booze tonight. On that thought, his eyes drifted back to Faith, still standing by the bar, holding a drink he'd bet was soda, and nervously running her finger up the side of the glass as she...*watched him?* Sam's lips curved up and Faith's gaze skittered away. She became adorably flustered whenever he visited Cole at the office, and though he probably shouldn't, Sam got a kick out of flirting with her.

Cole stepped into his line of sight, blocking his view of Faith and casting a threatening look at Sam, sending the message, *Don't even think about it.*

There were no two ways about it, Sam loved women and everyone around him knew it. He loved the way they smelled, the feel of their soft bodies against his hard muscles, their delicate features, the sounds they made in the throes of passion. But his mind refused to play the *any woman* game these days. It was drenched in thoughts of Faith, and he wanted to experience all those things about her firsthand.

"Sam!" Cole chided.

He shook his head to clear his mind, laughing under his breath, as he turned his attention back to the woman he was dancing with. His hands sank to the base of her spine. *Mm.* She felt good. His eyes were drawn to Faith again, who was staring into her drink. *Bet you'd feel even better,* was his first thought, but it was the second—*I wonder what you're thinking*—that took him by surprise.

I SHOULDN'T HAVE come to this wedding. Faith checked her watch for the hundredth time that evening. She'd told herself she had to stay for an hour after dinner. That was the respectable thing to do at her boss's wedding, even though she'd rather leave right this very second. Work obligations outside of the office were uncomfortable enough, but now she was not only surrounded by people she barely knew, but her stupid hormones were doing some sort of *I Want Sam Braden* dance. God, she hated herself right now. *Look at him, getting all handsy with the town flirt.* He'd been dancing all night with every other woman in the place. They practically lined up to be near him. Why shouldn't they? He was not only nice to everyone, but he was tall, dark, and distractingly handsome. The kind of handsome that made smart girls like Faith forget the alphabet. His arm was the most coveted spot in all of Peaceful Harbor, and damn it to hell, she did *not* want to be there.

Too badly.

I seriously need to dive into a tequila bottle. Or leave. Since driving home after drinking a bottle of tequila posed issues, she decided leaving was a better option.

She had the perfect excuse to cut out a little early, too. She was hosting a car wash tomorrow to raise funds for WAC, Women Against Cheaters, an online support group she'd started for women who had been cheated on.

By guys like Sam.

Sam glanced up and—*Oh God, shoot me now*—caught her staring. *Again.* She turned away, hoping he hadn't really noticed, even though his eyes were like laser beams burning a hole in her back. Of course he saw her. How could he not? She was practically drooling over him. She didn't want to have this stupid crush on the man who, if she believed the rumors, had slept with most of the women in Peaceful Harbor. If she took away his devastatingly good looks, he was the exact opposite of the type of man she wanted or needed.

Unable to resist, she stole another glance, and like every other set of female eyes in the place that weren't related to him, she was drawn in like a fly to butter. He was *gorgeous.* Manly. Rugged. And that smile. *Lordy, Lordy.* She fanned her face. His smile alone caused her toes to curl. All the Bradens were good-looking, but there was something edgy and enigmatic about Sam. *Dangerous.*

Too dangerous for her, which was okay, because she didn't really want him. Not in the *try to keep him* sense. A man like Sam couldn't be kept, and she wasn't about to be the idiot who tried. She'd be happy with leering and lusting, and pretending she wasn't.

Except, *oh shit*, he was coming over. He moved across the dance floor like he owned the place, confident, determined, focused, leaving the blonde, and a dozen other women, staring after him. If looks had powers beyond the ability to weaken Faith's knees, Sam would have eaten her up before he even reached her. His dark eyes were narrow, seductive, and shimmering with wickedness. His broad shoulders looked even wider, more powerful, beneath his expensive tuxedo. The top buttons of his shirt were open, giving her a glimpse of his tanned skin and a dusting of chest hair. He looked like he should be lounging on a couch with women fawning over him. Godlike.

Godlike? I am pathetic.

Faith was not a meek woman without a man in her life. She was single by choice, *thank you very much*. She stunk at choosing men, and besides that…men sucked. They cheated, they lied, and eventually they all tried to put the blame back on her. Ever since JJ, her last boyfriend, made good on the unspoken All Men Must Cheat promise their gender seemed to live by, she'd confined her dating pool to include only boring, slightly nerdy men.

"Faith."

Sam's deep voice washed over her skin and nestled into her memory bank for later when she was alone in her bed, thinking about him. She hated that, too. Why, oh, why, did he have to be a player? Couldn't he be like his brothers Cole and Nate? Loyal to the end of time?

He touched her arm, burning her skin.

"Oh. Hi, Sam." That sounded casual, right? He was so big, standing this close, and he smelled like man and sunshine and heat all wrapped up in one big delicious package.

Great. Now I'm thinking of your package.

"Would you like to dance?" he asked.

Yes. No! Stick to your boring-man rule, Faith.

Sam was anything but boring, taking every outdoor risk known to man and out carousing every night of the week.

Nope, she wanted no part of that.

"No, thanks." She sipped her drink, wishing it were tequila instead of Jack and Coke. Wishing she were home instead of standing beside the human heat wave.

His brows knitted. "You sure? I haven't seen you on the dance floor all night."

"Have you run out of girls already?" *Holy Jesus, did I say that out loud?*

An easy smile spread across his face, like he wasn't offended, but...*amused?* He looked around the room and said, "No, actually. There are a few I haven't danced with." Those chocolate eyes focused on her again. "But I want to dance with you."

She downed her drink to keep the word *Okay* from slipping out and set the empty glass on the bar. "Thanks, but I'm actually getting ready to leave."

"Now, that would be a shame." His eyes dragged slowly down her body, making her feel vulnerable and naked.

Naked with Sam Braden. Her entire body flamed, and he must have noticed, because his eyes turned midnight black.

"You look incredibly beautiful tonight, and it's Cole and Leesa's big day. You should stick around." He leaned in a little closer. "And dance with me."

It wasn't like her jelly legs could carry her out of there anyway. *Incredibly beautiful?* Faith had been told she was pretty often enough to believe it, but *incredibly beautiful?* That was pushing it. That was smooth-talking Sam, the limit pusher.

She had to admit, he had this pickup thing down pat. His eyes were solely focused on her, while she felt the gaze of nearly every single woman in the place on her like they wondered what she had that they didn't—or maybe like they wanted to kill her.

Yup. That was probably more accurate.

"The wedding was lovely," she managed. "I'm happy for Cole and Leesa, but I'm hosting a car wash at Harbor Park tomorrow afternoon. I should really get going so I have time to prepare."

Sam stepped closer. His fingers caressed the back of her arm, sending shivers of heat straight to her brain—and short-circuiting it.

"Harbor Park?" The right side of his tempting mouth lifted in a teasing smile. "Surely you won't turn into a pumpkin this early. You can't leave without giving me one dance. Come on. Think of how happy it'll make Cole to see you enjoying yourself."

He was obviously not going to give up. Maybe she should just give in and dance with him. She had no desire to be another in the long line of Sam's conquests, but it was just one dance, and then she could leave, and he'd go back to any of the other women there. That idea sank like a rock in her stomach.

Her stupid hormones swam to the surface again. *You did ask nicely.* Maybe she was reading too much into this dance. It was just a dance, not a date.

But his eyes were boring into her in that *I want to get into your panties* way he had. She'd seen him give that look to several other women tonight.

Several. Other. Women.

Ugh! Why was she even considering this?

It was his hand, moving up and down her arm, making her shivery and hot at once. And those eyes, drawing her in, making her feel important. She wasn't important to Sam. She knew that in her smart physician assistant brain, but her ovaries had some sort of hold on that part of her brain, crushing her smart cells.

Faith glanced at the dance floor and caught sight of Cole whispering something in Leesa's ear. They were such a handsome couple, and Cole was such a kind boss. Maybe she should stay a little longer. She didn't have to dance with Sam. She could just talk with him until he got bored and moved on.

Cole's eyes turned serious, and Leesa looked over, too. He said something to her and headed in their direction with a scowl on his face and an angry bead aimed at Sam. *Shit.* This was not good. He was her *boss.*

Oh my God. What was she thinking? She shouldn't dance with her boss's brother!

"Actually…" Panic bloomed inside her chest as Cole neared. Cole respected her, but she knew he'd noticed the way she got flustered around Sam. He'd seen her turn beet-red with Sam's compliments when Sam visited him at the office. She didn't need him seeing her all swoony-eyed over him now.

"I really have to go, but thanks for asking, Sam." She spun on her heel and hurried away before she could lose her nerve.

To continue reading, please purchase
RIVER OF LOVE (The Bradens at Peaceful Harbor)

Please enjoy a sneak peek of the first book in The Ryder series,
SEIZED BY LOVE (Blue Ryder)

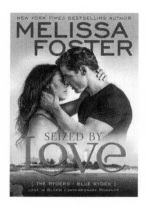

THERE WERE SOME nights when Lizzie Barber simply
didn't feel like donning an apron, black-framed glasses, and
high heels, covering her shiny brunette locks with a blond wig,
and prancing around nearly naked. Tonight was one of those
nights. Gazing at her reflection in the mirror of her basement
bathroom, Lizzie tucked the last few strands of her hair beneath
the wig and forced her very best smile. Thank God her elfin lips
naturally curled up at the edges—even when she wasn't smiling,
she looked like she was. And tonight she definitely wasn't in the
mood to smile. Her oven had been acting up for the last few
nights, and she prayed to the gods of all things sugary and sweet
that it would behave tonight.

Tightening the apron tie around her neck and the one

around her waist, to avoid wardrobe malfunctions, and tugging on the hem of the apron to ensure her skin-colored thong and all her naughty bits were covered, she went into the studio—aka the miniscule kitchen located in the basement of her cute Cape Cod cottage—and surveyed her baking accoutrements one last time before queuing the intro music for her webcast and pasting that perfectly perky smile back in place.

"Welcome back, my hot and hunky bakers," she purred into the camera. "Today we're going to bake delicious angel food cupcakes with fluffy frosting that will make your mouth water." She leaned forward, flashing the camera an eyeful of cleavage and her most seductive smile as she crooked her finger in a come-hither fashion. "And because we all know it's what's *beneath* all that delicious frosting that counts, we're going to sprinkle a few surprises inside the thick, creamy centers."

Lizzie had mastered making baking sound naughty while in college, when her father had taken ill and her parents had closed their inn for six months to focus on his medical care, leaving Lizzie without college tuition. Her part-time job at a florist shop hadn't done a darn thing for her mounting school loans, and when a friend suggested she try making videos and monetizing them to earn fast cash, she drew upon her passion for baking and secretly put on a webcast called *Cooking with Coeds*. It turned out that scantily clad baking was a real money earner. She'd paid for her books and meal plan that way, and eventually earned enough to pay for most of her college tuition. Lizzie had two passions in life—baking and flowers, and she'd hoped to open her own floral shop after college. After graduation, *Cooking with Coeds* became the *Naked Baker* webcast, and she'd made enough money to finish paying off her school loans and open a flower shop in Provincetown, Massachusetts, just like she'd always dreamed of. She hadn't intended to continue the *Naked Baker* after opening P-town Petals, but when her parents fell upon hard times again and her younger sister Maddy's educational fund disappeared, the *Naked Baker* webcast became Lizzie's contribution to Maddy's education. Their very conservative parents would have a conniption fit if they knew what their proper little girl was doing behind closed doors, but what other choice did she have? Her parents ran a small bed-and-breakfast in Brewster, Massachusetts, and with her father's health ping-ponging, they barely earned enough money to make ends meet—and affording college for a child who had come as a surprise to them seven years after Lizzie was born had proven difficult.

Lizzie narrowed her eyes seductively as she gazed into the camera and stirred the batter. She dipped her finger into the rich, creamy goodness and put that finger into her mouth, making a sensual show of sucking it off. "Mm-mm. Nothing better than *thick, creamy* batter." Her tongue swept over her lower lip as she ran through the motions of creating what she'd come to think of as *baking porn*.

During the filming of each show, she reminded herself often of why she was still doing something that she felt ashamed of and kept secret. There was no way she was going to let her sweet nineteen-year-old sister fend for herself and end up doing God knew what to earn money like she did instead of focusing on her studies. Or worse, drop out of school. Madison was about as innocent as they came, and while Lizzie might once have been that innocent, her determination to succeed, and life circum-stances, had beaten it out of her. Creating the webcast was the best decision she'd ever made—even if it meant putting her nonexistent social life on hold and living a secret life after dark.

The blond wig and thick-framed spectacles helped to hide her online persona, or at least they seemed to. No one had ever accused her of being the Naked Baker. Then again, her assumption was that the freaky people who got off watching her prance around in an apron and heels probably rarely left their own basements.

She was proud of helping Maddy. She felt like she was taking one for the team. Going where no girl should ever have to go. Braving the wild naked baking arena for the betterment of the sister she cherished.

A while later, as Lizzie checked the cupcakes and realized that while the oven was still warm, it had turned *off*—her stomach sank. Hiding her worries behind another forced smile and a wink, she stuck her ass out and bent over to quickly remove the tray of cupcakes from the oven, knowing the angle of the camera would give only a side view and none of her bare ass would actually be visible. Thankfully, the oven must have just died, because it was still warm and the cupcakes were firm enough to frost.

Emergency reshoot avoided!

Smile genuine!

A few minutes later she sprinkled the last of the coconut on the cupcakes, narrating as she went.

"Everyone wants a little something extra on top, and I'm going to give it to you *good*." Giving one last wink to the camera, she said, "Until next week, this is your Naked Baker signing off for a sweet, seductive night of tantalizing tasting."

She clicked the remote and turned off the camera. Eyeing the fresh daisies she'd brought home from her flower shop, she leaned her forearms on the counter, and with a heavy sigh, she let her head fall forward. It was after midnight, and she had to be up bright and early to open the shop. Tomorrow night she'd edit the webcast so it would be ready in time to air the following night—*and* she needed to get her oven fixed.

Damn thing.

Kicking off her heels, Lizzie went upstairs, stripped out of the apron, and wrapped a thick towel around herself. A warm shower was just what she needed to wash away the film of shame left on her skin after taping the webcast. Thinking of the broken oven, she texted her friend Blue Ryder to see if he could fix it. Blue was a highly sought after craftsman who worked for the Kennedys and other prominent families around the Cape. When Lizzie's pipe had burst under the sink in the bathroom above the first-floor kitchen while she was away at a floral convention for the weekend, Blue was only too happy to put aside time to handle the renovations. He was like that. Always making time to help others. He was still splitting his time between working on her kitchen renovations and working on the cottage he'd just purchased. He was working at his cottage tomorrow, but she hoped he could fit her in at some point.

Can you fix my oven tomorrow?

Blue texted back a few seconds later. He was as reliable as he was hot, a dangerous combination. She read his text—*Is that code for something sexy?*—and shook her head with a laugh.

Smirking, she replied, *Only if you're into oven grease.*

Blue had asked her out many times since they'd met last year, when she'd handled the flowers for his friends' quadruple beach wedding. Turning down his invitations wasn't easy and had led to more sexy fantasies than she cared to admit. Her double life was crazy enough without adding a sexy, rugged man who was built like Magic Mike and had eyes that could hypnotize a blind woman, but her reasons went far deeper than that. Blue was more than eye candy. He was also a genuine friend, and he always put family and friends first, which, when added to his panty-dropping good looks and gentlemanly demeanor, were enough to stop Lizzie's brain from functioning. It would be too easy to fall hard for a caring, loyal man like Blue Ryder. And *that*, she couldn't afford. Maddy was counting on her.

She read his text—*Glad you finally came to your senses. When are you free?*—and wondered if he thought *she* was being flirtatious.

Time to nip this in the bud, she thought. Her finger hovered over the screen while her mind toyed with images of Blue, six foot three, all hot, hard muscles and steel-blue eyes.

It had been way too long since she'd been with a man, and every time Blue asked her out, she was tempted, but she liked him so much as a friend, and she knew that tipping over from friendship to lovers would only draw her further in to him, making it harder to lead her double life.

That was precisely why she hightailed it out of her house on the mornings before he showed up to work on her kitchen. Leaving before he arrived was the only way she was able to keep her distance. He was *that* good-looking. *That* kind. And *that* enjoyable to be around. Not only didn't she have time for a relationship, but she was pretty sure that no guy would approve of his girlfriend doing the *Naked Baker* show. Of course, the mornings after taping her shows, she left him a sweet treat on the counter with a note thanking him for working on her kitchen.

Even though Blue couldn't see her as she drew back her shoulders and put on her most solemn face, she did it anyway to strengthen her resolve as she typed a text that she hoped would very gently set him straight. *After work, but this is REALLY to fix my oven. The one I cook with! Thank you! See you around seven?*

She set the phone down and stepped into the shower, determined not to think about his blue eyes or the way his biceps flexed every time he moved his arms. Her mind drifted to when she'd arrived home from work yesterday and found Blue bending over his toolbox, his jeans stretched tight across his hamstrings and formed to his perfect ass. Her nipples hardened with the thought. He'd been the man she'd conjured up in her late-night fantasies since last summer. What did it hurt? He'd never know. She closed her eyes and ran her hand over her breasts, down her taut stomach, and between her legs. She may not have time to date, but a little midnight fantasy could go a long way…

To continue reading, please purchase
SEIZED BY LOVE (The Ryders)

Please enjoy this sneak peek of the first
Love in Bloom novel, *Sisters in Love*
(You'll begin to meet the Bradens in *Sisters in White*, Book
Three of the Snow Sisters)

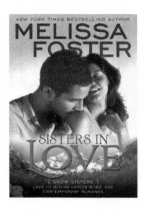

THE LINE IN the café went all the way to the door. Danica Snow wished she hadn't taken her sister Kaylie's phone call before getting her morning coffee. Living in an overcrowded tourist town could be a major inconvenience, but Danica loved that she could walk from her condo to her office, see a movie, have dinner, or even stop at a bookstore without ever sitting in a car. Every minute counted when you lived in Allure, Colorado, host to an odd mix of hippie and yuppie tourists in equal numbers. The ski slopes brought them in the winter, while art shows drew them in the summer. There was never a break. Every suit and Rasta child in town was standing right in front of her, waiting for their coffee or latte, and the guy ahead of her had shoulders so wide she couldn't easily see around him. Danica tapped the toe of her efficient and comfortable Nine West heels, growing more impatient by the second.

What on earth was taking so long? In seven minutes they'd served only one person. The tables were pushed so close to the people standing in line that she couldn't step to the side to see. She was gridlocked. Danica leaned to the right and peered around the massive shoulder ahead of her just as the owner of that shoulder turned to look out the door. *Whack!* He elbowed her right in the nose, knocking Danica's head back.

Her hand flew to her bloody nose. "Ow! Geez!" She ducked in pain, covering her face and talking through her hands. "I think you broke my nose." Each word sent pain across her nose and below her eyes.

"I'm so sorry. Let me get you a napkin," a deep, worried voice said.

Two patrons rushed over and shoved napkins in her direction.

"Are you okay?" an older woman asked.

Tears sprang from the corners of Danica's closed eyes. *Damn it.* Her entire day would now run late and she probably looked like a red-nosed, crying idiot. "This hurts so bad. Weren't you looking where—" Danica flipped her unruly, brown hair from her face and opened her eyes. Her venom-filled glare locked on the man who had elbowed her—the most beautiful specimen of a human being she had ever seen. *Oh shit.* "I'm…What…?" *Come on, girl. Get it together. He's probably an egomaniac.*

"I'm so sorry." His voice was rich and smooth, laden with concern.

A thin blonde grabbed his arm and shoved a napkin into his hand. "Give this to her," she said, blinking her eyelashes in a come-hither way.

The man held the woman's hand a beat too long. "Thanks," he said. His eyes trailed down the blonde's blouse.

Really? I'm bleeding over here.

He turned toward Danica and handed her the napkin. His eyes were green and yellow, like field grass. His eyebrows drew together in a serious gaze, and Danica thought that maybe she'd been too quick to judge—until he stole a glance at the blonde as she walked out of the café.

Asshole. She felt the heat of anger spread up her chest and neck, along her cheeks, to the ridge of her high cheekbones. She snagged the napkin from his hand and wiped her throbbing nose. "It's okay. I'm fine," she lied. She could smell the minty freshness of his breath, and she wondered what it might taste like. Danica was not one to swoon—that was Kaylie's job. *Get a grip.*

"Can I at least buy you a coffee?" He ran his hand through his thick, dark hair.

Yes! "No, thank you. It's okay." She had been a therapist long enough to know what kind of guy eyes another girl while she was tending to a bloody nose that he had caused. Danica fumbled for her purse, which she'd dropped when she was hit. She lowered her eyes to avoid looking into his. "I'm fine, really. Just look behind you next time." Not for the first time, Danica wished she had Kaylie's flirting skills and her ability to look past his wandering eyes. She would have had him buying her coffee, a Danish, and breakfast the next morning.

Danica was so confused, she wasn't even sure what she wanted. She chanced another glance up at him. He was looking at her features so intently that she felt as though he were drinking her in, memorizing her. His eyes trailed slowly from hers, lowered to her nose, to her lips, and then settled on the beauty mark that she'd been self-conscious of her entire life. She felt like a Cindy Crawford wannabe. Danica pursed her lips. "Are you done?" she asked.

He blinked with the innocence of a young boy, clueless to her annoyance, which was in stark contrast to his confident, manly presence. He stood almost a foot taller than Danica's impressive five foot seven stature. His chest muscles bulged beneath his way-too-small shirt, dark curls poking through the neckline. *He probably bought it that way on purpose.* She glanced down and tried not to notice his muscular thighs straining against his stonewashed denim jeans. Danica swallowed hard. All the air suddenly left her lungs. He was touching her shoulder, squinting, evaluating her face.

"I'm sorry. I was just making sure it didn't look broken, which it doesn't. I'm sure it's painful."

She couldn't think past the heat of his hand, the breadth of it engulfing her shoulder. "It's okay," she managed, hating herself for being lost in his touch when he was clearly someone who ate women for breakfast. She checked her watch. She had three minutes to get her coffee and get back to her office before her next client showed up. *Belinda. She'd love this guy.*

The line progressed, and Adonis waved as he left the café. Danica reached into her purse to pay for her French vanilla coffee and found herself taking a last glance at him as he passed the front window.

The young barista pushed Danica's money away. "No need, hon. Blake paid for yours." She smiled, lifting her eyebrows.

"He did?" *Blake.*

"Yeah, he's really sweet." The barista leaned over the cash register. "Even if he is a player."

Aha! I knew it. Danica thrust her shoulders back, feeling smart for resisting temptation.

To continue reading, please purchase
SISTERS IN LOVE (Snow Sisters, Book One)

More Books By Melissa

LOVE IN BLOOM SERIES

SNOW SISTERS
Sisters in Love
Sisters in Bloom
Sisters in White

THE BRADENS at Weston
Lovers at Heart
Destined for Love
Friendship on Fire
Sea of Love
Bursting with Love
Hearts at Play

THE BRADENS at Trusty
Taken by Love
Fated for Love
Romancing My Love
Flirting with Love
Dreaming of Love
Crashing into Love

THE BRADENS at Peaceful Harbor
Healed by Love
Surrender My Love
River of Love
Crushing on Love
Whisper of Love
Thrill of Love

THE BRADEN NOVELLAS

Promise My Love
Our New Love
Daring Her Love
Story of Love

THE REMINGTONS

Game of Love
Stroke of Love
Flames of Love
Slope of Love
Read, Write, Love
Touched by Love

SEASIDE SUMMERS

Seaside Dreams
Seaside Hearts
Seaside Sunsets
Seaside Secrets
Seaside Nights
Seaside Embrace
Seaside Lovers
Seaside Whispers

BAYSIDE SUMMERS

Bayside Desires
Bayside Passions

<u>THE RYDERS</u>

Seized by Love
Claimed by Love
Chased by Love
Rescued by Love

SEXY STANDALONE ROMANCE

Tru Blue
Truly, Madly, Whiskey

BILLIONAIRES AFTER DARK SERIES

WILD BOYS AFTER DARK
Logan
Heath
Jackson
Cooper

BAD BOYS AFTER DARK
Mick
Dylan
Carson
Brett

HARBORSIDE NIGHTS SERIES
Includes characters from the Love in Bloom series
Catching Cassidy
Discovering Delilah
Tempting Tristan

More Books by Melissa
Chasing Amanda (mystery/suspense)
Come Back to Me (mystery/suspense)
Have No Shame (historical fiction/romance)
Love, Lies & Mystery (3-book bundle)
Megan's Way (literary fiction)
Traces of Kara (psychological thriller)
Where Petals Fall (suspense)

Acknowledgments

I've been asked by beta readers if Cole is patterned after my own doctor-hubby, Les. All I can say is that I'm lucky enough to have a husband who is always willing to stand by my side and support my efforts, who doesn't judge based on what others say and do, and who is always kind enough to help with research, support my endless hours at the keyboard, and love me even when I fall for fictional men. I'm a truly lucky woman.

A special shout-out to all my fans and readers for sharing my books with your friends, chatting with me on social media, and sending me emails. You inspire me on a daily basis, and I can't imagine writing without our interactions. Some of you have even had characters named after you, which is always so much fun for me. Thank you for sharing yourselves with me.

If you don't yet follow me on Facebook, please do! We have such fun chatting about our lovable heroes and sassy heroines, and I always try to keep fans abreast of what's going on in our fictional boyfriends' worlds.
www.Facebook.com/MelissaFosterAuthor

Remember to sign up for my newsletter to keep up to date with new releases and special promotions and events and to receive an exclusive short story that was written just for my newsletter fans about Jack Remington and Savannah Braden:
www.MelissaFoster.com/Newsletter

For a family tree, publication schedules, series checklists, and more, please visit the special Reader Goodies page that I've set up for you!
www.MelissaFoster.com/Reader-Goodies

As always, heaps of gratitude to my amazing team of editors and proofreaders: Kristen Weber, Penina Lopez, Jenna Bagnini, Juliette Hill, Marlene Engel, and Lynn Mullan.

Melissa Foster is a *New York Times* and *USA Today* bestselling and award-winning author. Her books have been recommended by *USA Today's* book blog, *Hagerstown* magazine, *The Patriot*, and several other print venues. Melissa also writes sweet romance under the pen name Addison Cole.

Visit Melissa on her website or chat with her on social media. Melissa enjoys discussing her books with book clubs and reader groups and welcomes an invitation to your event.

Melissa's books are available through most online retailers in paperback and digital formats.

www.MelissaFoster.com
www.MelissaFoster.com/newsletter
www.MelissaFoster.com/reader-goodies